OTHER NOVELS BY CHRIS FABRY

War Room
(based on the screenplay
by Alex Kendrick and Stephen Kendrick)

Under a Cloudless Sky

The Promise of Jesse Woods

Every Waking Moment

Looking into You

Dogwood

June Bug

Almost Heaven

Not in the Heart

Borders of the Heart

A Marriage Carol (with Dr. Gary Chapman)

The Song (based on the screenplay by Richard L. Ramsay)

OVERCOMER
✦ ✦ ✦

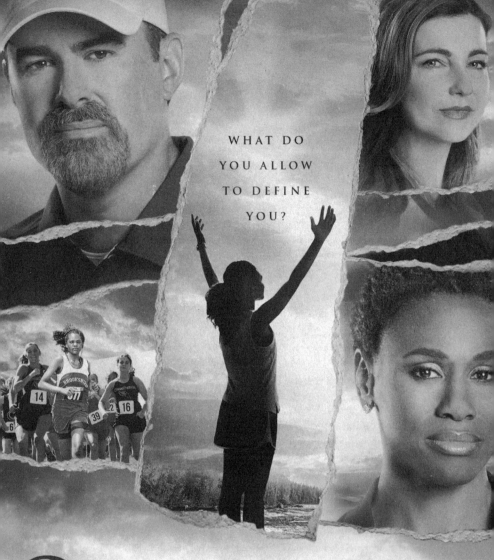

WHAT DO
YOU ALLOW
TO DEFINE
YOU?

OVERCOMER

A NOVELIZATION BY
CHRIS FABRY

BASED ON THE MOTION PICTURE BY
ALEX KENDRICK & STEPHEN KENDRICK

 TYNDALE HOUSE PUBLISHERS, INC., CAROL STREAM, ILLINOIS

Visit Tyndale online at www.tyndale.com.

Visit Chris Fabry's website at www.chrisfabry.com.

For more information on *Overcomer*, visit www.overcomermovie.com and www.kendrickbrothers.com.

Edited by Caleb Sjogren

Published in association with the literary agency WTA Services, LLC, Franklin, TN.

For information about special discounts for bulk purchases, please contact Tyndale House Publishers at csresponse@tyndale.com or call 1-800-323-9400.

Library of Congress Cataloging-in-Publication Data
Names: Fabry, Chris, date- author.
Title: Overcomer : a novelization / by Chris Fabry.
Description: Carol Stream, Illinois : Tyndale House Publishers, Inc., [2019] | "Based on the motion picture by Alex Kendrick and Stephen Kendrick."
Identifiers: LCCN 2019012201| ISBN 9781496438614 (hc) | ISBN 9781496438621 (sc)
Subjects: LCSH: Sports stories. | GSAFD: Christian fiction. | Movie novels.
Classification: LCC PS3556.A26 O94 2019 | DDC 813/.54—dc23 LC record available at https://lccn.loc.gov/2019012201

Printed in the United States of America

25	24	23	22	21	20	19
7	6	5	4	3	2	1

To Ryan, you are an overcomer.

—CHRIS FABRY

*Dedicated to my six children, Joshua, Anna, Catherine, Joy,
Caleb, and Julia, who have learned so many life lessons while
running cross-country. You are champions on the course and in
life. Keep chasing the Lord! I love you and am proud of you!*

—ALEX KENDRICK

Soon shall close thy earthly mission;
Swift shall pass thy pilgrim days;
Hope shall change to glad fruition,
Faith to sight, and prayer to praise!

"JESUS, I MY CROSS HAVE TAKEN," HENRY F. LYTE

PROLOGUE

✦ ✦ ✦

Barbara Scott paused at her front door and listened, hoping she would hear noise inside. The TV blaring. Her granddaughter crying. She longed for anything but silence. She had awakened that morning with a feeling this would be the day something good would happen, the answer to her prayers would come. When she got home from work and opened her door, all her fears would ease. She felt a pang of hope, a stirring she couldn't describe that was equal parts pain and expectation. Pain for the loss in her life. Expectation that today things would finally turn around. They had to get better, didn't they? Things couldn't get worse.

Barbara caught a reflection of herself in the window. At forty-five, it seemed Barbara had stood in front of a lot of doors. Some were locked. Others were wide-open and beckoned her inside. She knew she shouldn't walk through some doors, and others she didn't feel confident enough to enter. Life was a series of doors and regrets.

A warm summer wind whistled through the trees, but she felt an unexpected chill as she grabbed the wobbly doorknob. Some chills came and passed. This one went to the marrow. Was she coming down with something?

Her daughter, Janet, always talked about coming down with something. There was a word for that—*hypo-* something or other—but the word that came to Barbara's mind was *drama*. There was so much drama to that girl. Enough to last a lifetime. When would the drama end? When would Barbara be able to move ahead without all the worry and struggle Janet brought with her poor choices?

Please, God. Let her be here. That's all I'm asking. Let her be sitting on the couch. Let me hear that baby's cry. I just want them back. Is that too much to ask? I'll take the drama. Just bring them back. Let me hear from her today, Lord.

She pushed open the door and it swung, hinges creaking. She ought to spray them with some WD-40. Those hinges had borne the weight of that door like the weight she carried, her choices and the choices of others. She carried life like a cross. Her back was tired and her knees ached and her ankles were swollen from a full day's work. She was in the prime of her life, but she felt like every part of her had been wrung out like a dishrag, and her hopes and dreams had splattered on the tile, nobody but her to mop the mess. Why did she always have to clean up the mess?

That was a peculiar loneliness, when life lay on the floor and you were the only one to clean it. She didn't have the energy. It had left with her husband. Just flown like a bird carried off by a strong wind.

When the door banged against the hollow closet, Barbara took a step inside and scanned the living room. Perhaps Janet's suitcase would be there. Her jacket on the back of the couch. Janet holding the baby and walking up the hall from the back bedroom. She saw none of that. She heard no baby's cry. The room was no different from when she'd stepped out: cold, empty, and silent.

She put down her purse and keys and closed the door, then checked Janet's room. The bed was just as Barbara had left it that morning, made but empty. Her granddaughter's crib sat in the corner, also empty. The sight of it sent an ache deep into her soul. Where had Janet and Hannah gone?

Of course, Barbara knew. Not the exact location, but she knew who they were with. Barbara had driven to the man's old apartment on the other side of town, but his car wasn't there and there was no answer at the door. She'd called his work but they said he had quit. Nobody knew where he was.

Another closed door. Another dead end.

After Hannah's birth, there'd been a honeymoon period when Janet seemed buoyed by this new life. There was something about a baby in the house, even those wailing cries at 3 a.m., that told Barbara things would be okay, that though the world seemed like it had spun out of control, there was always a chance for life. She'd heard that a baby's cry was God's way of telling the world that He still had a plan. Now, standing in that empty room, she wondered if God's planning was off. Maybe He'd forgotten her prayers or hadn't heard them to begin with. And then the terrifying thought came. Maybe God wasn't there at all.

Months earlier, Janet had returned home penitent, deeply sorry for her mistakes and the trouble she had brought her mother. Barbara was glad Janet hadn't decided to end the child's life in the womb. She'd preached to her daughter that life was sacred and no child was a mistake. So they had walked through the last months of her pregnancy together, drawing a little closer each day, fixing up the back bedroom with a crib Barbara had found at a garage sale. She'd mended the broken slat on the rocking chair her own mother had used when Barbara was a baby. Oh, the worn arms on that chair and the memories it brought when she put her hand there.

Then, two months ago, Janet and Hannah left while Barbara was at work. No note. No phone call. Nothing. Just disappeared into thin air. And every day she came home hoping to hear the sound of that child.

Barbara wandered to the kitchen and noticed the red light blinking. The answering machine. Her heart fluttered as she hit the button and heard the computerized voice. "You have one message." Why couldn't the machine just play it instead of telling her how many there were and what time it came in? She just wanted to hear it.

That inner pang hit again. If she heard Janet's voice and knew she was okay and that little Hannah was all right, that would be enough. That would be the answer to her prayers. It would be like hope walking through the door. It would let her know that she hadn't asked too much of God.

"Mrs. Scott, this is Cindy Burgess at Franklin General." *The hospital. Why was the hospital calling?*

"We have an emergency here and need you to come down right away, ma'am. When you get this message, please call. My number is . . ."

Emergency?

The doorbell rang and she couldn't process the sound. She lifted her arm as if she could get the person to go away with just a wave. She looked for something to write on as the woman on the message repeated her number.

The doorbell again. Then a loud knock.

"Just a minute!" Barbara shouted, grabbing an unpaid bill from the kitchen table. She turned it over and wrote the number on the back.

"Please call me as soon as possible, Mrs. Scott," the woman on the machine said. "Better yet, just get here as soon as you can."

A banging on the door now. Someone shouted, "Open up!"

"Hold on a minute!" Barbara yelled, trying to scribble the last four numbers. Trying to think who might have been taken to the hospital and why they would be calling her about it. Trying to hope it wasn't who she thought.

The front door swung open and banged hard against the closet and Barbara looked into the face of the devil himself. The one everybody called T-bone. Why they called him that, she didn't know and didn't care.

T-bone held a blanket in front of him. It was the one Barbara had made for Hannah. Pink and soft and fluffy. He stepped inside.

"Don't you come in here," Barbara said. "I told you to never come to this house."

Her words didn't connect with him. His eyes were hollow and bloodshot. His cheeks sunken. He usually dressed nicely and had so much confidence—cockiness. But now he wore sweatpants and a stained T-shirt. He had a scruffy beard and wrinkled clothes that looked like they hadn't been laundered in a month.

"I didn't know what to do," T-bone said, stammering. "I just wanted to . . ." His voice trailed off.

What in the world was he talking about?

"Where's Janet and the baby? I haven't seen them in two months. Have they been with you?"

He nodded. "Yes." All the charm was gone. All the swagger he'd used to lure Janet had leaked out of him.

He looked like simmering death. He stooped and put the blanket on the floor in front of him.

The blanket moved and a little fist shot through the folds. Barbara gasped, then bent down and looked inside and heard her granddaughter give a raspy cry.

"Oh, come here, baby, it's all right," Barbara said, cradling the child to her chest. As soon as she held Hannah, she began swaying, moving back and forth to quiet and comfort the child.

"I called 911," he said weakly, absently.

"You did what?" Barbara said. "Why did you call 911?"

He didn't answer, his eyes darting as if he didn't know where he was. Then he turned and stumbled toward the door and she saw the untied shoelaces flapping.

"Where's my daughter?" Barbara yelled. "Is she at the hospital?"

Hannah wailed.

T-bone stopped on the first step and looked back with a fear she had never seen before. "I tried. I really tried. I didn't know what to do."

"What happened?" Barbara said, grabbing her purse and following him outside, holding the baby tightly.

He stumbled on the steps and fell, hitting his elbow on the concrete. He gave a muted yelp of pain. She didn't help him up.

"Where's Hannah's car seat?"

"I don't know."

"You drove her here without it?" Barbara snapped.

He managed to stand and took a few steps toward his car, walking like the ground was tilted at some impossible angle.

"If you've hurt my daughter, you're going to answer for it. Do you understand me?"

He tried three times to open his door, looking at her, mouthing something she couldn't hear. What did he say? She couldn't read lips but swore he was saying, "I'm sorry."

"When did this baby last eat?" Barbara yelled. "Where's her formula? And where are her bottles? You answer me, T-bone!"

He opened the door and fell behind the wheel of his nice car with leather seats. He started it and backed up, but he'd forgotten to close his door. When he gunned the engine, it slammed and his tires squealed. He raced out of the parking lot.

Heart beating wildly now, Barbara had to get to the hospital. Janet was in trouble. She could feel it in the voice of the woman on the phone. She could see it in T-bone's eyes. But what about Hannah? She couldn't drive without a car seat.

Lord, I need Your help like I've never needed it. Protect my girl. Keep her safe. And protect Hannah as we drive.

She wrapped the blanket tighter around Hannah and got in her car, holding the child in one arm as she drove to the hospital, praying like she had never prayed before. She didn't know what else to do.

Part 1

THE COACH

CHAPTER 1

✦ ✦ ✦

FEBRUARY 2014

ICSAA CHAMPIONSHIP GAME

Coach John Harrison told his Cougars the game would be a dogfight, and he was right. It was a seesaw, scratch-and-claw battle and both teams played well, making few mistakes and hustling for every loose ball. When the buzzer sounded to end the first half, the Cougars led the Knights by three points. In the locker room, John gathered himself and drew on his playing days. He knew exactly how those boys felt—the adrenaline, the aching muscles, and the drive to win. He wanted it just as bad—maybe more.

"We're going to keep driving to the basket," he said.

"We're going to attack their defense and force them to foul. This is our night. We are going to win this game."

John had decades of playing and coaching experience. He was forty-five but felt twenty-five, and a game like this brought out all the competitive juices. His dark hair had thinned a bit, but other than that and the few extra pounds he carried, he felt in his prime. He was made for games like this, for the challenge of going against a good team with a good coach.

However, in the second half, his confidence waned when the Knights pulled ahead. He regained some hope when his son Ethan hit a three-pointer with eight minutes remaining.

"This is it," John said in the time-out. "We're up by two. We don't take the foot off the gas pedal. Strong passes. Drive to the basket and get a good shot or pick up the foul."

John knew coaching was reminding. In the middle of the battle, players needed to hear a coach's words. Tell them, tell them again, and keep beating the drum. As he spoke, he sensed the momentum swinging their way. The crowd was with them, buoying them, and why wouldn't they be? They were playing in their own gymnasium. The league had made that decision a year ago because of its size and location. The Cougars were taking advantage of their home court.

John grabbed Ethan as the time-out ended. "How you feeling?"

"I'd feel better if we had a bigger lead," Ethan said.

John smiled. On the next play, the Knights broke toward

the basket and a Cougar player sacrificed himself and took the charge. The referee blew the whistle and called a blocking foul on the Cougars. John folded his arms, gave the ref a look, and called the next play.

Momentum is a cruel friend, and it turned on John and his team. With two minutes to go, they were down by eight points. In the huddle on the sideline, John desperately tried to make his team believe again.

"Look at me," John said intensely. "All eyes right here. This is exactly where we were last game with them, chasing them from behind. Remember what happened? They're scared we're gonna do it again."

"Let's do it again, Coach," Ty Jones said.

The team attacked the court with fire in their eyes. Ethan scored quickly, then stole the ball and put it in the basket. With less than a minute left, the score was 84–80. John yelled for full-court pressure and forced the Knights to call their final time-out.

"Come here, come here, come here!" John yelled, pulling his team together, the crowd going wild. The boys gathered around him, sweaty, lungs burning, fatigued. But he saw players hungry for his words. They knew they had a coach who believed in them.

"Okay, listen, they're going to try to hold the ball and run out the clock. You gotta keep the pressure up. Get in their face! When we get the ball back, run a double flex and look for Ethan or Jeff for a three. Then crash the boards. Stay in full-court press till it's over. Cougars on three."

John counted them down and their hands went into the air with a shout of "Cougars!"

John saw it in their faces. He had given them confidence by saying, "*When* we get the ball back . . ." There was no question or doubt in his voice.

The Cougars were built around three players: Ty, Ethan, and Jeff. John joked that they'd played together since they were in diapers. Other teams feared the Ty/Ethan/Jeff juggernaut because they worked with one mind, one heart. An opposing coach called them the "velociraptors" for their ability to coordinate.

John glanced at his wife, Amy, who sat in the stands with their younger son, Will. She'd been to every game this season, cheering him on but cheering twice as loud for Ethan, their older son. She looked his way, and he smiled, knowing she had his back.

Ty intercepted an inbound pass and the ball went to Jeff Baker, who drained a three-pointer. With only seventeen seconds left, the Cougars were in business.

No time to celebrate. John waved and yelled for a full-court press. They needed one more steal and one basket to pull ahead.

Instead of trying to run out the clock, the Knights drove to the basket but missed a layup. Another Knight rebounded and dunked the ball. The Knights went ahead 86–83.

As long as there was time on the clock, there was a chance.

"Ethan!" he yelled.

The ball came to his son. Three seconds left. Ethan dribbled twice, lunging toward half-court.

"Shoot it! Shoot it! Shoot it!"

Ethan launched a high, arcing shot. As the ball descended, the buzzer sounded, but instead of swishing through the net, the ball caromed off the rim and bounced harmlessly away.

The Knights celebrated. Ethan put his hands behind his head and knelt, totally spent. A hush fell over the gym and John looked at the scoreboard. He wanted to sink to his knees like a few of his players. But he couldn't. Instead, he clapped and urged Ethan from the floor as the home crowd chanted, "We are proud of you! We are proud of you!"

John shook hands with the Knights' coach and congratulated him.

"You've got a great team, Harrison," the man reciprocated. "We were lucky tonight."

"Luck didn't have anything to do with it. You fought hard. Good job."

As he walked from the court, he glanced at Amy and Will, locked in a hug, clearly crushed by the loss. They'd been sure this was the year. Instead, John was a runner-up yet again.

John found Ethan outside the locker room and he pulled his son in for a hug. He was almost as tall as John now. When they walked inside, they heard the chatter of defeated boys.

"We had 'em," Jeff said. "The refs gave them that game."

"I got hacked all night and the refs didn't call nothin'," Ty said.

John got their attention and took a deep breath, looking for words he hoped he could believe himself. What was supposed to be a celebration felt like a funeral. He had to help them see something they couldn't.

"All right, everybody, look at me," he began. "I wanted this one, too."

He looked at Ethan, then the others. Joining his voice with that great cloud of past coaches, he said, "I am proud of you."

The boys stared at him, believing. He saw it on their faces. And he knew the next words were not just for them, but also for his own heart.

"And here's the good news. That team is the biggest hurdle we'll face next year. They're graduating four of their starters while all of you are coming back. We'll also be that much stronger. Which means next season we take everything."

His words washed over them. Though devastated by the loss, they nodded and accepted the challenge. He had given them hope in the midst of defeat. Too bad that hope for next season didn't come alongside this year's trophy.

CHAPTER 2

✦ ✦ ✦

Hannah Scott waited in the principal's office at Franklin High School. She'd seen those TV shows where the police left a suspect alone in a room to stew, to think about the crime. When detectives returned and pushed the suspect, the story flew from the lips of the accused. She vowed she wouldn't admit anything. Being left alone helped her think, gave her time to figure out some plausible way to explain. It was like those puzzles she had done when she was little where you trace your way through the maze until you come to the end. But every time Hannah came up with a reason why she had a full envelope of cash in her backpack— money gathered by her Spanish teacher for food and even a piñata for a class party—she hit a solid line. There was no believable explanation.

Hannah closed her eyes and a Spanish word appeared in her mind: *ladrón*. She doubted the teacher would be impressed with her expanding vocabulary.

What would her grandmother say? How would she react? Had they called her at work? Was she on her way? This would send her over the edge. Her grandmother became angry so quickly, fire dancing in her eyes. She never struck Hannah or physically hurt her. She didn't have to. All it took was a word or a look. And those came all too often.

Hannah hated putting her through this. Her grandmother had enough hurt in her life. Hannah needed to find a way out of this herself.

The door opened and the principal walked in, not making eye contact, and right behind him was her Spanish teacher, who did. Hannah didn't know which was worse, the man who looked at the floor or the woman who caught her eyes and held them.

Mrs. Reyes had dark hair and a kind smile and bright-red lipstick. She taught most of the class in Spanish, getting students to repeat what she had said so they could experience the language rather than just read it on a page. She was a good teacher. She seemed to enjoy what she did, even though some students didn't try. Hannah liked having a teacher who was her height. She didn't have to look up. The woman had taken extra time after class, helping Hannah understand assignments. Some of the class seemed to learn the language easily, and Hannah wondered if they had siblings or a parent who helped. She was alone with her questions.

The principal, an older man with skin that hung from his neck in folds, placed his pudgy hands on the desk in front of him like he was about to get a manicure. "Hannah, we've called your grandmother and left a message, but so far—"

"She's at work," Hannah interrupted.

"Yes. We called her cell phone and her work line."

Great, Hannah thought.

Mrs. Reyes sat forward. "There must be a reason why that envelope ended up in your backpack."

Hannah looked at her hands.

"Do you need money for something? If you need help, you can tell us."

Hannah knew opening her mouth would only lead to more trouble. Her grandmother had taught her from early on to always tell the truth because when you lied, you had to remember all the things you'd said to keep the story straight. The truth was a better way to live. But for Hannah, the truth could also lead to a lot of trouble.

"Did you take the envelope from Mrs. Reyes's drawer?"

"No, sir."

That part was true. If she'd taken a lie detector test, she would have passed that question, because the envelope wasn't in Mrs. Reyes's drawer—it was in the side of her purse on the floor behind the desk.

"Hannah, look at me," the principal said.

She sat up straight like her grandmother taught her. There was something in his eyes that made her want to look away, so she concentrated on the crease between his eyes that deepened as he furrowed his brow. Did he always have that or did it come from his years of being a principal? Did it come from dealing with students like her?

"How did the envelope get into your backpack?" he said.

She swallowed hard. Tears came to her eyes and she felt her chin quiver. She hated that. It made her feel . . . what was the word? *Culpable.* It was a word in both Spanish and English that meant "guilty."

"I don't know," she said, bending to reach into her backpack.

"Hannah, Mrs. Reyes left you alone in the room for a few minutes, and when she came back, you were gone and so was the envelope."

"Somebody else took it."

"Hannah, tell the truth," Mrs. Reyes said. "It's better than trying to make something up."

Hannah thought of her grandmother's face and brought her inhaler to her mouth and took a puff. She wasn't doing it for sympathy—she really felt like her lungs were contracting, but that could have been because of her nerves. She'd learned in health class what happened in your brain when feelings and hormones mixed. She didn't understand it, but she felt it.

"Somebody else must have put it in there," Hannah

said, her voice thin. "I don't need money. My grandmother works hard. She . . ."

She trailed off as she heard a voice in the other room. Then came a knock at the door. Her grandmother walked inside and glanced at her.

"What have you done now, baby?"

She said it sweetly, with compassion, but Hannah could see the fire in her grandmother's eyes. She would talk about this for weeks. All the trouble Hannah caused. The last time she was here, the principal had used the word *expulsion* for the next infraction.

She could hear her grandmother's questions.

Where are you going to go to school now? I can't enroll you in some private school. I don't have that kind of money. Do you think it grows on trees? Hannah, what were you thinking?

She closed her eyes and imagined herself with a word tattooed on her forehead. *Ladrón.*

Thief.

CHAPTER 3

✦ ✦ ✦

John Harrison sat in his wife's classroom, playing back the
championship game on his iPad. He'd always been able to
keep stats and totals in his head, his mind a statistical vault,
and this game was no exception. Each missed foul, missed
call, and missed opportunity of his team was a thorn on the
season's rose.

"I thought you told the guys to put that game behind
them," Amy said, a twinkle in her eye. "You said to not
obsess over the loss."

"Easier to say than do. Plus, you have to learn from
your mistakes, right? I'm telling you, next season . . ." He
shook his head and pointed at the screen. "Look at that.
His feet were moving. No way that was a charge."

Amy was John's biggest cheerleader. His success was hers and her successes were his. Sadly, the same went for his failures. In fact, she had taken some losses harder than he had.

Their marriage had always been a for-better-or-worse-no-matter-what union, both of them committed to working out the rough spots whenever they came up. Theirs was the kind of love that said, "If you ever leave, I'm going with you."

He remembered one long night of the soul after they'd been married only a couple of months. Tears and a whole box of tissues and staring at Amy's shoulders shaking. It would have been easier to withdraw and chalk it up to "emotions," but he didn't. He moved toward her, and when she moved away, he didn't give up. Once he finally peeled the onion of her emotions, he realized fear was at the core. She was scared about the future. Something he had said, some offhand comment had put a pinprick in their marital balloon. The clock said 3:12 when he finally found the leak and patched it.

Amy was a words person. She needed to hear things from him, and since that did not come naturally to John, he had to work harder to let her know what he was thinking. He could bark orders to kids on the team all day, but that wasn't communicating when it came to his wife. Every time there was distance between them, words were the bridge, the path that drew their hearts closer.

Today, something wasn't right between them. Was it the loss of the game? Maybe it was something tied in with the hopes they both had for Ethan. They wanted him to attend a good college and get a good job and find a good wife and have a good life. Every parent had hopes and dreams. The next step for Ethan was college, but on two teacher salaries a scholarship was his best hope. That question hung over their family and John wondered if somehow Amy felt he hadn't come through. He should have done more, become more successful, more financially secure.

But that couldn't be it. Amy never counted on money for her happiness or contentment. Still, he felt a little inadequate. If only they had more in the bank, a basketball scholarship lined up for Ethan, things would be better.

Maybe it was a season they were in. They'd been married nineteen years and every marriage went through ups and downs. That was it. The distance, the unsettled feeling was normal. This was their reality. So he needed to go with the flow and stop thinking so much about it.

John stared at the screen. A time-out he should have called one pass sooner, all coulda-shoulda-woulda. It was impossible not to replay the game and see a different outcome.

"See, right there, that is eight calls they missed. And he just walked!"

"You going to show the refs your video?" Amy said with a smirk. She was prepping for an experiment in her next chemistry class.

"I'm thinking about it."

They both groaned, knowing that wasn't true. John wanted to talk about Ethan. What they might be able to do before his senior year to help him—a camp, strength training, anything to make scouts more interested. Before he could bring it up, Keith Wright, head coach of the football team, stepped into the room.

"Hey, John, Amy, you might want to come see this."

The look on Keith's face was unsettling. Was there some disturbance in the hall? Another news story of a school shooting?

"You go," Amy said. "I need to finish this up for fifth period."

"All right, I'll be back."

John followed Keith to the teachers' lounge, where a group of faculty and staff had gathered, grim-faced, staring at a television. A news reporter mentioned Tarsus Steel, the largest employer in Franklin. The company had decided to close the plant, which meant the loss of six thousand jobs.

Immediately John thought of all the men in his church who worked for Tarsus. In a town of twenty-four thousand, the shuttering of the oldest and largest employer in the region would be an economic earthquake.

As the news anchor switched to a live report on-scene, John saw Brookshire's principal, Olivia Brooks, in the corner with her head down, a pained look on her face. The fallout of this would greatly affect the school.

The reporter said families were given the option to

move with the company and that the transition would be completed by July 1.

"Unbelievable," Cynthia Langdon said. She taught English and was a favorite of students. "And we just renovated the school."

Keith turned to John. His voice was low and resigned. "There goes the football program."

"You don't know that," John said.

"John, most of my players have parents who work at the plant." He shook his head and looked back at the screen. "This ain't gonna be pretty."

Keith put a hand on John's shoulder before he left the room. It felt like an omen, a good-bye of sorts. Was he overreacting?

"The news is spreading rapidly throughout the city of Franklin," the reporter said. "Local businesses are also learning of the closure and bracing for what lies ahead."

When the room emptied, John went to Olivia. She was one of those rare administrators whose no-nonsense demeanor combined with deep compassion for students and faculty. Her parents had been teachers and had passed on a desire to help change the world one student at a time.

"What do you make of all this?" John said.

Olivia was near tears. "I've heard rumblings from a friend who's on the school board. I knew the company was considering a move. But you know how rumors go. They've been talking about this for years. I heard they were consolidating—actually thinking about moving workers to Franklin. Instead, we've got this. John, it's going to be devastating."

"Keith agrees. He thinks the football program is toast."

Olivia looked away.

"Olivia, tell me he's overreacting."

"I don't know what to say. You know I'm not gloom and doom. I like to believe the best and see the silver lining. I honestly don't see one."

John returned to Amy's classroom and noticed the iPad on the desk. Suddenly the replay of the game didn't seem quite as important. Funny how a crisis could reorient your world. Amy's jaw dropped when he told her the news.

"What's this mean?" she said.

"Keith thinks the football program is done. Olivia looked like she'd been tackled by a linebacker. I don't think anybody really knows all the fallout. I sure don't."

Amy stared at the experiment she had prepared. The fifth period bell rang and students filled the hallway. John wondered how empty that hallway would seem in the fall.

CHAPTER 4

✦ ✦ ✦

Barbara Scott felt defeated every time she looked at Hannah. She didn't want to, but she did. For weeks she had inquired about getting the girl into a new school, but doors closed. Hannah had a reputation she couldn't shake. Barbara inquired at private schools in the area, but when she heard the cost per semester, she politely thanked them and hung up the phone.

In late July, as the enrollment period was coming to an end, a woman named Shelly Hundley left a message. She said she was in the financial office of Brookshire Christian School and wanted to speak about Hannah. On her break at work, Barbara returned the call.

"Thank you for calling me back, Ms. Scott. I was told you were interested in Hannah attending here?" The woman spoke in crisp tones. She sounded like she had her life together. Not a care in the world.

"I did inquire there, but when I heard the cost, I knew I couldn't make it work. But thank you for—"

"I understand, Ms. Scott. And you're right—Brookshire isn't cheap. But we think our school is worth the investment. There are some great people here who really care about our students."

Barbara couldn't believe the sales pitch. "I'm sure they do, ma'am. But I can't afford it."

"I understand. But there may still be a way," Shelly said quickly, before Barbara could hang up.

"What way is that?"

"Why don't you and Hannah come by the office tomorrow afternoon?"

Barbara wanted to say, *What's the point?* Instead, she said, "I work until six."

"How about in the morning, before you go to work?"

"I work two jobs to make ends meet. I start at five tomorrow morning and I'm not done until six in the evening."

"I see," Shelly said, pausing. "What if we met tomorrow night at seven thirty? That would give you time to get home, have dinner with your granddaughter, and then bring her here."

Barbara shook her head. This woman wasn't giving up. And how did she know Hannah was her granddaughter?

All of that swirled in her brain until Barbara had enough. "Look, I appreciate you offering to stay late, but I don't see a reason to trouble you. Even if you cut the rate in half, I can't afford it."

"Please. Just bring Hannah to the school tomorrow evening. I promise it will be worth the effort."

Barbara reluctantly agreed, though she doubted the woman's words. Everybody had an angle. Everybody was looking for something from somebody and if you trusted them, at best you'd get hurt and at worst you'd have your heart broken. Many times over, as Barbara had learned. What if she took Hannah there and she actually liked this school? Why get the child's hopes up when there was no chance?

But Barbara had exhausted every other option already. And a hopeless possibility was still better than no possibility at all. The next evening, after a quick dinner, Barbara and Hannah headed to Brookshire.

"I don't understand why we're going there if we can't afford it," Hannah said.

"You and me both, baby. Somebody wants you to see the school. And I'm guessing they want you to see it and like it enough to get me to pay. It's not gonna happen. Not in a million years. But at least we can hear the woman out."

Hannah put her earbuds in and Barbara motioned for her to wait. "Don't get too attached to this place. Act coy. Do you know what *coy* is?"

"Not really."

"It means . . . don't get excited. And if you do, don't let her know. Play it cool."

"Okay."

Barbara hated to admit that every time she looked at Hannah, her stomach churned. Every time she saw those deep-brown eyes, she saw her daughter's face. She saw the way Janet had squandered her life. She saw Hannah making bad choices and mistakes that would follow her, maybe for the rest of her life. Hannah was running for something just out of her reach.

The problem, Barbara knew, was that when she looked at Hannah and saw Janet, she also saw herself. Three generations along the very same path, though making very different kinds of mistakes along the way. Life for Barbara had become a nonstop loop where she worked all day and came home to her little house by the bend in the river. She had scraped up the down payment and moved in only to be too tired to enjoy the accomplishment. On so many levels her life was one step forward and one step back down a flight of stairs. Here she was again at the bottom landing trying to pick herself up.

Her marriage had been like that. She'd found a man she thought could make her happy. The outcome wasn't good. At first, the marriage had gone well. Everything *seemed* fine. She called him "honey" and he called her "love." The trouble came when she discovered she wasn't his only love.

Barbara had inklings something wasn't right from their first date. He made her feel warm and cherished and cared for, unlike other men who didn't open car doors or act gentlemanly. But something was off. Something didn't quite fit. It was just a hint of a question mark, a twinge of doubt, that Barbara pushed down. Strangely, the doubt about him became a doubt about herself. Every time she had the feeling that something was off, she kicked herself and heard an accusing voice: *What are you thinking? He's a good man. He'll be a good provider. A real catch. Why are you sabotaging your chance at a good marriage?*

She heard that in her head as she walked the aisle and said, "I do." And she did. She pushed all the questions and doubt away and plunged in.

And then, one summer day five years after the wedding, things fell apart. It happened, strangely enough, with the idea of cleaning her house, top to bottom. While Janet was content in her playpen, Barbara rolled up her sleeves and chose to start with the spare room upstairs. She opened the closet and removed clothes she didn't even know she had. In ten minutes she had her first load ready for Goodwill and felt she was making progress.

She took everything from the shelf above the clothes—photo albums, magazines, a strongbox with birth certificates and important papers, and mementos collected from their honeymoon. With everything clear, she noticed a square piece of wood in the ceiling slightly askew, probably the entry to the attic crawl space. The panel sat funny, revealing a hole, like it had been recently moved. She tried to reach it, but even on tiptoes she couldn't. She carried the crooked, paint-scarred stepladder from the garage, checking on Janet. She climbed the ladder and pushed at the board, but instead of aligning it, she became curious. What was up there? She took another step up and peeked over the edge of the opening.

What Barbara saw sent her life into a spiral. Videos. Magazines. Those were bad enough. What took her breath away were pictures in a plastic bag. She opened them and looked through them. These were not old pictures but recent. As she stared at them, all the doubt she had felt while dating and in the last five years rose like a mushroom cloud. The man she thought she had married, the one who called her "love," was not who she thought he was. He wore a mask. And the pictures showed the face behind it.

Standing on that ladder, seeing the truth, had crushed Barbara. But she also resolved then and there that she would never be taken in by anyone. She would never let someone convince her they were something they weren't. She had learned the hard way you couldn't trust anybody. If you did, they'd let you down.

Now, driving to Brookshire, seeing Hannah in her peripheral vision, she felt like she was on some rickety ladder. She had gone through unimaginable hurt and pain with Janet, who sneaked around with T-bone, who lied about where she was going and what she was doing. All she had left of her daughter was a photo album and a gravestone.

The summer sun was still up when they arrived at Brookshire. The school grounds were immaculately trimmed.

"Sure looks different than Franklin High," Hannah said.

Shelly met them at the front door and insisted on giving a guided tour. They walked through the halls and into the gymnasium. She showed them the track and other athletic fields. Sports seemed to be a big deal, though the recent closing of the steel plant had caused a diaspora.

That's it, Barbara thought. *Enrollment is down and the school is desperate to get new students.*

Shelly took them to a beautiful library, a media center, the cafeteria, and an auditorium that looked amazing. Barbara wanted the tour to stop, but she followed the woman through the halls. After a half hour, Shelly led them to her office. The room was furnished nicely but wasn't over-the-top.

"So what did you think, Hannah?" Shelly said, smiling and folding her hands on her desk.

Hannah glanced at Barbara, then back at the woman. "It's nice."

"How would you like to go to school here?"

Barbara leaned forward. "Ma'am, I told you there is no way I can afford—"

Shelly raised a hand and opened a folder on the desk. "There's a friend of the school who heard of Hannah's situation and wanted to help."

"Friend?" Barbara said. "Who?"

"A person who wishes to remain anonymous," Shelly said. "Hannah's tuition has been paid. For the entire year."

"What?" Hannah said, glancing at Barbara with eyes as wide as saucers. She put a hand over her mouth as she stared at her grandmother.

Barbara's jaw dropped, too. Tears came to her eyes. *Who would do such a thing?*

"I don't know what to say," Barbara finally said.

Shelly looked at the folder. "Now, there is the situation of the expulsions at the former schools. There's a code of conduct we ask our students and their parents or guardians to sign. You'll see the dress code, as well. I have a welcome packet that explains all of that. So if you agree, you simply sign the forms and return them."

"We can sign that now," Barbara said quickly.

Shelly smiled. "It's another month before school starts. Take the packet, read it carefully so you know the rules and what's acceptable and not acceptable."

"I can assure you Hannah will abide by all the rules," Barbara said. "That trouble she had, that's over and done with. Right, Hannah?"

"Yes, ma'am," Hannah said, her voice a little too soft for Barbara's liking.

"We are grateful for this opportunity, Ms. Hundley. And you can trust that Hannah will be on her best behavior."

Shelly looked at Hannah. "I think you're going to find the teachers and staff here warm and welcoming. The

students all want to learn. We have a great athletic program, though to be honest, we're not sure which sports will
be available in the fall. What are your interests outside of
the classroom?"

Hannah seemed confused by the question.

"She ran track last year," Barbara said.

"Cross-country," Hannah said, correcting her.

Shelly nodded. "That's great. You should go out for the
team."

As they left, Barbara paused in front of the school and
studied the list of names on a plaque. That's when it came
together. That's when she realized what had happened.

In the car, Hannah stared out the windshield, dumb-
founded. "Did that really happen?"

"I can hardly believe it myself, but it really did, baby."

"I wonder who gave the scholarship."

Barbara swallowed hard and stared at the road. "That's
not important. What is important is for you to study hard,
work hard, and avoid any of the trouble you got into at
Franklin High. You understand me?"

"Yes, ma'am."

Barbara drove toward home and a memory jumped out
of nowhere. She and her daughter would celebrate when
something positive happened. If Barbara got a raise or
if Janet got a good grade on a test or a part in the school
play, Janet would pull out the same song and play it over
and over. At home, she turned up the speakers and danced
around the house. The memory made Barbara smile.

Instead of turning left as they neared their house, she took a right.

"Where are you going?" Hannah said.

"'Celebrate good times, come on,'" Barbara sang, dipping her head and snapping her fingers.

"What are you talking about?"

"It's something your mother used to sing. Anything good happened and she'd play that song and dance. And we'd go to Anna Banana for ice cream."

Hannah smiled and seemed to enjoy the sight of her grandmother singing and dancing behind the wheel. Barbara thought it was a breakthrough. Things were beginning to turn around.

CHAPTER 5

✦ ✦ ✦

After a long day of prep and planning at school, John stopped at a bakery and bought a dozen cinnamon rolls, a store specialty. Tonight was their first small group study since summer break and he was looking forward to connecting with people they had met with for five years.

Ethan and Will shot baskets in the driveway until John asked for help straightening the house for company. The boys obliged. Amy was busy with dinner, though she had spent the day planning for the start of the school year as well. John felt like they were in constant motion, from one event to the next. Life was a treadmill and their lives were little boxes on a calendar filled in by someone else—duties as assigned. Once school started, the treadmill would accelerate. This weekly gathering had become an oasis, a chance to connect with others and step away from the rat race, if only for a couple of hours.

The group had morphed over the years but now they were five couples and Larry, which sounded like a musical group from the 1960s. Larry was single and took care of his aging mother. He'd been in the military and something had happened between basic training and a deployment. Most nights he kept quiet, unless someone asked his opinion. Amy said Larry was deep water.

Tough times in the group forced their roots deeper and drew them closer. A cancer diagnosis was thankfully caught early, and a couple going through infertility brought news of a pregnancy, then a miscarriage. Instead of creating distance and isolation, the highs and lows bonded them in a way John couldn't explain or fully understand. God had used the broken places to help them grow.

By the time John showered and came downstairs, Bill and Peggy Henderson had arrived. Bill and Peggy were anchors in the group and the church. Bill and their pastor, Mark Latimer, visited the hospital and nursing homes together. He worked for a concrete company, doing mostly flat work for new construction. He'd poured the concrete for John and Amy's driveway. The two sat in the kitchen, not touching the cinnamon rolls. That was a clue something was wrong. Nobody said no to those rolls.

"I thought we could survive with repair jobs and such,

but the owner told me today he's closing," Bill said. "New construction's dead. It'll be a long time before it picks up, if it ever does. He's taking the business out of state."

"Feels early to close shop, doesn't it?" John said. "Things could turn around."

Bill rubbed his rough hands. "Seems drastic, but I understand the decision. It's bad, John."

"What will you do?" Amy said, putting a hand on Peggy's shoulder.

"We're not sure," Peggy said. "I'm trying to stay strong. You know, trusting God in the dark. I'm just not there yet."

Bill stared at his coffee. "We wanted you to know before we got started tonight. We have some hard decisions to make."

"When one hurts, we all hurt," John said.

There were tears and a lot of prayer that night. People shared their fears. Larry read something from a journal he'd kept, prayers they had prayed in the group a few months earlier. Prayers they had forgotten, some they hadn't even noticed God had answered. Amy was right about the deep water.

It was John's nature to fix things, but he was learning to hold back. It was enough to hear the pain and struggle of his friends and simply listen to the doubts and disappointments. He also held back from sharing his own questions and fears. And he could feel them floating, right under the surface of his life.

CHAPTER 6

✦ ✦ ✦

Hannah was equally nervous and excited about Brookshire. She welcomed a fresh start at a place where other students knew nothing about her past. Her grandmother kept talking about what a great opportunity Hannah had with a "clean slate." A fresh start, like the new clothes she'd been given to start the year.

Her grandmother's expectations made her nervous. What if she messed up this opportunity? And how would the other students treat her? After all, it was a Christian school and they would expect her to obey all the rules. She assumed the school would have people who watched you like a hawk to see if you were doing anything wrong.

Hannah considered herself a Christian, of course. Her grandmother had taken her to church and she'd gone to Sunday school classes. She had even occasionally tried to pay attention to sermons, even when they went on and on and she nodded off. These days, her grandmother worked so hard all week that by Sunday she was exhausted. It was easier for both of them to stay in a warm bed on Sunday mornings.

Hannah finished her day at the Y and headed home. She'd picked out her favorite shirt that morning, the one that said, *Hello Weekend*. There was something about wearing a shirt you liked that made the day seem more bearable. The *Hello Weekend* shirt was like putting on short-sleeved hope.

Instead of heading straight home, Hannah walked toward Webb Park. It was a peaceful place with playgrounds and fields surrounded by woods. There was a bench by a little pond where geese landed and honked and she liked to imagine them having conversations. Even geese seemed to have one bird who was on the outside, a misfit. Hannah wished she could be a bird and reach out and make friends. Maybe give it a bit of hope.

She sat on the bench a few minutes, listening to kids on the swings, the *squeak-squeak* of metal on metal, the back and forth, legs pumping, striving to go higher. When the geese didn't come, she headed toward a knoll that led to the apartments near her house. She would cut through there to get home.

There were people at the tennis courts and bikes

propped against fences, and nearby some guys played three-on-three basketball, celebrating each shot made, each pass intercepted. It was the sound of summer ending on every court in the country where kids dreamed of being special. She looked for the boy who seemed like he didn't belong. There was usually one who didn't quite fit, slower or shorter or without the same hand-eye coordination. A kid who didn't have the swagger, the mojo. But the six seemed evenly matched. The tall ones hung around the basket. The shorter ones dribbled low and cut toward the lane and then passed to the open player.

Hannah listened as she walked between the basketball court and baseball field. Passing the court sideline, she noticed a bench with a red boom box on it. There were a couple of skateboards, a water bottle, orphan backpacks strewn like trash, and a pair of headphones.

She stopped.

Nice headphones. Expensive. Name-brand. She had earbuds that worked fine. She didn't need the headphones. But it wasn't about what she needed.

She glanced at the boys, who were so engaged with the game, concentrating so hard on defense or making a strong pass, that they didn't notice her. Focused like a laser. In that moment, in that split second, something clicked inside.

As one player made an easy layup and the ball was taken out at half-court, Hannah stepped toward the bench and with one swift movement took the headphones and walked away. Her heart beat fast. She expected someone to yell,

"Hey, those are mine!" All she heard was the bounce of the ball and the shoes on the court and guys yelling at each other.

She folded the headphones, slipped them into her backpack, and quickened her pace toward the woods. The clapping and banter subsided. Then there was an uncomfortable lull, like the calm before a storm. She kept her head down, walking resolutely toward the trees.

Don't look back.

The lull continued.

Don't look back.

She couldn't help it.

She looked back.

Headphone Guy stared at her. He knew. And she knew there was one thing to do. Run for home.

She sprinted. The guys yelled behind her. Angling right, she skirted the baseball fence and made for a path through the woods. In the open field she probably had no chance of escape. But if she got on uneven ground, using the trees to hide her, she had a chance. Her heart beat furiously as she reached the trees.

Don't look back.

She knew turning her head would slow her down, but she had to know how close they were.

They were too close.

She hit the dirt path and her speed kicked in. The backpack felt like it weighed a hundred pounds, bouncing behind her, but she kept going, one foot in front of the other.

Zigzagging through the trees, she heard the lead guy yell something about "dead." Whatever he said, it didn't matter. She couldn't let them catch her.

Down a hill, around a turn that blocked her from sight for a moment, she considered getting the headphones out and dropping them. But she figured even if the guys happened to spot them, they would keep chasing her.

Footsteps behind her. The lead guy yelling something.

If she could make it to the apartments, she could hide behind a Dumpster or crawl under a car, but they were too close. She heard their shoes slapping the earth.

And then she heard something else. Her breathing. The tightness in her lungs. The dry wheeze of an asthma attack.

Her vision blurred. She panicked. It felt like the walls of her lungs were collapsing and there was nothing she could do to stop them.

At the edge of the woods was a boulder and she fell behind it and sat there, trying not to gasp, trying to even her breathing and calm her heart. She found her inhaler and pulled it out just as the guys stopped no more than ten feet behind her. A few more steps and she'd be found.

"Did you see her?" one said, out of breath.

"No."

She waited. *Don't come any closer,* she thought. It was a prayer of sorts.

If they came around the edge of the rock, her life was over.

She had her inhaler in hand, but if she used it, they'd hear her. If she didn't use it, she might collapse. Black out.

She felt herself slipping. She couldn't wait. She put the inhaler to her lips and gave one pump. Relief came over her. The tightness relaxed a little.

"Listen," one guy said.

She tried to keep still. No movement. Just lean against the rock and hope.

"I bet she ran into those apartments."

"Who was she?"

"I don't know. But if I see her again, she's gonna pay!"

Headphone Guy yelled it like he meant it. They retreated, and she put her head back, breathing deeply now. She had to wait for them to get out of sight, and then she would wait some more.

When she was sure they were gone, she stood and ran down the hill, between the apartment buildings and onto the sidewalk, not looking back, headed home like an arrow.

She was never more happy to see that little house. She opened the front door, stepped in, closed it, and for the first time since she'd picked up the headphones felt she could relax. She sighed, finally safe.

"Baby, where have you been?" her grandmother said with an edge to her voice. "I thought the Y closed at four."

Hannah tried not to react, not to jump out of her skin at her grandmother's voice.

She took off her backpack and told her grandmother she had gone to Webb Park and her grandmother asked why. Hannah shrugged. Why did she go through the park? Seemed like a good idea. But she didn't say that because she knew how her grandmother would react.

Next came the look. And when your grandmother looks at you that way, the way she's looked a thousand times before, you know something bad is on its way. She held something up and with a voice that sounded like she had practiced all day she said, "Where did this come from? I found it in your jeans pocket."

Hannah stared at an iPod. She had meant to hide it in the box in her nightstand. She'd forgotten that detail. She knew she had to say something, so she grabbed the first idea.

"I found it."

Of course this was true: she had found the iPod, but she found it lying on a girl's purse in the locker room at the Y.

"Hannah Scott, don't you lie to me. I already bought you one of these." There was guilt in her words, with a bit of shame and anger mixed in like yeast to rise with a high temperature. She handed it to Hannah. "Take it back."

Hannah took the iPod and for an instant saw herself going to the Y and slipping it into the lost-and-found bin, under someone's hoodie or in some gloves left from the previous winter.

"I'm already late for work," her grandmother said, grabbing her purse. "Your dinner's on the stove. I'll be home by ten."

When she reached the back door, she turned. "Hannah, I mean it. Take it back."

"Yes, Grandma."

Hannah put on her backpack, grabbed her fried egg and cheese sandwich and chips and something to drink, and retreated to her room. It was a small space with paneled walls, but it was her haven, a place to shut out the conflict and struggle and people running after her. The wall behind her bed was filled with photos and cards and clippings from magazines. The images made her smile. Musicians and runners. A cuddly panda. And a horse. She didn't remember why she had chosen all those pictures, but now they kept her company on the wall, and when she saw them, they made her happy.

She sat on the bed and pulled out the headphones, then opened the drawer in her nightstand and removed the old shirt hiding the blue box. Inside were her treasures, things she had "found." A pair of sunglasses, a watch, bracelets, a camera. The box excited her and brought a wave of guilt. These headphones weren't hers, but they were now. She hated herself for taking these things. She didn't need the headphones—she had her earbuds and another pair at the bottom of the box she didn't use. So why did she take them?

The new headphones fit neatly inside. She put on the lid and covered the box with her shirt and closed the drawer. Hidden away.

On her nightstand was a small TV she'd gotten for Christmas the year before and underneath it was a magazine ad she'd saved. She didn't pin it to her wall because it didn't fit with the other pictures. It didn't make her feel the same way they did. There was something about the man in the ad, the way he smiled, the way he held the hands of the little girl on his shoulders.

The ad said, *Create Lifelong Memories*. She studied the girl's smile. It looked like she could launch from her perch on her father's shoulders, just fly off in any direction, and that made Hannah warm inside.

Maybe that's why Hannah didn't have the picture on her wall. It gave her a warm feeling but also reminded her of what she didn't have. No, what she couldn't have. There was hope for becoming a better athlete or owning a horse or looking pretty. But there was no hope for having a mother or father. That dream was dead. Both her parents were phantoms. She remembered neither of them. She had only a handful of pictures and the few words her grandmother gave. And her grandmother never spoke of her father.

She folded the page and took a bite of her sandwich. Her grandmother knew exactly how to get it crispy but not burned on the outside. How did she do that? When Hannah tried, the bread smoked and turned black. Probably the temperature of the pan or not enough butter.

When she finished, she went to the kitchen and washed and dried her dishes. That would make her grandmother happy. It was still light outside. Her grandmother didn't like her going out alone in the evening, but what could be wrong with a quick run?

She changed into her running shorts, laced up her shoes, and went to the front porch to stretch. That was one thing her coach at Franklin High had drilled into her, always stretch before a workout. She had taken that advice and hadn't injured herself like other runners.

She hopped down from the front porch and heard voices up the street. Teenage boys. She thought she recognized one of them. She couldn't make out exactly what they were saying, but one guy sounded super angry.

And then she realized it sounded like Headphone Guy. They were a few houses away. She jumped up, darted inside, and closed the door, standing behind it, hoping they hadn't seen her. Were they canvassing the neighborhood? Had they called the police? Fear coursed through her. She listened as they walked past, then peeked out the window, catching a glimpse of them. Were those the guys from the basketball game? It didn't matter. There was no way she was going for a run.

CHAPTER 7

✦ ✦ ✦

In John Harrison's mind there was no problem, no struggle, no amount of distance between him and his sons that couldn't be overcome by a game of H-O-R-S-E. Focusing on something together, even a competition, helped open conversations.

He waited as long as he could for Ethan, then began a game with Will. Will was into the bounce-it-off-the-backboard, kick-it-high, catch-it-in-the-air-and-shoot-it approach. John chuckled as his son seemed to make up each shot as he went along.

Amy called out the window and told them dinner was ready. John looked for Ethan's Jeep. He worked part-time at Race2Escape, an escape room that recently opened in town.

At the table, Will picked up a hot roll and dropped it on his plate as Ethan walked in with a worried look. "Dad, did you hear Coach Wright is moving to Fairview?"

It was more of an accusation than a question and John calmly buttered a roll. "Well, he went from thirty-two players to thirteen, so I think he saw the writing on the wall."

Ethan spoke up, his voice tight. "So no football on Friday nights."

John sighed. He was just as frustrated with the end of the football program as Ethan. "You know most of those boys will play baseball or soccer in the spring. They'll be fine."

Amy sat. "Well, they could run cross-country. Gary would love that."

"Whatever," John said, unable to hold back his disdain for cross-country.

"Hey, what about our team?" Will said, referring to Brookshire basketball.

"We're in good shape," John said. "There's your brother, Ty, and the twins, so we've still got our best players."

Ethan sat, still fuming about the football program.

Amy turned to Ethan. "How was work?"

"It was fine. We had two groups come in but neither of them escaped."

"Because the rooms are too hard," Amy said.

Ethan nodded and stared at John. His voice was softer,

more gentle when he said, "Do you know how many students we'll have?"

"I think about 240." He said it quickly, almost convincing himself it was a good number. Then he let out some of the disappointment. "We had 550 last year."

Amy shook her head. "Don't say that. That makes me so sad."

John reached out and the four of them joined hands. "Well, I think we'll be fine as long as no one else leaves."

As he bowed his head, Ethan said, "Then you haven't heard about the Hendersons."

"What happened?" Amy said.

"Ty said there's a For Sale sign outside their house. Went up yesterday."

John rubbed his forehead. "That's a big blow to the church. Bill does so much."

"Did," Ethan said, correcting him.

John nodded and bowed again, praying for the Hendersons and all they were going through. In a way, he felt like he was praying for himself, too.

A week before school started, John walked into Olivia Brooks's office. She had that no-nonsense demeanor as he sat. She had asked to meet with him and he could tell there was more bad news. A cut in salaries? Layoffs? Another sport cut from the school? He took a deep breath and prepared for the worst.

The first news was that he would be picking up a civics

class left by a vacancy. That wasn't so bad. But who had taught that class last year? He couldn't remember.

"John, I think our kids deserve a chance at as many sports as we can offer."

"I agree."

"And I don't want to end any programs I don't have to."

"You're preaching to the choir, Olivia. What's going on?"

She plopped a folder on her desk. "Gary is leaving."

That was it. Gary taught civics. And he coached the cross-country program. Though John had doubts about the sport, John respected him and his knowledge about endurance running and getting the best from his team.

"Why is Gary leaving?"

"He took a job in Texas. So now I'm down three coaches and two teachers and school starts next week. At this point, I don't think I can save football, but I do think I have a solution for cross-country."

"Who?"

Olivia put her hands on the desk in front of her and gave him a look that said it all. And she didn't blink.

The look finally broke through and he realized what she was asking. "Olivia, no!" As he said it, he couldn't believe how much like his boys he sounded when he or Amy asked them to do some undesirable chore.

"I believe you could do it," Olivia said confidently.

"I'm not a cross-country coach. I hate running. Amy bought me a treadmill three years ago." He paused. "Never use it."

Olivia wasn't having it. She softened her voice and leaned forward. John thought she probably learned this tactic at some persuasion seminar for principals.

"I don't want to have to cancel another program. You are my best option."

Something stirred inside. What was it? A sense of injustice at what had happened? School enrollment had been cut in half. Football was toast. Who knew if basketball or any other sport would survive.

Instead of playing defense, John went on the attack. "Cross-country's not even a real sport."

"That's not fair. Come on, now. I've never seen your basketball players throwing up after a game."

"Exactly," John said. "I don't want to see that. Nobody wants to see that."

He thought she would smile. She didn't. So he went for the coup de grâce. "And cross-country overlaps with basketball, so . . ." Three-pointer. Swish.

"Not by much," Olivia said. "John, I have heard you give some very inspirational speeches to your players. About stepping up under pressure and going the extra mile. That is exactly what I need from our staff right now."

As she spoke, John couldn't believe he was in this position. He rolled his eyes. He did anything but look at her. She was using his own words, his own locker room speeches against him. He wanted to blow the whistle or toss a yellow flag onto her desk. She sounded so convinced, like she'd made up her mind decades before he walked into the room.

"Did I mention that you're my best option?" she said with resolve.

John looked out the window. He didn't know the first thing about cross-country. But then what was there to know? Just show the kids the route and blow a whistle. What a waste of his time and energy.

"What do you say?" Olivia said.

He shook his head. "All right. It looks like I don't have any other option. I'll do it."

"Good." She told him who to contact in order to get the schedule set, plus information about uniforms, waivers, and other material he would need. He couldn't listen. He didn't want to deal with schedules and skinny kids with shin splints. He held it together until he walked out of the office. He wanted to scream and yell. Instead, he walked into the hall and flailed his fists in exasperation. When he finished, he turned to see Jimmy Meeder, the janitor, staring at him.

John composed himself and walked past the man as quickly as he could, saying hello.

That night John told Amy and the boys to get in the car. They were going to make something good happen for a change. But when they pulled up to the Sac-O-Sushi restaurant, there was a For Lease sign on the front door. Could things get any worse?

CHAPTER 8

✦ ✦ ✦

Hannah walked onto the well-kept campus on her first day at Brookshire not knowing a single student. She kept looking for a face she'd recognize from the Y or perhaps someone who had attended one of her former schools. That brought up a worse fear than loneliness—someone who knew her past. Shelly, from the financial office, was the only person at Brookshire she knew by name. And that made Hannah wonder who had given her a scholarship. Why had she been chosen? It still felt hard to believe.

Her grandmother's shift at the restaurant started early. The campus was only a mile from her house, but her grandmother wouldn't hear of her walking on the first day, so Hannah arrived an hour before the opening bell. She sat outside the entrance waiting for students and teachers.

She hadn't slept the night before, tossing and turning, nervous about just how much she'd stand out from the other kids at Brookshire. Her grandmother said not to worry, that everything would be fine and she would make friends. Easy for her to say. Hannah didn't make friends easily. She wasn't sure why. Life just felt less complicated that way.

Her grandmother had given her a talk about her "problem." She reminded Hannah of the pledge she signed and of the consequences of any infractions, wagging a finger, looking at her as if she had stolen a school bus and had it in her back pocket.

"Yes, Grandma," was her ready answer to everything. She said it in her sleep. Even though her grandmother didn't know about her blue box, it felt like she was expecting Hannah to fail, and that expectation pressed on her like a hundred-pound weight.

Hannah was quiet, some would say timid, but she was always thinking, always swirling something inside. Her grandmother seemed to understand this and expect the worst possible thing. And her grandmother was usually right—Hannah felt she probably would do something wrong. In reality, Hannah saw herself as a bad girl. She didn't make wrong choices or do bad things—*she was bad*. She was a walking mistake, with a mother and a father who loved drugs more than her. They loved them so much they had died taking them, and that made Hannah feel hollow inside. She carried that truth in her life's backpack and stowed it in the blue box of her heart. There was no escaping that truth. And when she looked in the mirror, she saw someone who might make the same kind of mistakes they had made. That same realization was reflected on her grandmother's face each day. Disappointment. Frustration. Life was a series of letdowns for her grandmother, and Hannah was the biggest of all.

She sat on a bench beside the flagpole, the Stars and Stripes flapping in a slight breeze above. Students arrived by bus. Others either drove their own cars or were dropped off by parents. And most of their cars were nice and shiny, not like her grandmother's. Hers was old and square and boxy, which was at least one good thing about being dropped off an hour early. She loved her grandmother, but she didn't want to be seen in an old car driven by an older woman. Was that normal?

Moms dropped daughters, dads dropped sons, and there were even cars where both mom and dad let kids out. How did they get so lucky? Students bounded out of cars and streamed toward the school with confidence. They acted as if something good was about to happen. Even the way they walked showed they belonged and had confidence about what was on the other side of those doors.

Hannah had none of those feelings. Still, the fact that she was at Brookshire meant something. Someone had paid a lot of money to allow her to attend.

"Baby, do you see what they're giving you?" her grandmother had said, pointing a finger at a form with her signature. "Now don't you squander that. You squeeze all the learning you can out of what you're being given. You hear?"

"Yes, Grandma."

Hannah pulled out her class schedule. She tried to memorize teachers' names and room numbers and she had drawn a map on the back of the page. She'd gone over it so many times the paper was wrinkled and worn and she clutched it as she walked inside before the opening bell.

She wondered how different Brookshire would be from Franklin High. When some kids at her public school talked about Brookshire, they rolled their eyes. Christians, to them, were people who made rules they could keep so they could look down on others. They thought they had halos around their heads because they didn't curse or smoke or whatever it was they didn't do. No, she wouldn't fit in at Brookshire. She didn't belong.

Hannah compared her backpack with everyone else's. She compared her clothes, her shoes, her hair. She walked close to the wall as if looking for a safe room if she needed to retreat.

A scrawny-looking kid in front of her stuck out his foot and tripped a boy who wasn't paying attention and the kid fell flat on his face. The scrawny kid laughed and the boy beside him joined in.

"Freshmen are losers," the bully said.

Hannah helped the boy up and asked if he was okay. He adjusted his glasses and brushed off his shirt.

"Stop it, Robert!" someone said behind her. It was a tall boy who looked like an athlete.

Robert and his friend scurried away like night bugs when a light shines. The athlete shook his head as he watched the two hurry away, laughing.

Glasses Boy looked at Hannah. "Thanks."

Someone spoke on the intercom and directed students to the gymnasium. Hannah turned toward the wrong end of the school, then retreated and joined the stream of students that flowed to the gym and onto the bleachers. Her heart beating wildly, she sat in the first open row she found and settled, taking off her backpack. A big sigh. Now she could relax. Then she realized she was sitting in the section marked for seniors. She saw the *SOPHOMORE* sign and had to walk across the gym floor and climb over people to get a seat. One of them was the scrawny kid, Robert.

"Look who has no idea where to sit," he said, rolling his eyes.

Hannah tried ignoring him, but she felt her face get warm. The principal called them to order and the gymnasium quieted.

Mrs. Olivia Brooks welcomed students to a new school year. She was a stately African American woman with a bright smile. She stood tall and scanned the faces on both sides of the gym, holding the microphone perfectly so people could hear her clear, crisp voice. Hannah thought it would be a dream come true to have the confidence to speak that way.

"Let's welcome our freshmen to Brookshire," she said, and a roar rose from the students. Seniors on the opposite bleachers actually stood. It was strange because at Franklin High the freshmen were treated like gum on the bottom of shoes. Was it an act? She'd already seen one freshman get picked on, and the school day hadn't even started. With each class the noise crescendoed and Hannah began to believe there was something different here. And it appeared the support started at the top.

Mrs. Brooks recognized teachers and staff. She then introduced a man she said was "the most important person at the school." Hannah scanned the stage, but it wasn't a head coach or an administrator. Instead, she had a bearded man in a gray uniform step forward.

"This is our head custodian, Jimmy Meeder, who keeps this school shining every day. And I want you to help him and his staff by doing your part to keep it that way."

"Jimmy! Jimmy! Jimmy!" the seniors chanted, and the rest of the students picked up the cheer. The man remained stone-faced, nodding toward the seniors, then took his place by a rolling trash can by the wall.

"Now, to all our new students this year," she continued, "I want you to know you are welcome here. If you have questions or can't find a room, ask someone. Come to the front office. We're here to help each other, especially as you get started. We want this to be the best year in our school's history."

The applause was a bit quieter. Mrs. Brooks paused, then continued in measured tones.

"As you know, our town is going through a tough time. Last year, we had to place chairs on the gym floor to fit everyone. Many of our friends have moved and we're going to miss them. Because of this, we've had to cut some extracurricular activities and sports."

Students groaned, especially the juniors and seniors.

"Here's our commitment to you: We will pull together and do everything with excellence so that you will receive the best education possible. And you will do the same. If your sport was cut, we'll help you find another one so you can join a team and make a difference. Whatever you do, work at it with all your heart. Music, sports, and yes, homework—whatever you do, give it everything you have and let's see what can happen. Okay?"

Hannah felt something inside. There was excitement in the room about the new year and even though circumstances weren't the best, Mrs. Brooks exuded hope that leaked and trickled down on everyone like dew on the morning grass.

When they were dismissed for first period, Hannah stood and put on her backpack and reached for her class schedule. She'd been holding it tightly but now it was gone. She sat and looked underneath the bleachers. The gym emptied and she felt tightness in her lungs.

See, you always do something stupid, she thought.

She ran to the senior section where she first sat. Her schedule wasn't there. She tried to stay calm. She had memorized that page and those classroom numbers, but for the life of her she couldn't remember her first class.

The teachers were gone. Jimmy, the janitor, was gone. The last students trickled through the doors and she was alone. Everyone knew where they were going. Everyone was in their place and walking confidently. Only Hannah was late.

Mrs. Brooks said to come to the office if anyone needed help. But Hannah couldn't do that. Asking for help meant you were weak. She had to figure this out herself. And just like that, she remembered. Geometry. Mr. Bailey. Room 219.

She hurried to the stairwell, found the room numbers above each door, and scooted into 219 just as a balding man was closing it. "Got in under the wire," he said, smiling.

The seats in the back were taken. She walked all the way across the room and sat in an empty chair by the window. Mr. Bailey read the list of names on the sheet with each student raising a hand. He looked up after each name to make eye contact, then wrote something down.

"Gillian Sanders," he said.

A redheaded girl behind her said, "Here," in a squeaky voice.

"Rory Simpson," he said.

Something felt off. Had he missed her name on the list? She panicked.

"Rachel Thompson," he said.

Hannah's heart sank. Then her brain kicked in and she remembered. Geometry was her second period class. She was terribly late for first period. She grabbed her backpack and walked toward the door.

"Is something wrong?" Mr. Bailey said.

"I'm sorry," she said. "Wrong room."

Before the man could say anything, she was in the hall, trying to get her heart to stop beating like a marching band. Where should she go? She felt so embarrassed, like such a loser. All she had to do was find the right rooms, just hang on to the schedule, but she had dropped her compass and here she was without direction. And the more she tried to remember where she was supposed to be, the more the walls closed in.

The door to Mr. Bailey's class opened and she darted into the bathroom. She found the first empty stall and locked it. She stood there, a feeling washing over her. She remembered the playground when she was three or four, her grandmother telling her it was okay to climb the stairs to the slide, and Hannah looking back at her grandmother on the bench urging her forward.

Hannah got in line with the others and used the rails along the narrow steps to climb higher than she had ever been on her own. And when the kid in front of her sat and took the plunge, it was her turn, and Hannah made the mistake of looking at the ground. It was scary high. The slide looked steeper from here. Her breath became short and she held on to the rails.

"Hurry up!"

"Just go, will you!"

She couldn't close her eyes and slide down that smooth, silvery surface. Her grandmother said something. Then Grandma was at the bottom of the slide looking up at her. "It's all right, baby. You'll be fine."

Hannah gasped. Something inside wouldn't let her move. But no one could see the struggle—they only saw how she was in their way. She turned and nervously walked down, navigating the narrow steps meant for one person at a time.

When she made it to the ground, her grandmother took her hand, told her it was all right, that everybody got scared. But Hannah didn't feel all right. Hannah felt like she was the only one. Everyone else laughed, slid, reached the end, and scurried to get in line again. What was wrong with her?

She took off her backpack in the stall and hung it on a hook. She didn't come out until the bell rang for second period.

CHAPTER 9

✦ ✦ ✦

John Harrison put a notice on every bulletin board in the school about cross-country tryouts. In each of his classes he made the same announcement, but the response was tepid.

He wrote his name on the chalkboard and called roll for his American history class. He loved teaching history because he believed those who didn't remember it were condemned to repeat it, like the famous writer said. His son Ethan had changed the quote slightly to say, "Those who don't remember history are condemned to a makeup test."

John stifled a wince at the empty seats and remembered the words of Olivia Brooks. He chose to see the class half-full rather than half-empty. Still, there was pain for him and pain for the students who were sitting among empty chairs vacated by friends.

He invited each student to say a little about themselves. It was hard for some, easy for others. Near the end of the class he handed out a syllabus and information about how their grades would be determined. He encouraged students to keep up with their daily reading, which was pivotal to learning history.

He checked his watch. "Before we dismiss, I just want to let you know that tryouts for guys and girls cross-country are tomorrow afternoon. So if you're interested, come on out. And I would appreciate it if you would help me pass the word."

Only one student looked at him.

"Why are they making you coach that?"

The question sounded like an indictment. John faced his son Ethan, who spoke with a scowl. John could have made a joke or ignored it, but he felt his son had provided an opportunity.

"That's the wrong question, Ethan. Most of the faculty are taking on extra responsibilities for the time being." He glanced at the rest of the class who sat silently watching the family conflict. "Look, if we're going to keep moving forward, we have to stop thinking about negative things. Okay?"

His words sounded hollow, even to himself. The truth was, he had the same feeling as Ethan, he just didn't want to admit it. And the question had stirred something inside him. There was so much he had taken for granted in the town and school. Before the bell rang, he assigned a chapter on the Great Depression, which felt more than ironic, and after the bell he motioned for Ethan to stay.

John had been trying to figure out how to gently prod his son to go out for cross-country. Ethan was a leader and if he showed up, others would follow. Of course, Ethan would need to step aside when basketball season started, but just him being there on the first day of tryouts would be a shot in the arm for the program. From the time Ethan was old enough to bounce a ball, John had tried hard to not pressure him, whether in sports, academics, church, or anything he wanted to do. As a player and a coach John had seen overbearing dads force their kids into situations that were clearly more about the dad than the child. John wanted his sons to do their best, but he never wanted his expectations to burden them. He didn't want to exploit Ethan to bolster the cross-country team, but this wasn't a matter of using anyone—he was encouraging Ethan to lead.

The room emptied and John sat on a desk and faced his son. He tried to keep the edge from his voice as he asked why Ethan had questioned him during class.

"I'm sorry. I just think it's a joke you have to keep the cross-country program alive. Nobody cares."

That hit another nerve. He measured his response. "Okay, it's been assigned to me, so I have to figure it out until somebody else can take it. But don't shoot it down while I'm trying to build it up."

Ethan thought a moment and stared at John. Finally he said, "Please don't ask me to try out."

His son's honesty and the look on his face was like a rug being pulled out from under John. He tried not to show his frustration, but he could tell by Ethan's response and the way he trudged toward the hallway that he had failed.

This year was going to be a struggle on a lot of levels. What would FDR do?

The next day, John made his way past the buses and down the concrete stairs to the field for tryouts. He was surprised to see about a dozen students waiting at the landing. They talked and shared videos from their phones. All his efforts at promotion had paid off.

"Hey, guys, you all here for tryouts?"

They stared at him like he was from another planet.

"Tryouts?" one kid said, looking up from his phone.

"Cross-country," John said.

"No, sir, we're just hanging out."

John looked from face to face to see if there was any other reaction. "None of you are here to try out?"

Shaking heads and scowls.

"No, sir, sorry," a girl said, and one by one the group disbanded and walked past him up the stairs.

It felt like a defeat. At best the students were apathetic about the sport. He thought of Ethan's words in class and knew what he had to do: find Olivia Brooks and tell her there wasn't a cross-country team.

As the students walked up the steps, he glanced at the field. A lone figure sat on a small set of bleachers. She wore shorts and a T-shirt and stared at the ground. John took a deep breath and started the long walk toward her.

"Hey, are you here for cross-country?" John said as he reached the bleachers.

"Yes, sir."

A small voice. Reserved. She had a scared pup look to her.

He looked around. "Do you know anybody else coming to try out?"

She stared with brown eyes as if it were a question she had no idea how to answer. And why would she?

"No, sir."

John asked her name and the girl opened her backpack and handed him a form she'd filled out. "Hannah Scott."

John scanned the page. Hannah was a sophomore. She'd run at Franklin High the year before. Born on February 14. A Valentine's baby. He saw the emergency contact information was for a Barbara Scott and she was listed as Hannah's grandmother.

John heard a sound, a puff of air, and he looked up to see Hannah pulling an inhaler from her mouth. "I'm sorry, Hannah, is that . . . ?"

"It's for my asthma," she said.

John stared at her, incredulous. "You can run with asthma?"

Hannah shrugged. "Sometimes."

John looked back at the form and wondered what to do.

He checked his watch and looked up the hill for stragglers. The stairs were empty.

He thanked Hannah for coming and was going to hand her a sheet with their practice schedule but thought better of it.

"When does practice start?" she said.

"I'll get back with you on that," he said. "Why don't you come by my office tomorrow?"

"So you're not going to have me run today?"

"I can tell you're good enough for the team. Just come by the office and I'll give you an update, okay?"

"Yes, sir."

John headed for the stairs and turned to see Hannah walking to the far end of the field. She disappeared into the trees and he made a beeline for the main office. He met Principal Brooks on the sidewalk in front of the school.

"Olivia, there is no cross-country program."

"What do you mean there's no program?"

"I had one girl show up and she's got asthma."

A look of recognition showed on her face. "Oh, you mean Hannah Scott."

John was surprised she knew her. "Yes."

"Does she want to run?"

"Yes, but we can't allow that. How could she compete?"

Olivia explained that a doctor's note had been provided by Hannah's grandmother. "She just has to keep her inhaler with her."

Ethan's words came back to him. *"Nobody cares."* John tried to hold back his contempt. "Okay, but we still don't have a team, so what does it matter?"

"I thought that one runner could still medal without a team," Olivia said.

"Technically," he said, wincing. "But why have a season with one runner?"

His voice sounded like a whine, even to himself, and he realized he and Olivia were not on the same page. Not even in the same chapter. It made no sense to keep a program going for only one runner when other programs had been cut. Surely Olivia would be open to reason and cut the cross-country albatross from his neck. But the way she looked at him told him she wasn't backing down.

"One runner matters," she said.

John turned away, unable to hold back his frustration. He wanted to call a time-out and yell at a ref.

"John, you are a good coach and a good teacher. I already told you that I don't want to have to cancel another program. If she wants to try out, then let her."

It felt like he was wearing gray and standing on the steps of the Appomattox courthouse. John simply said, "Okay," and Olivia kept moving, walking away from the confrontation while he stood with a weight he didn't want to carry. He took off his hat and smacked his leg with it and stared at the sky. His life felt out of control, and no matter what he did, others had more say. He hated that feeling. It was why he had looked forward to the basketball season. They finally controlled their destiny—and just when everything had fallen into place, another rug was pulled.

John drove home and found Ethan and Will playing basketball in the driveway. John saw Ethan guarding Will tightly and thought about his team and how hard they'd worked at defense. When Will, a full foot shorter, stepped back and took a shot and made it, Ethan celebrated like he'd scored himself.

John wanted to talk more with Ethan about what he'd said in class, but this wasn't the time or the place. Besides, here was a high school senior spending time playing one-on-one with his younger brother. There was something special happening on that driveway.

He found Amy in the kitchen preparing dinner and said, "Ethan's a good big brother."

"He is a good big brother," Amy said, smiling. "So how were tryouts?"

He dropped his keys on the counter. "Well, I gathered everyone together—" he paused for dramatic effect—"and I said to her, 'Thanks for coming out.'"

"No," Amy said.

"Yeah."

"One person," Amy said.

"Hannah Scott. She's a sophomore. She's got asthma."

"Hannah Scott," Amy said, repeating the name. "Yeah, I have her in science."

"I caught Olivia afterward. She still wants me to coach her."

A car pulled into the driveway and Amy looked out the window. "Hey, I think Neil Hatcher just pulled up."

Neil was the father of Tommy and Kevin Hatcher. The twins were part of the backbone of John's hopes for the upcoming season. John slowly made his way outside and shook hands with his friend.

"What brings you to the neighborhood?" John said.

"I wanted you to know before you heard it from someone else."

"That sounds a little ominous."

"I did everything I could, John. You know I grew up here. The family farm is just down the road. This town is all I've known and I thought we'd all grow old and—"

"Where are you going?"

"Sharpsville. I thought I could make a go of it, thought I could stay, but the company made me an offer. It tears my heart out to break up the team like this."

John looked away, then back at his friend. "I know this was tough for you, Neil. I totally understand. It's life, right? You have to deal with it as it comes."

"I was praying on the way over here you'd say something like that."

"I want the best for you and your family. Your sons."

"The boys are really upset. They said they were looking forward to a championship. And playing with Ethan one more year before he heads off to college."

"Yeah. Sharpsville is going to have a pretty good team themselves, it looks like."

Neil put a hand on John's shoulder. "I want you to know I appreciate what you've done. You're a good coach. You're a good man."

Neil drove away and John felt like he was watching more leave than Neil Hatcher. Was this part of God's game plan for their lives? He had believed God was in control of everything. He didn't totally understand God's hand in history as he read it and taught it, but he believed God was there and working behind the scenes. But with the events of the past few weeks, he wondered if those were just words. Were they the correct answers to score well on a test, or were they something he could really live and believe?

He walked through the yard, avoiding his sons still playing ball on the driveway, and returned to the kitchen to tell Amy what Neil had said. In frustration he slammed his hat on the table. "What's happening to my team? This was supposed to be our year!"

"Well, is there anybody else who can play?" Amy said.

It felt like she was trying to fix things. But he could tell she cared. "Maybe," John said. There was no conviction to his voice.

Ethan spoke through the open window. "Hey, what did Mr. Hatcher have to say?"

John gave Amy a look and trudged outside in a daze. He told Will to head inside and wash up for dinner. Will complained but seemed to sense something was going on.

"Is it about Tommy and Kevin?" Ethan said.

John walked past him into the backyard, trying to think

of a way to spin the news. Instead of softening the blow and putting a silver lining on it, he nodded and told him straight-out what he'd heard. Man-to-man.

Ethan paced in the freshly mowed grass, then stopped. "What is happening to my senior year? You think Ty's going to stay when he finds out everyone's leaving? He's already got two colleges looking at him."

"You don't know that he'll leave," John said.

"He might. That means we'll have four players, Dad. Why would a scout come look at me when we don't even have a team?"

Exactly, John thought. His son saw the truth and was feeling the emotion that John couldn't fully express because . . . well, he had to keep things together. He had to stay strong. Stiff upper lip.

Ethan thought a moment and John saw the wheels turning in his son's head. A different path. A way it all could make sense, perhaps.

Ethan lowered his voice and spoke seriously. "What if I finish up at Franklin High?"

"You want to go to Franklin High?" John said, incredulous. "We still have a shot. You and Ty can carry the team. I just have to come up with a couple more players."

"Who?" Ethan said. "No one else can play."

John glanced away and saw Amy and Will at the window staring at them. He tried to think of something to say, something that would bring them together instead of further apart.

"I hate this!" Ethan said and he walked into the house.

"So do I." John said it to himself. He said it like a prayer, wondering if God heard him.

CHAPTER 10

✦ ✦ ✦

That scrawny kid, Robert Odelle, was in two of Hannah's classes, and he had decided to hound her. Every time a teacher called her name, Hannah cringed. He had picked her out of the herd, and after she was called on in class, he waited until the teacher wasn't looking and mimicked her voice.

She had never found her class schedule in her backpack and assumed she had lost it until one day Robert said, "Why didn't you make it to science on that first day, Hannah?" He never showed her the worn paper. He didn't have to. The smirk on his face was enough to tell her he had taken it or picked it up when she dropped it. There

was glee in his eyes and she couldn't understand why anyone would want to be that mean to somebody they'd barely
even met. Why did he take pleasure in someone else's
pain? Hannah had seen much worse than Robert Odelle at
Franklin High, but she hadn't expected it here. Wasn't this
place supposed to teach the Golden Rule, that you were
supposed to do unto others what you would want them to
do to you? Robert seemed to flip that rule around, and it
irritated her more than any bullying she'd experienced at
the Y or at other schools.

Her teachers were fond of quoting a Bible verse that
said, "All have sinned." Hannah knew that described her
in so many ways and it made her cringe. She felt terrible
about stealing, but she just couldn't stop. Robert never
seemed to feel bad about how he treated her. Maybe he
was the same way. Maybe he just couldn't stop.

On the first day of cross-country practice, Robert followed her out a door. "How are you supposed to run when
you can't breathe?"

Hannah didn't look at him. She just walked toward the
field.

"Have fun gasping," Robert called after her.

Hannah had told her grandmother she'd made the team
the night before. Her grandmother said she hoped Hannah
would make friends with her new teammates. Hannah
didn't have the heart to tell her she was the only one on the
team. And she didn't tell anyone about Robert.

Coach Harrison met Hannah at the practice field where

the cross-country course began and showed her a layout. She walked the course alone, making mental notes of the rise and fall of the terrain. When she finished, she was surprised to see Mrs. Harrison and her younger son sitting on the bleachers.

Coach Harrison had his laptop open, studying the times of other athletes, and he sat beside her on the bench. He focused on what it would take to win a medal, pointing out the current state champion, Gina Mimms, who ran for Westlake Academy. Her time for the 5K was under twenty minutes, which seemed lightning fast. Out of reach.

"Have you been timed lately?" Coach Harrison said.

"No, sir."

He said they would begin there. "I'm going to get the golf cart while you stretch. Do you have your inhaler?"

"I'll just run with it."

Will looked up from his homework. "Can I run too?"

"It's three miles, buddy," Coach said.

"You need to finish your homework," Mrs. Harrison said.

Will begged and Hannah silently watched their interaction. She always imagined other families were a lot like hers. Kids spent time alone. They stayed at the Y and went to after-school programs and checked in with next-door neighbors. Even when her grandmother was home, Hannah watched TV alone and ate alone because her grandmother was exhausted from her two jobs. She learned about families from the ones she saw on TV shows and in the movies. So when she saw Coach Harrison and his wife, she again wondered what it would be like to have two parents who cared about each other and spent time with their kids.

To her surprise, Will's begging worked. He promised to finish his homework later and Coach Harrison glanced at his wife and that was it. Just a glance and they seemed on the same page. Will would try to keep up with her and she wouldn't be running alone.

"I'll bet you can run this in twenty-four minutes," Mrs. Harrison said to Hannah.

"I can do it in twenty-four," Coach Harrison said.

Mrs. Harrison laughed. "I doubt that."

"Watch me," he said.

"John, you don't have to prove anything. You don't just run three miles without—"

"Watch me," he said, grinning.

Hannah smiled and the three of them lined up. She began with an even pace, focusing on the uphill climb at the beginning of the course. Walking it, the incline didn't seem steep. Running it was a different proposition. Almost immediately her legs burned and her chest tightened. She could hear Will breathing hard behind her, his feet clopping like a Clydesdale. Coach Harrison lumbered behind him, trying to keep up.

She had learned from her coach at Franklin High not to run on her heels but to strike the ground as if running on her toes. There was so much to think about with any sport, but today she thought about Coach Harrison and his focus on a medal. What if she couldn't run faster than twenty-four minutes? What if she never got under twenty-two or twenty-one minutes or came close to Gina Mimms?

The more her mind churned, the harder the course became and she remembered Robert's jab about not being able to breathe.

"Have fun gasping."

She pulled out her inhaler, pumped it once into her mouth, and immediately felt her lungs relax. She glanced over a shoulder at Will, who was all arms as he ran. Farther back she saw Coach Harrison in the trees, his Brookshire shirt already drenched with sweat like he had jumped into the deep end of a swimming pool.

The last part of the course sloped down, and as she neared the field and the finish line, her legs felt like deadweight. Mrs. Harrison saw her and yelled encouragement to push to the finish. Sweat dripping and breathing hard, she passed Mrs. Harrison and heard her say, "23:15."

Mrs. Harrison told her to keep moving and stay loose. The woman zeroed in on her, not just looking at her but seeming to look into her. "You okay?"

It was a simple question and short, but for some reason Hannah had never felt that kind of care. She couldn't get over the feeling of having someone really see her, really understand her struggle. Hannah nodded and filed the moment away.

"Look at you, Will!" Mrs. Harrison yelled as Will came through the trees. He finished at 24:10, his hair wet and flopping like a mop. Pretty impressive for a sixth grader who hadn't trained. He bent over, elbows on knees, glasses fogged.

"That was amazing, Will," Mrs. Harrison said.

"That was terrible," Will said, gasping. "Why would anybody want to do this?"

Will gave Hannah a weak high-five and they both drank water and eventually sat on a bench across from Mrs. Harrison, who nervously looked at the woods, then at the stopwatch.

"Dad's not going to be happy with his time," Will said.

"I think he'll be happy to just finish," Mrs. Harrison said.

"The problem with this sport is there's no ball," Will said. "There's no dunking or goals or anything."

"Well, I think this sport is about endurance, sweetie."

There it was again, something subtle Hannah picked up. It was an easy conversation between mother and son. Will didn't even have to think twice about talking with his mom or expressing something that came to mind. That wasn't how conversations went with her grandmother. She did call Hannah "baby," which Hannah liked at times, but at others didn't. Hannah usually tried to gauge her grandmother's mood to decide if she should share something. Most of the time she held back.

Mrs. Harrison stood, looking up the course. "Finally."

Hannah caught sight of Coach Harrison swinging his arms and trying to get enough momentum to make it to the finish line. He gasped for air and when he reached level ground and noticed he was being watched, he sprinted, lifting his legs high and trying hard to make the finish look as good as possible.

He flopped to the ground, rolled onto his back like an insect, and said, "That was terrible! Why would anyone want to do this?"

When he asked his time, Mrs. Harrison studied the stopwatch as if it were a bad diagnosis.

"32:02."

"What? I didn't even break thirty?"

"I'm just surprised that you finished."

The coach playfully tossed his hat at her and said, "Go away."

She laughed and there it was again. That connection. Laughing together, sweating together, tossing hats, listening, looking, freely speaking what was inside. It was all of that and more.

"Hannah, do you have a ride home?" Mrs. Harrison said as they packed up.

"It's just a mile. I can walk."

"No, we can take you home. We'd love to meet your parents."

A familiar ache settled in Hannah's gut. Her situation wasn't normal—she wasn't normal. Especially at a place like Brookshire.

"It's just me and my grandma. My parents have passed."

"I'm sorry. I didn't know." Mrs. Harrison's voice was

tender and full of compassion. "We'd be happy to take you home. I can call your grandmother and let her know."

"I'm okay. I don't mind walking. Thanks anyway."

Hannah walked away, glad for the extra time to stretch and recover from the run and grateful for the time alone. She could think through the course and how she might get faster the next time. Maybe she could get under twenty-three minutes. But the real reason she had passed up the offer of a ride was something that had happened after she completed the race and Mrs. Harrison was focused on Will.

While pacing in front of the bleachers, she had noticed Coach Harrison's watch. He'd removed it just before he ran. Without thinking, without hesitation, Hannah took it and slipped it into her pocket without anyone noticing.

Part 2

THE QUESTION

CHAPTER 11

✦ ✦ ✦

John dried dishes in the kitchen as he and Amy processed the events of the day. There was a discipline issue in one of her classes. John's mind was fixed on the basketball team and the loss of the twins and all of their collective uncertainty. Drying silverware caused his mind to wander and he realized he wasn't paying attention. When Amy turned the conversation to cross-country, he regained his focus.

"There would be a lot more interest and the team would get bigger if some of the popular kids ran, don't you think?"

"Popular?" John said.

"You know who I mean."

John dried a salad bowl. "Ethan could do it if he wanted

to." But he'd already made it pretty clear how he felt about that.

"He sure could. You know, John, I don't understand why he won't run. He's your son and he's so athletic. He would do really well out there. And then we could be out there together."

John thought about Will. He wasn't a fan of running himself, but he was on board to cheer for Hannah. Maybe Ethan could get with the program. "I could go talk to him."

"Okay, that's good," Amy said.

John took the stairs to Ethan's room and found him studying in bed. He knocked lightly on the door and Ethan kept his head down in the notebook, working out a precalc problem. The room was all Ethan. Trophies and memorabilia of seasons past. Above his bed was a miniature basketball hoop and backboard.

John sat in Ethan's desk chair and faced him. He slowly said, "Can I appeal to you to think about something?"

"What's that?" Ethan said.

"I know you don't want to do cross-country. But there are advantages to it."

Ethan looked at his notebook, something close to a scowl crossing his face. "Dad . . ."

"Just hear me out," John said, interrupting. He checked his tone. Gentle. Inviting. "I'm not going to twist your arm. Running will help you stay in shape."

Ethan chuckled. "You make the team run as punishment."

He had him. "Yes, that's true. But it'll help with discipline, it'll show a lot of school spirit, and I think you'd be really good at it."

The scowl turned to a softening of Ethan's features. It looked like he was capturing a vision of something. Then Ethan spoke confidently. "You know how you've always practiced basketball with me?"

"Yeah."

He put the notebook down and sat straight. "Well, even though I would hate it, if you'll run with me to train, I'll do it."

John stared at his son, unable to speak.

Downstairs, John took a deep breath and found Amy in the kitchen. "He's not running."

"Aww, John. Why not?"

"Amy, it's okay. He doesn't want to and we just need to be supportive."

Amy's face tightened and she shook her head. "Okay, you know what? I'm going to go talk to him."

"No, no, no, no," John said, blocking her exit. "We just need to give him space. You know, and love him." She looked unconvinced. "And we don't have to bring it up anymore."

"Really?" Amy said.

John's cell phone rang. Saved by technology. The screen said, *Pastor Mark.*

As soon as he answered, Amy's eyes widened. "Oh, I forgot to tell you . . ."

He tried to hear Pastor Mark and Amy at the same time

but it didn't work. Too much information from two different sources.

". . . and I told him you would do visitation at the hospital . . ."

". . . could you be there in about an hour?"

"Uh, yes, I will be there in an hour," John said into the phone, giving Amy a bewildered look.

"Thanks for volunteering," Mark said.

When he hung up, Amy said, "You know what, I'm sorry. I forgot to tell you."

He headed for the shower.

"You're a good man, John Harrison," Amy called to him.

"Whatever," John said.

John drove to Franklin General, reflexively looking at his left wrist to check the time. Where had he put his watch? He could have sworn he'd taken it off and put it on the bleachers before he ran that day, but he couldn't find it when they packed up. He'd look for it again when he got home.

Normally it was Bill Henderson who accompanied Pastor Mark, but this was part of the fallout of all the changes in town. John hated losing Bill's friendship, but he also hated the void left by someone who contributed so much to the church. Bill was great at these hospital visits, and he seemed to enjoy it, so until now John had never felt the need to step up. Would spreading out the Hendersons' responsibilities allow others to get involved and perhaps grow deeper in their faith? Would it help him? Maybe getting outside his comfort zone was what he needed.

Mark met him in the hospital lobby and thanked John for coming. "The first person we need to visit is Ben Hutchins, fourth floor."

John winced when his pastor took the stairs. Mark said he needed the exercise. John felt every step in his calves and thighs.

"You know Ben is one of our founding members," Mark said.

It made sense. Ben was older and had a kind smile, was a pillar at church, always present, always engaged with people's needs. When they reached the room, a nurse requested that only one of them go in because other family members were visiting. John offered to wait in the hall and Mark entered the room.

When John turned around, he met two nurses wheeling an empty bed straight toward him. He stepped back but lost his balance for a moment and leaned against a door. It opened and he stumbled into a room where a man lay listening to music.

"I'm sorry, sir. I didn't mean to disturb you."

The man didn't look at John but at a spot on the wall near the ceiling. "Who's there?"

"I'm just waiting to visit a church member next door," John said, motioning toward the next room. The man didn't follow his movement or look at him. Instead, he pointed his remote toward the CD player and paused the music.

"Are you a minister?"

"No, sir. I'm just here visiting a few people with my pastor." John wanted to get back into the hall, but something made him linger.

"Well, if you're just waiting, maybe you can visit me, too." He said it with a slight grin and a little hope in his voice.

John stepped into the room, tentative, looking toward the hall and leaving the door open behind him. "Sure. My name's John Harrison." He stepped closer to the bed and studied the man's face. He was African American with a graying mustache and beard. He had a slight build and looked pretty sick, judging from the number of machines hooked to him.

The way the man reached out a hand it was clear he couldn't see. It hung in the air like a wandering kite string. John stepped forward and took the man's hand and shook it. When he did, the man smiled as if he had found something he'd lost.

"Thomas Hill," he said. He gripped John's hand as if they'd known each other all their lives. "Nice to meet you."

"Nice to meet you, Thomas." What to say next? What would Bill do in this situation? Or Pastor Mark?

"Umm, have you been here very long?"

"About three weeks," Thomas said. "I've been trying to keep diabetes from getting too greedy. Took my sight a few years ago. Now it wants my legs and my kidneys."

"I'm sorry to hear that," John said. "Do you have family here?"

Thomas paused and it seemed a cloud was passing over him. The sound of the heart monitor filled in the silence between them.

"I'm more or less on my own. I grew up in Franklin, though. They brought me back here from Fairview to get dialysis here."

John chuckled. "You might be the only one coming *from* Fairview. I think everybody else is heading that way."

Thomas smiled and there was a light to his eyes, even though he couldn't see. John sensed something in the man. It was like someone thirsty for words had just jumped into a clear, fresh pool of springwater and was splashing around.

"That's what I hear," Thomas said.

Because of Thomas's condition, John didn't worry about keeping eye contact. He turned and looked out the door, wondering if Mark was finished. Thomas's voice caught his attention.

"So tell me about yourself, John."

John turned. "Well, I'm the basketball coach at Brookshire Christian." A pause. Under his breath he said, "I hope, anyway."

"You don't sound too sure."

John scratched the back of his neck. "There's a lot of things I'm not too sure about right now. I also teach history and I've been assigned the cross-country program."

"Cross-country," Thomas said, his face lighting up even more. He chuckled. "That was my sport."

"Yeah?"

"I was third in the state in my day."

"Really? Then I might need some advice because I don't really know what I'm doing."

Thomas laughed. It was such an easy sound that seemed to work its way up from his toes. That a blind man on dialysis could generate a laugh and light like this held John back from excusing himself and walking into the hall.

John had come because Amy had volunteered him. He'd come partly out of obligation to support his pastor, but here he was pulling up a chair beside Thomas's bed. John believed God was involved in every aspect of a person's life. Amy talked about "divine appointments" when she "just happened" to run into a student or a friend at an opportune time when they needed encouragement.

John sat and told Thomas about the changes at the school, the loss of the football program, and the fight to hang on to as many extracurriculars as possible.

"Frankly, I don't know why we're keeping cross-country. There's not a lot of interest."

Thomas grew quiet. "For the kids who do come out, cross-country can teach a lot. I learned about endurance. The importance of training."

John sat forward. "That's the thing. There's just so much I don't know. Give me five guys and a basketball and I can diagram an offense or a defensive scheme with the best of them. But the running thing is like speaking a foreign language."

"I think you'll be surprised at the similarities," Thomas

said. "You prepare your basketball team for each opponent you come up against, their strengths and weaknesses, right?"

"Sure."

"It's the same with cross-country, but the preparation is less about what other runners are doing and more about what's up here." He pointed to his head. "And in here." He pointed to his heart. "I think I might be able to help. What are your practices like?"

John told him his approach to training. Thomas listened and moved his legs when he talked as if remembering the feeling of running. His answers were insightful and John wished he had a notepad to write down what he was hearing.

John's questions covered everything from diet to the race day warm-up. "How do you train to have that big kick at the end of the race?"

"Oh, that kick," Thomas said, shaking his head.

Someone knocked gently at the door and John turned to see his pastor.

"John, I'm sorry to interrupt. Visiting hours are almost over."

"Sure," John said, missing his watch again. "Thomas, I should probably say hello next door."

"No problem." Thomas grew somber and searched for words. "Hey, John . . . I don't get many visitors I can talk shop with. Feel free to come back anytime."

The heart monitor beeped, a series of numbers and lines showing what was happening inside the man, and it made

John wonder what was going on in the man's soul. What were his doubts and questions, fears and hopes?

John wanted to leave Thomas with something pastoral, something a Christian should say to someone confined to a hospital bed. He smiled and said, "It's good to meet you, Thomas. I'll be praying for you."

"I'll take it," Thomas said.

On the way out of the hospital, Mark asked about Thomas and John told him he had stumbled into the room and started a conversation. "It was a fluke."

"It's funny how the Lord works out some of these connections," Mark said. "Maybe God's up to something in Thomas's life and He used you to encourage him."

"I feel like he encouraged me more than I did him."

"Well, maybe God is up to something in both of your lives."

John thought about that as he drove home. The boys were in their rooms and he stuck his head in and told them good night. Amy apologized again about volunteering him and John waved her off. He told her about meeting Thomas and the insights he gave.

"Maybe he can help you with Hannah."

John nodded. "He's in pretty bad shape, though. I honestly don't know how much time he has left."

John rummaged through his nightstand drawer and went to the bathroom sink. "You haven't seen my watch anywhere, have you?"

CHAPTER 12

✦ ✦ ✦

"I'll just leave this here and you can pay me when you're ready," Barbara Scott said, forcing a smile to the customers in the corner booth. "No hurry."

"Well, it certainly wasn't any hurry getting our food out here," the man said, wiping his hands on a napkin.

"Harold," his wife scolded across the table.

He shook his head and threw down the napkin. "The English muffin tasted like it came right out of the box. Couldn't you at least have thrown it in the toaster for thirty seconds? Was that too much to ask?"

She was surprised by his venom. The truth was, Barbara had delivered the food to their table as soon as the order was ready. And she *had* toasted the English muffin, but he had said he didn't want it burnt. She didn't respond with any of these thoughts, of course. *Don't argue. Be polite. Don't blame the slow kitchen.*

"I'm sorry about that, sir. Can I freshen your coffee?"

"No, I'm done," he said, waving her away like a fly at a picnic. Some customers were like that. You could do everything in your power to make their meal a pleasant experience and they'd find some reason to complain. The good ones, even if something had gone wrong with the order, treated you like you were a person, not a robot in a uniform. The good ones tipped well. But a customer like Harold, whose face looked sour, sent her spiraling down. It took only one to ruin a shift, to keep you thinking about what you might have done differently.

"Do you want me to get the manager?" she said without emotion.

He pulled his wallet out and threw a twenty-dollar bill on the table. "No, I want to get out of here. Keep the change."

His wife touched her on the arm as if apologizing without words. Barbara knew the bill was more than nineteen dollars with tax and took the money to the cash register.

"Sounds like you got a bad one?" Tiffany said, putting two pieces of bread in the toaster. She was the newest server and half Barbara's age.

"For some people being mean is a full-time job," Barbara said under her breath.

"Don't let it get to you," Tiffany said with a wink.

Barbara smiled because that was exactly what Barbara had said to Tiffany every time she had fought back tears. Tiffany was giving her a dose of her own medicine. Barbara put the change in her pocket and wiped down the table.

"Don't let it get to you."

That was a lot easier to say than to live, Barbara thought. Her whole life had been an exercise in not letting it get to her. Whatever the *it* was, she tried to stay out of its way. But it always had a way of coming back in the door and sitting in her section.

Barbara knew worrying was counterproductive. She remembered a sermon years ago, when she was still going to church, and the pastor had quoted Jesus and how worry couldn't add a single hour to your life. The pastor had read another quote that said, "Worry does not empty tomorrow of its sorrow, it empties today of its strength." That stuck in her soul, but it was like trying to cut down on salt when salt was already in everything. It's hard not to worry when it's already baked into your heart.

Barbara worried about her finances. She usually had too much month and not enough money. She constantly worried about keeping her jobs because her bosses weren't the easiest to work for and the slowdown in town meant fewer customers and more pressure to perform. She worried about keeping her car running and paying the insurance bill.

And then there was her worry about Hannah. She couldn't be there during the day, and some nights she didn't get home until the girl was already in bed. She worried about Hannah's grades. She'd tried to help with homework, but what she encountered in the textbooks was incomprehensible. What they taught in high school these days was college material when she was a teenager. This caused Barbara to question whether she could effectively raise her and help her become who she was meant to be. A heart that questions itself is a heart that finds it difficult to love.

Barbara tried to drown the doubt by keeping busy. She worked not just to pay the bills but to occupy her mind so she didn't replay what happened fifteen years earlier. Mostly, she was successful with that, but at times, like when she cleaned tables or drove from one job to another, she thought of her mistakes. All the might've beens of life. Could she have somehow kept Janet from her mistakes? Maybe if she'd done one of those interventions she saw on TV? Maybe if she had driven through one more neighborhood, she'd have found Janet. One more search could have rescued her.

The past was a loaded serving tray and Barbara struggled under its weight. Each morning she looked in the mirror and lived with the regret of her daughter's death. She hadn't been there when Janet needed her most. And now, with Hannah looking so much like her mother, every glance at the girl opened the old wound.

Barbara had sent a note to Brookshire Christian School from the doctor that said Hannah could run cross-country even though she had asthma. When she'd looked up the mailing address in the directory, seeing the principal's name on the cover brought back painful memories. Hints of the past bubbled as she studied the name.

Getting the doctor's note reminded Barbara to renew the prescription for Hannah's inhaler. She discovered her insurance coverage had changed and the co-pay had gone up fifty dollars, something in the fine print she hadn't seen. Another fifty dollars gone that couldn't be used for groceries or gas or the mortgage.

As Barbara scrubbed at a spot of dried syrup on a table by the windows, she wondered about Hannah's future. Barbara didn't want her granddaughter to have to scrape up just enough money each month to keep the bill collectors off her doorstep. All the more reason for her to get a good education and then a good job and not be stuck on the hamster wheel. If Hannah could get good grades and finish high school, perhaps Barbara could afford to send her to community college for an associate's degree. Then Hannah could get a loan and finish her bachelor's at a state university. It made Barbara's head spin to think of the cost of tuition, books, and fees.

But more than that, what if Hannah got herself kicked out of school again? She'd been caught stealing several times, and it sure looked like that hadn't stopped. It was only a matter of time before it got the best of her.

Barbara recalled a garage sale trip when Hannah was six. They were looking for a bike with training wheels so Hannah could learn to ride, and the one they found was rusty and too wobbly. Barbara took Hannah's hand and returned to the car. On the way home, she glanced in the rearview and saw Hannah playing with something.

"What do you have there, baby?"

Hannah quickly hid what she was holding and Barbara put her hand out over the seat. "Give it here."

"I don't have anything," Hannah said in that squeaky, sweet voice.

She pulled over, got out of the car, opened the back door, and gave Hannah the *look*. The child wilted and handed over a small stuffed animal with a tag on its ear. A fast-food restaurant had given these to children with their meals years earlier.

"Where did you get this?"

"I don't know."

"Yes, you do. Did you get it from the garage sale?"

No response.

"Baby, look at me. Did you get this at the garage sale?"

"Mm-hmm."

Barbara got back in the car, turned around, and returned to their last stop. She marched Hannah up to the table outside the garage, pulling her by one arm. Hannah's head was down but Barbara was sure this was a teachable moment. She would nip this stealing penchant in the bud.

"My granddaughter had this with her in the car and she's here to return it."

The woman took the toy from Barbara and leaned down. Hannah had a finger in her mouth.

"What do you say, Hannah?" Barbara said.

She said something unintelligible.

"Take your hand out of your mouth and apologize."

"Sorry," Hannah said, making the word three syllables.

Instead of helping, instead of reinforcing the lesson, the homeowner said, "Oh, that old thing. We have about a hundred we didn't sell. Why don't you take this and pick out another one."

Barbara's mouth dropped open. "No, no, no! She's got to learn that she can't take things that belong to others."

"I understand," the woman said, "but look at that face. She's sorry for it, aren't you, sweetie?"

Hannah nodded like a bobblehead doll with a tight spring, then wandered into the garage and came back with two more stuffed animals. Barbara didn't know what to say. She told Hannah on the way home that she could have gotten into big trouble.

"Never do that again."

"Yes, Grandma," Hannah said.

Then it was a pack of gum at a gas station. Barbara found the remnants of a chocolate bar in one of Hannah's pockets. Most often she had a plausible story about whatever she hadn't paid for. And now Hannah was going to a school with a zero-tolerance policy on stealing. What would happen if they caught her?

It was the worry that ate Barbara alive. It was all the things Hannah might be squirreling away. Was there something in the girl's DNA that made her susceptible? Perhaps someday they'd come up with a pill she could take.

But that was ridiculous. There was no cure. This was a choice. Barbara wanted to make it for Hannah, but she couldn't. And she couldn't watch her every minute of the day.

From what Barbara could see, Hannah wasn't boy-crazy yet, but that would probably come, just like it had for Janet. Then she was in for a whole new set of worries. And so far, it didn't look like Hannah had gotten involved with any drugs. But Janet hadn't started using until after high school.

"What happened with that customer?"

Barbara nearly dropped a tray of dirty dishes when her manager, Doyle Odelle, came up behind her. She gathered herself and tried to explain, but the look on his face said it all.

"Business is bad enough. I can't afford to have unhappy customers."

"I did everything I could to hurry things up in the kitchen."

"So it's the cooks' fault?"

"No, sir. You know there are some people who aren't happy with anything. His wife all but apologized to me for the way he treated me."

Doyle frowned. "You need to do more to make them happy. Maybe smile once in a while? Try that."

"Yes, sir."

"I'm changing the schedule. You won't have as many hours next week."

Barbara wanted to protest but instead she bit her tongue. It was just one more thing to worry about.

CHAPTER 13

✦ ✦ ✦

John had designs on a free hour to grade papers when he saw Troy Finkle. Troy taught English and drama, and he had a look in his eyes as he headed straight toward John. It wasn't hard to say no to Troy—the man just never heard the word. John tried valiantly, but Troy roped him into being a drama monologue judge. He set it up like a TV show with judges behind a table providing critique.

The stereotype of coaches was they didn't appreciate art or creativity. But students were energized by different things, and John was as happy with a student excelling in drama as one who threw touchdowns on Friday nights. Well, almost. You could only take the drama thing so far.

What could have been an invigorating time of literature and poetry became a painful hour of students reciting lifeless material, remembering words but displaying no heart. Two students performed the old Abbott and Costello "Who's on First?" They had memorized every syllable but couldn't translate the words into a performance. And that was the trick in sports, music—any discipline, really—to bring the material to life and deliver it in such a way that it became a gift to the world. John was pleased with that image. Who said coaches can't be creative?

Toward the end of the cringe-worthy performances, Troy turned to John and said, "Do you know anyone in this school who can speak with one ounce of passion?"

John thought a moment and looked at Troy. "You."

The deflated drama teacher immediately brightened. He held up a fist and John bumped it. It was something how one little word could provide a boost to someone who needed it.

Back in his class, furiously grading before the next period, John heard footsteps in the hall and then a slight knock. He looked up to see Ken Jones and his son, Ty. It was a moment he'd hoped wouldn't come.

"Coach Harrison, got a minute?" Ken said.

"Hey, Ken, how are you?" John said, standing and shaking the man's hand. He shook Ty's hand and felt a dead fish. Ty studied the floor tiles.

All around the room were visible reminders of leaders,

maps representing the history of the country and the world. The rise and fall of empires. Conflict and struggle that informed every living thing. And John couldn't help thinking these two were part of his own history. Ty had played basketball with Ethan seemingly since they could walk. The two of them, along with the twins, would have been unbeatable. *Would have been.* John tried to put that out of his mind and focus on Ty and his dad.

Ken stumbled over his words at first and tried to get them out. John could tell there was real pain in the man's practiced speech.

"We just wanted to come tell you that we've decided to move Ty to Cornerstone."

There it was. The final nail in the team's coffin. The words took John's breath away. He tried to look Ken in the eye, but he could only dip his head and take a deep breath. He wanted to argue, to shout that they could still make Ty's senior year a great one, still win that championship. It would be the comeback story of the year—the little team that could. He held back and looked at Ken.

"He's got a good chance of getting a scholarship there," Ken continued. "And after we've lost so many players here, well . . ."

John summoned the strength to speak from his heart and give something, one dad to another, from coach to valued player. "I understand."

Ken's face showed relief and gratitude. John hadn't tried to change their minds or yell or make this about himself.

"Look, you're an excellent coach," Ken said quickly. "And none of this is your fault. We just have to do what's best for his future."

John nodded. He did understand. Even though it hurt, he knew he had to give something to Ty. He turned to him and remembered the skinny kid who cracked gum and bounced the ball higher than his head. He had lightning speed and with his growth spurt, he had become one of the best players in the state.

"You're a great player, Ty. I'm going to watch you on TV one day."

"Thanks, Coach. I enjoyed playing for you."

Ken and Ty left John alone with his thoughts and the maps, posters, and pictures. A portrait of Abraham Lincoln hung behind him, the man looking down like a specter. Lincoln had gone to battle to keep the Union together instead of letting it break into two countries. Abe had a vision for unity of North and South, and there was great bloodshed and struggle in the fight to remain one nation, under God, indivisible. He'd eventually paid for it with his life.

John sat hard in his chair and stared at the pages. One of them was Ty's. He had written about the role sports played in helping people get through the Great Depression. He used prizefighter Jim Braddock and a horse named Seabiscuit as examples of the hope that sports could give people who were in a deep struggle.

When John had looked into Ken's eyes, he had seen

himself. He wanted to give Ethan the best shot at a scholarship and a good start at life. That was his main goal.

But was it really? Was he more concerned about himself and how the team made him look as a coach? If he had really loved his son and wanted the best, should he have suggested Cornerstone for Ethan or considered Ethan's idea to switch to Franklin?

The internal struggle continued as John picked up this year's basketball schedule. Their first game was at home against Cornerstone. What would it be like to see Ty hit a jump shot and watch two points go up under GUEST on the scoreboard? They would play that team four times this season.

But they wouldn't play at all. Not now.

John had tried to hold on to hope for their town, their church, their school. He'd tried to think positively, to buck up and see the silver lining. What didn't kill you made you stronger. Hurdles were there to help you leap higher. Blah, blah, blah. Reality stared back at him from the schedule. And he knew beyond doubt the season had just walked out of his room in jeans and sneakers.

The season had left the building.

He crumpled the page in frustration and slammed it into the trash can. And it struck him that this was the only shot they'd probably make this year.

CHAPTER 14

✦ ✦ ✦

Hannah stretched and performed lunges on the field before
Coach Harrison arrived with his clipboard. He glanced at
it, then at the clouds, everything but her eyes. Teachers and
parents complained about teenagers daydreaming, but she
had seen plenty of preoccupied adults. Coach Harrison
seemed anywhere but on the field.

Before he could speak, Hannah said, "Why do you wear
that?"

He looked down at his shirt and sweatpants, bewildered.

"That shirt," she said. "It says Brookshire Basketball.
When are you going to wear a Brookshire Cross-Country
shirt?"

"It's not because I don't want to," he said. He thought a moment, finally looking her in the eyes. "I'll ask Mrs. Brooks about a coach's uniform."

Coach Harrison went over Hannah's times and charted her progress from each practice. It felt like numbers meant everything to him. She didn't realize he had kept these details, but she couldn't argue with the facts. She had made progress, though not as much as she wanted. Heading into her first race, her coach seemed reserved.

"We have to be realistic about this competition. I don't want you getting out there and feeling like you need to keep up with Gina Mimms."

Why not? she wanted to ask. *Gina Mimms is all you talk about.* Instead, Hannah sat straight and said, "Will she be there?"

Coach Harrison nodded. "Westlake has two other runners who are like lightning. But remember, Gina's a senior. She's eighteen. She's got a full-ride scholarship to an SEC college next year. She's major league. You don't want to—"

"And I'm minor league?" Hannah said, interrupting.

He frowned. "I didn't say that."

"T-ball?" Hannah raised her eyebrows and smiled, but inside, she felt an ache. She wanted to make her coach happy. She wanted to see him smile when he looked at her numbers. She wanted to make him proud.

Coach Harrison took a breath. "What I'm saying is, I don't want you running her pace. I want you to find your own. I talked with a coach at Miller Academy, and she says Mimms starts really fast and gets others to pace with her. They run out of gas before they finish the first mile. Mimms pulls away in the second mile and she slows a bit on the third, but nobody catches her."

"Smart," Hannah said.

"Yeah, it's shrewd. You're not going to bite on that, though. I don't want you to get halfway through the course and collapse, you know, with your . . ."

He looked at her and she could tell his preoccupation was gone. "I won't let you down, Coach."

"I know you won't. I just want you to run *your* best race. And the only way you can do that is to be you. You don't have to be Gina Mimms. Your goal is to get better with each practice and each race. Got it?"

"Yes, sir."

Mrs. Harrison brought a stadium chair and sat grading papers as Hannah ran. She took the longer run today, a five-mile course instead of three, which built her endurance.

She wanted to show Coach Harrison she could beat Gina Mimms. Like David knocking down Goliath. All she needed was a chance. And maybe a sling and a few stones. She would get better with each practice.

She attacked the first mile, imagining Gina right in front of her. Her legs felt strong and she pushed herself, thinking of the look on Coach Harrison's face when he clicked the stopwatch. His mouth would drop open. Mrs. Harrison would hug her. They'd do a happy dance in the field because of the time.

The second mile changed that dream. Her legs felt dead, her body heavy. She wanted to stop and lean against a tree to stay upright, but she couldn't. That was the worst thing she could do. She slowed her pace somewhat and focused on leaning forward more, allowing her momentum to carry her. Then came the wheeze. It's how the tightness started—with a whistle in her throat. When she couldn't breathe fully, the wheeze was the first sign and the sound scared her. And with the fear came more tightness in her lungs. And with the tightness came the feeling of drowning. She kept moving, though she sounded like a chugging steam locomotive rather than a well-oiled machine.

Hannah's grandmother chided her every time she left her inhaler behind. She'd catch Hannah leaving without it and each time she'd ask, "You don't have asthma today? Decided to take the day off?"

The truth was, Hannah wanted to forget the disease. She wanted the gasping and wheezing to end. When she was little, some adult had said she could grow out of asthma, that when her lungs developed fully, she might not feel the walls closing in and her vision blurring. She couldn't remember if it was a doctor or perhaps an adult at a playground who said that, but she took it as a prophecy. She wanted the statement to be true.

That desire also brought questions. Had she done something to deserve asthma? Was it punishment from God for something her parents did? Or perhaps God saw the things she stole and the bad thoughts she had about others and He had zapped her. If God knew everything, perhaps He had a scorecard or chart like Coach Harrison, detailing her sins. Maybe at some point all the things she'd hidden in her blue box had tipped the scales and God had shaken His head in disgust and given her asthma. Was that how it worked? God smacked you with something bad and whacked you harder when the wrongs piled higher? Did He punish parents with drug overdoses?

These thoughts swirled as she began the third mile. Hannah slowed, pulled out her inhaler, gave herself a puff, and let the medicine sink into her lungs. She jogged on a little knoll and through the trees saw the flag flapping above the school. She kept running. One foot in front of the other. Chug, chug, wheeze, wheeze. The lack of oxygen caused her legs and arms to ache. They felt like dumbbells she couldn't lift.

She stopped and blinked, the trees shifting in her vision. This was a bad one. Like that time in elementary school when she had been playing tag. She was the fastest on the playground and everybody knew it, so they tried to catch her, and the faster she ran, the less she could breathe. And then the air was gone and she was on the ground in the field, a teacher's face over her. Then the school nurse. Kids crowded around. Some cried.

Men in uniform and an ambulance.

An oxygen mask over her face.

Her grandmother looking at her with a furrowed brow. She was supposed to be at work. How had they reached her? Her grandmother scolded her after the hospital visit. Something about a co-pay and insurance and a payment plan. Hannah promised it would never happen again.

She tumbled now, grabbing at a small tree on her way to the ground. She picked herself up and cut through the woods toward the school. She took another puff. Was she getting the medicine? Sometimes the canister was empty but the sound was the same.

When was the last time she'd changed the canister? Was it a month ago? Had she gone through it faster since practice started?

She stumbled through leaves and pine needles. The soccer goal was to her right. Finally she couldn't stay on her feet. She pitched forward, putting her hands out to keep from falling face-first in the dirt. Somebody yelled nearby. Air. She just needed air. And it was gone.

"Hannah, are you okay?" Mrs. Harrison said, kneeling beside her.

You can't talk when you can't breathe. Coach Harrison arrived.

"Just stay still. What do you need?"

She wanted to say she needed to catch Gina Mimms. She wanted to hear her coach say he was proud of her time. But you can't be proud of a failure. There is no pride in losing.

"Breathe," Mrs. Harrison said, putting a hand on Hannah's arm.

Easy to say. People take breathing for granted. Hannah

took another puff of the inhaler and her heart slowed a bit and her airway opened a fraction and it felt like the worst was over. Hannah glanced up at Coach Harrison. He looked pained and she knew what he was thinking. If Hannah couldn't even finish a practice without collapsing, how would she run a race?

"I think that's enough running for today," he said.

"Well, we're giving you a ride home," Mrs. Harrison said. "No argument, okay?"

Hannah nodded. She sat on the ground for a few minutes, her failure so heavy she couldn't move, couldn't think. She couldn't look them in the face when the Harrisons helped her to the car and drove her home.

CHAPTER 15

✦ ✦ ✦

John Harrison had a few unwritten rules. Never let them see you sweat. Don't let others know your secret fears or that you have any. Winning isn't everything, but it's close. And life is about becoming self-sufficient. The less help you need, the better off you are, the more mature. But here he was farther from winning than he'd ever been and desperate.

He was a coach, an educator, a husband and father. He told others it was good to reach out for help. Somehow when he had to face his own failure, though, asking for help made him feel weak and pathetic.

He wandered to the backyard and stared at a pile of bricks that vexed him. Every time he saw them out the back window, they reminded him of things left undone.

Dinner was ready. Amy had called the boys. But he wasn't hungry and through the open kitchen window he heard Will say, "What's up with Dad?"

He shook his head and picked up a brick. One thing that was up was the letter from the school board that had arrived. It revealed his and Amy's pay had been cut 10 percent. He'd expected this news and was prepared for a cut closer to 20 percent. But the cold, hard facts in black and white hit hard. Why send a sterile letter? Why not tell them face-to-face?

Ethan had brought up Ty's decision to move schools as soon as John got out of the car from cross-country practice. On the drive home he had seen one For Sale sign after another. There was a moving truck parked just down the street. People were leaving, businesses closing, property values plummeting. Their house was their biggest investment, and instead of growing in value, it was quickly sinking. Another letter contained the bad news about John and Amy's retirement accounts. At least, he assumed it was bad. He didn't have the heart to open it.

Amy had asked in May what he was going to do about the brick pile. Which he interpreted to mean, "Do something with those bricks." They were leftovers from a back patio install two summers previous. John wanted to create a backyard fire pit. He and the boys could build it together. But his good intentions turned into an eyesore, and here he was, tossing bricks into a wheelbarrow. A few tosses and he realized he needed gloves, but when he looked in the garage, he couldn't find them. Ethan or Will had probably used them and forgotten to put them where they belonged. He wanted to say something through the open window but held back.

When all of life is in turmoil and you're not up to a task, John found it best to pick something he could accomplish. Many times that meant yard work. Mowing the grass was the only job he ever really finished each week. And it had to be done again the next. Now, with two boys who could mow, John looked for something to tackle that would assuage his brewing storm—something he could handle on his own.

"Hey, John, your plate's getting cold," Amy said as she stepped outside.

He didn't answer. He set his jaw and kept loading.

"You want me to put it in the refrigerator?"

"Sure."

She went inside. He brushed off the dirt from the bricks, though he wasn't sure why. Where was he going to pile them next? By the garage?

The door closed and Amy appeared, arms crossed. "Why are you doing that now?"

"Is it bothering you?" he said with an edge.

"Yes. What's the urgency? Those bricks have been lying there for months."

He thought of correcting her. They'd been there more than a year. "And they've needed to be cleaned up for months."

"So you have to do it now."

John looked up. "Do you need me to be doing something?"

"Yes, actually I do." Arms still folded. It felt like he was being accused of a capital crime. "I have papers to grade and laundry to take care of and Will needs help with his homework." She paused and walked toward him, the frontal assault advancing into his demilitarized zone, then stopped a yard away, looking down on him like a commanding officer at a deserting soldier. "So can this wait or do you still need more time to pout?"

He felt the internal gears ratchet, a stirring of juices he could normally hold in check. Not today. He rose, locking eyes. "Excuse me?"

Amy held up her hands and smiled. "You know what? I get it. You're a basketball coach without a team. And now you have to coach cross-country. But it's not the end of the world, John."

Sweat trickling down, he stood firm and the words tumbled. "Oh, is it that simple? I'm glad it's so clear to you. But you forgot the 10 percent pay cut, no scholarship option for our son, no possibility of winning with one runner with asthma. All I'm left with is a job that's totally pointless. I'm glad I have your understanding."

"Stop it!" There was emotion in her voice. "No one asked for this. But this is what we've got. So stop playing the victim here."

John furrowed his brow, the storm raging. "Are you trying to help me? 'Cause you're not!"

As soon as he said it, he knew. It was a moment every married man had experienced, the feeling of justification for lashing out. The fire hydrant that built pressure until, at the turn of a valve by someone who loved him, the water exploded.

Amy's eyes welled with tears. Why didn't she just leave him alone? Why couldn't she keep her words to herself, hold back judgment and challenge until some other time? Why couldn't he just deal with his anger and disappointment how he wanted?

She turned and walked angrily into the house, slamming the door behind her.

They had been to counseling years before, after Will was born. She had gone to a pastor to help deal with some of her struggles, some sleepless nights, anxiety. John had accompanied her to try and help "fix" her and in the process had seen some things about himself, about the way they communicated. Amy was more in touch with her feelings, which meant she realized when she was angry and tried to understand why. John, on the other hand, didn't admit he was angry until the dam broke. And even then he was likely to yell that he wasn't angry.

He picked up a brick and felt the weight in his hand. Something was going on with the conflict with Amy, the situation in town, the school, the basketball team, the church—all this struggle dragged him in some unwanted direction. They'd worked hard to build something and it felt like a pile of bricks.

In a fit of rage, he lifted the brick above his head and hurled it down onto the concrete, smashing it to bits. It felt good. Bricks don't cry. But as he stared at the broken pieces, the detritus of what was once whole, he looked at his life, his wife and family. Were they being reduced to dust because he was unable to give up his fears and self-pity?

He had always told his players it's not the circumstances that are most important; it's how you respond. If a team-mate got into a shooting slump or was injured, others could choose to criticize or encourage.

You could toss bricks or build something.

An old voice came to him with accusation and condemnation. *Who does she think she is? What does she know about the pressure you feel to provide and take care of the family?*

All of this weighed on him. And Amy was telling him to get over it? To stop playing the victim? Wasn't she the one, along with her counselor, who told him he needed to *feel* things? That's what he was doing! And what had he gotten? Criticism.

"No one asked for this. But this is what we've got."

Amy's words echoed. She was right, of course. She was always right about the big picture of their lives. You had to see what you had instead of what you didn't have. Start from where you are, not from where you want to be.

But if God was in control . . .

He sat on a cooler, on the top where it said, Do Not Sit, and put his elbows on his knees. He believed in God and that He was in control. If that was true, at the very least, God had allowed all of this. He'd allowed the team to scatter like dry leaves in the wind. He'd allowed John's vision about his son's future to blur. He'd allowed John to become coach of a one-runner, asthma-laden cross-country team.

Then he thought of Hannah. He'd seen her earlier that day struggling to breathe. Had God allowed that in her life for a reason, or was it all chance? Was it just a bad draw of genetics, or was there more to the story?

"All I'm left with is a job that's totally pointless."

In the corner of his eye he saw movement, and he turned as Amy stopped by the fence beside the driveway. They were both in the shadow of the rim and backboard. As soon as he saw her, he knew what would happen. She would attack. She would list the ways he'd wounded her with his words. So John built a wall to protect himself. He had to shield himself from any pain she was about to inflict.

She picked up a metal stool and placed it a few feet away from him and sat. She didn't smile, didn't try to make things better. He was sure fangs and claws were about to appear. She pulled the stool closer, scraping it hard across the concrete, making him wince at the sound. She was way too close, invading his space.

Then she scooted so close their knees touched. He recoiled, trying to retain a shred of dignity. He was about to receive a tongue-lashing and he probably deserved it.

She dipped her head and gathered herself as if she needed momentum for the jump she was about to take.

"So I have this problem that pops up sometimes. I see things about my husband that I don't really like and so I want to try and fix them. But I'm not very good at it." She chuckled through the emotion. "And maybe I'm not supposed to be. Because he gets really angry with me."

John stared at her. She should be yelling at him. She should be throwing a brick of her own, a fastball pitched in retaliation. Instead, this felt like a loving curve aimed straight at his heart.

"But the thing is, I really, really love him. He's a very good husband. And he's a great dad. And he wants to provide for us and protect us, and I am so very grateful for that. And I know I don't tell him enough."

Amy's words, her demeanor, her emotion caught him in some unreachable place and the wall he had built, the ice that had formed on his heart, began to melt.

She reached out and touched his face. "So when he's discouraged and hurting, I want to try and help. And it's not always easy to know how. So maybe if I just tell him and remind him that I love him and that I'm praying for him and that I'm here for him, I'm right here for him . . ."

John knew he had a choice. He could hold back, wipe his face, and smile . . . or he could surrender to the emotion. Surrender to the love his wife had offered. Surrender to the curveball she had thrown.

"Can I do that?" she said.

What could he say to a heart poured out? His soul softened as he listened and he swallowed hard and choked out, "I love you."

Amy's face lit and a tear ran down her face. "I love you, too."

John put his hand on her head and drew her close, touching foreheads with her, crying together. She told him she loved him again.

"I'm sorry I've been a jerk," he said. "Please forgive me."

They sat a few moments, and John could feel the inexorable draw of his heart to hers. As he collected himself, John stared at the broken brick on the concrete. Parts of his life seemed in pieces and ground to dust. But he had married way above his class. And he thanked God for a wife who could encourage and inspire him even when he'd hurt her with his words and actions.

"What are you going to do now?" Amy said.

"I'm going to tell our sons what kind of woman to look for if they ever get married."

CHAPTER 16

✦ ✦ ✦

Hannah put her tray down at an empty lunch table just as Robert Odelle spoke behind her. She would have avoided him if she had seen him. He had a way of sneaking up on her and jabbing with his words. Were some people born bullies? Or had kids been mean to him in elementary school? Was he just doing to others what they had done to him?

"Sitting with your imaginary friends, Hannah?"

She rolled her eyes and took a deep breath, trying to ignore him. Why didn't a teacher see what he was doing? The school talked about making everyone feel welcome. She believed that, but when Robert lobbed his verbal bombs, all that talk felt hollow, just empty words.

He scurried away and she stared at the empty chairs around her. Some girls attracted friends easily, and the more they made, the more showed up. It was like rich people who made money because they had money. For her, making a friend was the most difficult thing in the world. Mrs. Harrison had talked about magnets and polarization in science class. Hannah was a magnet polarized the wrong way. She repelled instead of attracted others.

"Hey, Hannah, can I sit with you?"

Hannah looked up to see Mrs. Brooks, the principal. Her smile made Hannah feel warm and nervous at the same time. Had she done something wrong? Did Mrs. Brooks know about her "problem"?

"Sure," Hannah said, picking at her carrots on the tray. Suddenly she didn't feel hungry.

"I hear you're running in your first cross-country race tomorrow. Are you excited?"

Nervous was a better word. Her insides felt tight. And she felt sick to her stomach every time she thought about Gina Mimms. She could see the girl racing ahead, crossing the finish line, yawning and doing her nails when Hannah crossed the line. Hannah's fear was that she'd be dead last— or worse, not even finish. She had a recurring nightmare that she would cross the line and it would be dark, no one left, no cheers, just crickets.

"A little," Hannah said. "We don't really have a team."

Mrs. Brooks scrunched up her face. "Girl, that makes

me admire you even more. You still represent our school. Do you enjoy running?"

Admire? Mrs. Brooks admired her? For what? Clearly she didn't know her.

Hannah shrugged. "It's really the only thing I'm good at."

Mrs. Brooks studied her. "Come on, that's not true. Mrs. Harrison said you're a whiz at science. Your grades in your other classes are good."

"That doesn't count," Hannah said.

"Why not?"

"I don't know. Because everybody's supposed to try in class. It's just something you do."

A hint of a smile. Mrs. Brooks took a bite and chewed. Something about seeing her eat—such a small thing—gave Hannah permission to do the same. The woman wiped her mouth with a napkin. "You're doing your best in all your classes—even the ones you don't feel are your best subjects. That's what your other teachers tell me."

"You've been asking them?"

"I talk to teachers about a lot of things. And new students are at the top of the list. I want to make sure you feel welcome."

There were those words again. But this time, somehow she knew the woman meant what she said. Hannah thought this was the perfect time to bring up the subject of Robert and how the skinny bully was doing whatever he could to make her life hard. But she held back. She didn't want Mrs. Brooks to think she complained about everything. Plus, she could handle Robert. She didn't need the principal's help. Everything would work out. Just give it time.

"That verse I mentioned at the start of the school year—you were at the assembly, right?" Mrs. Brooks said.

"Yes, ma'am."

"Whatever you do, work at it with all your heart, as if you're working for the Lord and not for people. That's basically what it says. And it means that whether you're running cross-country or writing an essay in English or eating lunch, you can do it with everything in you."

Hannah wasn't sure what she was supposed to do with those words, so she took another bite and nodded. Nobody expected you to talk when your mouth was full.

"What do you think of the Bible class you take? Is it helping you?"

"It's interesting."

Mrs. Brooks smiled. "What does that mean?"

"I don't know. I've never really read the Bible much outside of church."

Mrs. Brooks nodded as if filing something in her brain. "So when you say you're not good at anything else, tell me what you mean."

So many questions. But the woman seemed interested. "I don't know. I guess I mean I'm not good at anything that counts."

"Want to know something that counts?" Mrs. Brooks said. "You. And I can't wait to see you in that new uniform tomorrow running your heart out."

"You'll be there?"

"Wouldn't miss it."

The next day, Hannah was up before the sun and had dressed in her uniform. She stood in front of the mirror and turned, studying the bright-blue and white colors. She put her hands over her head as if breaking the tape at the finish line. Would she finish? When she walked into the kitchen, her grandmother's mouth dropped.

"Look at you, Hannah—such a pretty blue! You're going to be the best-dressed at the game."

"It's a meet, not a game. And they don't give medals for best-dressed, Grandma."

Her grandmother chuckled and the twinkle in her eyes made it look like she was seeing something more than just Hannah standing there.

"Well, I don't know a whole lot about races and such, but they ought to give a medal for best-dressed. Might make it more exciting. And you would win first place, no doubt. You look pretty as a picture."

When the Harrisons pulled up outside, Hannah was out the door and down the steps. Her grandmother thanked them for giving Hannah a ride and they drove away.

Hannah checked about a hundred times for her inhaler and it was there, right where she had put it.

Coach Harrison looked in the rearview. "Nice day for a long run, eh, Hannah?"

"Yes, sir."

Mrs. Harrison turned. "You feeling okay?"

Hannah nodded. Her asthma wasn't a problem now, but Mrs. Harrison seemed to be asking something more.

"I think you're going to win," Will said. "First place."

"I just don't want to be last," she said.

Will smiled and put his headphones on, his head bopping to his music.

Hannah watched the traffic, cars speeding up and slowing down at stoplights, and she remembered her bus rides when she ran for Franklin High. The memory made her wince.

She was a freshman and felt she didn't belong. The coach and the other girls weren't mean. They just didn't notice her. Hannah was usually last to finish in practice, and when the coach gave tips and pointers for improvement, he never said anything to her. She felt invisible.

The best runner at Franklin High had been a senior, Jessica Simons. All the talk of Gina Mimms by Coach Harrison paled in comparison with the attention given Jessica at Franklin High. She was fit, pretty, popular, always smiled, always dressed nicely, and was headed to some school out west that had given her a scholarship. The team was afflicted with what Hannah termed *Jessica envy*, a malady with symptoms that included dressing like Jessica, parting their hair like hers, and edging closer to her. Hannah felt it too, but she was forced to observe from a distance.

At the last race of the season, Hannah decided to get

noticed. When the gun sounded, she sprinted to the front and ran stride-for-stride with the leaders. It felt good to have runners behind her for a change. Four minutes into the race she actually thought she had a chance at a top-ten finish.

Her vision of staying in front was cut short when she reached the first hill. Runners passed her like she was standing still and she felt an ache in her lungs and legs. She topped the hill and as she entered a narrow stretch of path on the other side, she slipped on loose gravel and reached out to gain her balance. At that very moment, Jessica Simons was passing on Hannah's left. Hannah fell hard, one leg tangling with Jessica's. Both girls tumbled.

Hannah rolled to the right side of the path, gathered herself, and knelt. Runners passed between her and Jessica. Then a Franklin High runner stopped. Jessica wasn't getting up. Her right leg was turned at an odd angle. She was clearly in a lot of pain.

Hannah dodged the next wave of runners and rushed to help.

"Get away from me!" Jessica shouted.

Hannah fell back, startled. She retreated to the top of the ridge to alert others to avoid a fallen runner. It seemed like a kind thing to do. When the stragglers passed and Jessica still lay in a heap, Hannah ran to find her coach.

The result of Jessica's fall was a torn ligament. Surgery was scheduled for the following week. Doctors said she would regain full range of motion, but the rehab stretched for months. Every time Hannah saw Jessica on crutches in the hallway, she hid.

Hannah wondered if Franklin High would be in today's race. And she wondered if Jessica had recovered or if her dreams had died. If so, that was Hannah's fault.

They pulled into the parking lot and Coach Harrison and Will set up the canopy tent while Hannah stretched. Girls with backpacks talked, laughing nervously. Teams warmed up together, lunging, stretching, and some even prayed with arms draped around each other. Hannah noticed Coach Harrison talking with another coach but she couldn't hear the conversation.

When it was almost time for the race, Coach Harrison approached her. "So, Hannah, what was the best advice your coach gave you last year?"

Hannah thought a moment. Her coach hadn't given her advice individually, of course, but she picked something she'd heard him say to others.

"To pace myself and save some energy at the end?"

Coach Harrison looked relieved. "That's exactly right. We're going to keep that in mind when you run today. You're going to do great." He patted her shoulder. "Why don't you head to the starting line?"

Hannah walked away and heard Mrs. Harrison say, "That's all you got?"

She reached the starting line knowing Coach Harrison wasn't any more confident in her than she was. Once there, she jumped and stretched. Parents and siblings on the sideline clapped and cheered. Hannah scanned the crowd for any sign of her grandmother, but she knew better. Her grandmother had to work, and with her schedule, she probably wouldn't see Hannah run all year.

Then Hannah spotted Mrs. Brooks in the bleachers. She wore her Brookshire jersey and waved, giving Hannah a thumbs-up. It calmed Hannah's heart to know the woman had kept her promise to be there.

Before the start, Hannah spotted Gina Mimms to her right. The girl looked strong, fierce, determined. She was focused, like a prizefighter ready to pounce on a weaker opponent.

When the gun sounded, Gina shot from the starting line. She sprinted ahead and Hannah lost her in the wave of runners between them.

Pace yourself, she told herself. But it was hard to hold back and not follow the crowd running at full tilt, especially with the level of cheering from the sideline. She glanced at Coach Harrison, who held up his stopwatch.

"It's not how you start. It's how you finish."

She'd heard that from the coach at Franklin High. She tried to block it out and run.

The course was a winding, undulating path through pine trees. The air felt thick with the smell of freshly fallen needles. Hannah ran past a section of the course where people played Frisbee golf. She'd never played. Seemed like something rich kids would do.

Though she kept what she thought was a good pace,

runners passed her easily. It was hard not to speed up and try to match their pace, but each time she did, she tired quickly. Teams ran together in a line and she heard them encouraging each other. Halfway through, her legs were on fire and breathing became more difficult. She wondered what running without asthma would feel like, and just that thought sent her in a downward spiral. Wanting something she couldn't have always did that.

People cheered loudly at the finish line. Unfortunately, Hannah heard the sound through the trees because she still had half a mile to go.

Colorful flags showed the way and she tried to kick for the final push. By then, her tank was empty and several girls passed her in the last hundred yards.

Mrs. Harrison was the first to her, congratulating her on a great race. Will gave her a high five. "You were awesome."

"You were wrong," Hannah said, gasping. "I didn't finish first."

"Yeah, but you weren't last," he said.

"That's a great start to the year, Hannah," Coach Harrison said. "You should be proud of that race."

"What place did I get?"

"I wouldn't focus on that as much as your time. From my notes, I think that was a personal record for you."

"What place did I get?" she said again.

He lowered his voice. "I think you wound up thirty-fourth. Again, not bad for your first race of the year."

How he said it, the catch in his voice and the way he

glanced down at his clipboard, made her feel ashamed. His words said, "Great job," but his face said something else.

Hannah watched teams gather and thought it was funny that such a solitary sport was done in a crowd.

As they loaded the car and drove away, Hannah spotted Gina Mimms with a medal around her neck, hugging her teammates and smiling for pictures.

Could she ever feel good about her performance if she didn't make the top ten? Coach wanted her to compete against the clock, but clocks didn't win medals. Only fast runners did.

CHAPTER 17

✦ ✦ ✦

John Harrison had wrestled with what to say to Hannah before her first race. Amy had encouraged him to give Hannah a pep talk, something that came naturally before every basketball game he'd ever coached. The words flowed easily in those situations, but with Hannah, his well of encouragement was dry. When she crossed the finish line, Amy had asked what his plan was for her future, and her question haunted him.

Sundays were a day of rest for the Harrison family. They went to church and relaxed in the afternoon, sometimes watching sports or playing games. Will had gone to a friend's house and Ethan said he and some friends were playing a pickup game in the Brookshire gym when John got an idea.

"Where you headed?" Amy said.

"Going to come up with a plan for my team like you suggested." He hugged her and drove to Franklin General Hospital and took the elevator to the fourth floor. He found Thomas Hill lying in bed, staring into the distance at something he would never see, clutching the CD remote. John knocked on the open door.

"Thomas?"

"Yes."

"Hey, it's John Harrison."

A look of recognition filled the man's face. "Oh, it's the maybe/maybe-not basketball coach," he said with a smile. Even blind, there was such a light in the man's eyes.

"Yeah, it's looking more like maybe not," John said. "You got time for a visit?"

"Let me check my calendar," Thomas said. "Yeah, I guess I could squeeze you in."

John sat and explained his coaching frustration. "I watched from the sidelines as every runner finished. And I thought, I need to do something different. I need a plan for my team but I don't have one. I was wondering if you could coach me so I can be a better coach."

Thomas thought a moment and John saw a smile on his face. It looked like he was reliving his running days. "First step in becoming a good coach is understanding what you don't know. It's humility, really. So I commend you for even asking the question."

"Well, it's taken me a while to get here, but I'm ready to learn." He clicked his pen and Thomas turned his head at the sound.

"Best coach I ever had didn't know a whole lot about the sport. He was kind of tubby, actually. He only had one thing he could give."

"What was that?"

"He believed in me. Believed I could run. See, I can give you ideas for your team, ways to train, techniques to make your runners faster and help them progress. But first you have to believe. You have to see what's possible and then give them your vision. Understand?"

"I'll admit my vision for what we can accomplish is pretty low."

"Having a coach who believes is simply gold. Think of it in basketball terms. You go up for a three-pointer toward the end of the game. Do you want a coach saying, 'No, pass it,' or do you want a coach saying, 'I know you can make it'? For a runner, when you hit the wall—and in every race you will hit a wall and you'll think you can't run another step—you reach out and grab on to someone else's hope. Someone else's belief. That can propel you in ways you'd never imagine. That's the kind of hope you need to have and give your team."

"I'm glad you had that kind of coach, Thomas."

"You know what? I believe in you, John Harrison. Just you asking these questions means you can be that kind of coach."

Thomas told John how he would approach the next week in practice, the drills and incremental training that would build endurance. John furiously took notes, trying to keep up, and when Thomas began to talk about threshold speed, John stopped him and asked for an explanation.

"So your threshold speed is the fastest you can run at a consistent pace. Anything beyond that becomes anaerobic, which you save for your kick at the end."

John had his head down in his notes and barely noticed a nurse arrive to take Thomas's vital signs. When she was finished, she said, "Okay, Mr. Hill. I got what I needed. Can I get you anything?"

"I'm good now. Thank you, Rose."

"All right, I'll check on you later."

There was an easy communication between the two and John used the pause in the conversation to finish a couple of notes. When Rose left, Thomas turned his head and picked up where he had stopped.

"Interval training is also good. Run one minute fast, then one minute slow. Then increase to two minutes fast, one slow. Three fast . . . you get the idea."

"Oh, this is good," John said, drinking in the information.

When Thomas spoke, he waved the CD remote like a conductor waving a baton. "It should go without saying that them eating healthy and getting good sleep is crucial for your team."

John felt bad that he hadn't told Thomas the whole

truth about his team. Now seemed like a good time. "Well, I only have one runner and she's got asthma, so I have to figure out—"

Thomas interrupted him with a wave of laughter. "Wait a minute, hold up. You lost your ball team. You changed sports. And you still got no team. Well, that's sad, even for me." He cackled to himself.

John took the ribbing in stride. "You see why I'm so frustrated."

"Yeah, actually I do."

The passion rose in John. "This year I had the players, I had the schedule. I mean, this was going to be our year." He stopped, catching himself as the tension rose. He wasn't here to talk about his shattered dreams. They'd simply come tumbling out. "I'm sorry. I don't mean to dump on you."

Thomas quieted and became serious. "Well, look. I'm sure you've thought about leaving town, too."

"I don't know where I'd go," John said.

This man who was broken and secluded had entered into John's pain. It wasn't fair to burden him, but somehow Thomas seemed ready. And with every blip from the heart monitor, it seemed this friendship drew closer. Slowly, deliberately, he turned his head.

"John, if I asked you who you are, what's the first thing that comes to mind?"

He thought a moment. "I'm a basketball coach."

"And if that's stripped away?"

"Well, I'm also a history teacher."

"Okay," Thomas said. "We take that away, who are you?"

There was something about Thomas and how he spoke that let John put down his defenses. "Well, I'm a husband, I'm a father . . ."

"And God forbid that should ever change, but if it does, who are you?"

That question unsettled him. Like some of his arguments with Amy, Thomas had touched a nerve. The third rail of his heart. He'd come for coaching help. Suddenly the spotlight had turned to his own life.

"I don't understand this game."

"It's not a game, man," Thomas said. "Who are you?"

John uncrossed his legs and sat forward. "I'm a white American male."

Thomas threw back his head and laughed. "Yeah, that's for sure."

John checked his notes—he wanted to get Thomas back on the cross-country trail.

"Is there anything else?" Thomas said, not letting up.

John searched his mental biography. "Well, I'm a Christian."

Thomas grew quiet. "And what's that mean?"

"It means follower of Christ," John said matter-of-factly.

"And how important is that?"

A flash in John's memory. He was on the floor in his dorm room. Helpless. An injury had brought him to the end of himself. A friend had been there to help point him in the direction of who he really was.

"It's very important," John said.

"Interesting how it's so far down your list."

John sat back, feeling like he'd just been fouled going for a layup. "Okay, wait a minute. I could have easily said Christian first."

"Yeah, but you didn't."

John knew Thomas couldn't see, but it felt like he was staring straight through him.

"Look, John, your identity will be tied to whatever you give your heart to. Doesn't sound like the Lord has first place."

"You're calling me a bad Christian?"

"Let me be a little direct," Thomas said.

A little? John thought.

"Last time you were here, you said you'd pray for me."

The words sank deep and John knew what was coming. He wanted to stop Thomas, protest, explain he wasn't a professional minister, he was busy with work and family, and he'd taken the time to talk out of the goodness of his heart and here he was using . . .

He decided not to go there. Instead, he listened and heard words that cut like a knife.

"Did you?" Thomas said softly.

Simple questions often lead to hidden passages. The world turns and hearts find their way when simple questions are given the space for honest answers. John tried to avoid it, but he knew Thomas would call him out. It was the most painful word John had ever said.

"No."

"No," Thomas repeated, somehow absorbing the pain and showing his words had never been an accusation. He now spoke slowly, with compassion.

"For someone who knows the Lord, you're acting like somebody who doesn't. Which makes me wonder. What have you allowed to define you? When you lost your team, it didn't just disappoint you—it devastated you. *Something* or *someone* will have first place in your heart."

John stared at Thomas. There was a feeling of freedom here. He realized no matter how he responded, Thomas would accept him. With his next words, Thomas's face changed, like he was seeing something new—something John couldn't even grasp.

"But when you find your identity in the One who created you, it will change your whole perspective."

Thomas's eyes moistened and John saw life in the man. He was sick, he was dying, but he was also expressing something from a deep well of his life and offering it as a gift.

"You've given me a lot to think about," John said, moving the chair back and standing.

Thomas stuck out his hand and held it aloft. When John took it, Thomas squeezed tightly. "I hope I didn't come down on you too hard, John Harrison. And I have a confession."

"What's that?"

"I've been praying for you ever since you stumbled into

my room. I pray for everybody who comes in here. And I'm going to keep praying for you. I wanted you to know that."

John walked out of the room and took the stairs, slowly making his way to the first floor and out a side exit. In his truck, the emotion came. He saw the truth now. Thomas and Amy had seen something and were trying to help pull back the curtain, but only God could open the eyes of the blind.

John had tried to follow God and live well. But somehow he had made life about what he could accomplish. And Thomas had challenged him to a new perspective. He had shown him the emptiness of chasing success.

John put his hands on the steering wheel. He'd never felt further from God and at the same time closer to God. Layers of his life were peeling away and showed what he really trusted.

The only words he could say were "I'm sorry." And instead of judgment and condemnation, he felt an embrace.

"I'm sorry, Lord. You're first. You are first."

As cars pulled out around him, John thanked God for His kindness and for revealing what was most important. That hospital parking lot became a new starting line to his life. God had used a blind man to show him what he couldn't see. That made John smile through his tears.

CHAPTER 18

✦ ✦ ✦

Hungry and exhausted, Barbara walked through the door with a handful of bills. It felt like every time she paid one bill, two took its place. It was like trying to plug a hole in a boat already filled with water. She put down her purse and saw the disarray in the kitchen. The trash overflowed, so she wrapped it up and got it to the curb.

She returned to a sink full of dirty dishes. There were more on the counter. The dishwasher had stopped working a year earlier and she couldn't even afford the trip charge for the repairman to diagnose the problem, so the dishes had to be done by hand. Why couldn't her granddaughter do her part?

"Hannah?" she said loudly.

No response. She was probably in her room with music blaring in her earbuds. She had warned Hannah about damaging her hearing, but *lonely* didn't care about decibel levels. Or sometimes Hannah studied with the television on. Hearing voices on the television, she said, helped her not to feel alone. That pierced Barbara's heart, but what could she do?

Barbara took a deep breath as if diving underwater for sunken treasure and cleaned the counter. She hated leaving Hannah alone while she worked, but the girl was too old for a babysitter. Their neighbor, Mrs. Cole, checked on her and gave Barbara a report every now and then. Hannah spent time in school and ran cross-country and there was the Y program. All of that was to keep her busy and out of trouble.

There was always more Barbara could do. She kept a mental list of things she ought to do to keep Hannah from becoming . . .

The old wound again. It didn't take long to return there, to wander back to her ground zero of pain. The only good thing about memories like these was it made Barbara move faster and get more done. Keeping busy pushed the hurt away and kept it at a distance. The harder she worked, the easier it was to sleep. But her last waking thoughts were usually regrets. Things left unsaid and undone and the guilt that lingered.

Hannah's backpack sat on the table and her shoes were by the front door, where she'd kicked them off. She'd told the girl to hang her backpack on the hook she'd installed by the door instead of slinging it onto the table or the couch. The unzipped pack fell open when she grabbed it to clear the table, and something caught her eye. She lifted the flap and among the notebooks and papers and textbooks was a man's watch with a black band.

Her heart sank. The air went out of the room. She pulled out the watch and studied it. "Oh no she didn't," she said to herself. Then she raised her voice. "Hannah!"

No response.

She stomped toward Hannah's room, each step stirring more hurt. Her heart beat wildly. If Barbara had an anger tank, it was full to overflowing.

"My cup runneth over," she thought.

She stood in the open bedroom door and saw the girl on her bed, earbuds in, reading a running magazine. Her biology and history books sat like lonely soldiers on her nightstand. Barbara yelled Hannah's name with such force it surprised even her.

Hannah looked up, doe-eyed and frightened. She'd been lost in what she was reading and listening to.

"Where'd this come from?" Barbara said, holding out the watch.

Hannah removed the earbuds. "I didn't know you were home."

Barbara held out the watch as evidence, like a prosecuting attorney, and shook her head. She wasn't going to let

157

the girl change the subject. Before she spoke, she noticed what Hannah's earbuds were plugged into.

"That is not the iPod that you were supposed to be taking back . . ."

Hannah stared at her, caught in her own trap.

"I'm not doing this, Hannah," Barbara said, feeling at the end of her patience, the end of her ability to love. "I cannot do this by myself. I'm doing everything I can to support you, and you keep doing things like this." Her knuckles turned white holding the watch. "Why?"

Barbara felt transported to another bedroom years earlier. She had used the same passion and words with Janet. And here she was again, repeating herself, walking the same tightrope over a canyon so deep she couldn't see the bottom.

Quietly, softly, Hannah said, "I don't know."

"You don't know?" Barbara said, her eyes like fire. "Baby girl, let me tell you something. This is wrong! You know better than this."

Hannah stared, unmoving. Fear and shame had a hold on her.

"Girl, you're going to fool around and get your behind locked up and there's nothing I can do about it."

That was Barbara's greatest fear. Hannah would be sent to juvenile detention. Or her luck would run out too late and she'd be caught and tried as an adult.

Barbara glared at Hannah, holding her gaze, then tossed the watch on the bed beside the girl and walked out. She wanted to scream. She wanted to handcuff Hannah and keep her from doing one more stupid thing with her life. She was going to get expelled from that new school. And then what would Barbara do with her?

She wandered into the kitchen and sat at the table and put her head in her hands. Her hunger had given way to frustration and despair. The hopelessness she felt almost drove her to pray.

Almost.

CHAPTER 19

✦ ✦ ✦

John found Ethan alone at the Brookshire gymnasium and watched him from the shadows. Ethan had such a pure shot. And he had a way of seeing so much of the court. He anticipated the movements not only of his own teammates but his opponents as well. It was the kind of thing you couldn't coach. You just shook your head in admiration. Now, watching Ethan shoot, John remembered Thomas's words and his perspective on life.

John walked past half-court as Ethan sank a sixteen-foot jumper.

"You know, you can still be a walk-on somewhere."

Ethan put the ball on his hip, his cheeks flushed, his forehead sweaty. "That won't pay for college."

John nodded. "So earn it. Lots of guys get a scholarship when they're already on a team. Or make the grades."

Ethan stared at the ball, then looked up, something in his eyes. "What if I can't do it?"

John looked away, hearing the doubt in his son's voice. He wanted to give him confidence. "I'll help you where I can. But you may have to get a job and work your way through like most people."

Ethan looked down the court and John thought of all the games they'd shared in this gymnasium. He wanted to say something profound, something his son would remember years from now. Instead, he put up both hands, requesting the ball. Ethan rifled a pass to him, the Wilson *pinging* in his hands.

John held the ball and turned it, studying the craftsmanship. Then it came to him. Echoes of what Thomas had said. He looked up at Ethan.

"If you never play in college at all, I love you. And I'm already proud of you."

Ethan drank in the words. He looked into John's eyes and nodded like he'd received them and filed them away for future use.

John slapped the ball with a hand. "But to keep you humble, I'm about to tear you up in one-on-one." He bounced the ball to his son. "Check."

A big grin. "Come on, Dad. Don't do this to yourself."

"Give me the ball. You're going down."

Ethan bounced the ball to John. "You can't beat me."

John took a quick twenty-footer just beyond the three-point arc and sank it. "Oh, you're going to let me do that right in front of you?"

Ethan got the rebound and took it to the back court.

"No, no, no, it's make it, take it. Give me the ball."

Ethan shook his head. "Are you serious?"

John got the ball, and this time Ethan was on him, swiping at the ball, pushing his shoulder as he tried to drive toward the basket.

"Foul," John said, still dribbling.

"No foul!" Ethan said, moving his feet and protecting the basket.

John threw up a turnaround jumper that miraculously went in and he gave a whoop and lifted both hands in victory.

"It's a long way to twenty, old guy," Ethan said, laughing.

John took the ball out and drove again, this time Ethan stripping it from him, the ball bouncing off John's knee and out of bounds.

"My ball, top of the key," Ethan said. "Let's see your defense."

It was a game John would never forget. Something had lifted from his shoulders talking with Thomas, and he was passing that to Ethan in a way he couldn't explain but felt keenly.

At dinner, John and Ethan recounted the matchup playfully. Amy wanted to know who won. Ethan said he did but John countered with the number of fouls Ethan had committed.

"Dad, you taught me to be aggressive."

"Yeah, but not against me," John said, deadpan. "I'm your dad—you've got to respect your elders."

Amy laughed. "It sounds like he beat you."

"Well, in some ways I kind of feel like I won," John said.

"Hey," Ethan said. "You said that feelings don't determine facts."

"You did say that," Amy said.

John stared at his plate of spaghetti. And after a long pause he said, "Yeah, he won."

Ethan beamed. "Thank you."

As they finished the meal, John sat back and looked at each member of his family. It was time to put words to what had happened inside. "I need to say something that's been kind of gnawing at me. Losing the basketball season was disappointing. But it shouldn't have crushed me. I think it's because I've had some things out of order."

Ethan and Will stared at him. Amy gave a slight smile, knowing more about the process he'd gone through than the boys. His voice trembled a bit when he said, "My faith in God should be the most important part of who I am. I think I let less important things get in front of Him. So I need to say I'm sorry and that I've asked God to help me keep my priorities straight."

John had been nervous about opening up in front of his

family. But he received nothing but support. They were on his team. They wanted the best for him, as he did for them.

"I can't worry about what I can't control. So I've got to trust Him no matter what."

Will looked at him and said, "Cool."

"Cool?" John said, smiling.

"Cool," Amy said.

Ethan looked at his plate, smiling with the others, but clearly he still had questions.

"All right, cool," John said.

CHAPTER 20

✦ ✦ ✦

"I wish you could have seen him," John said as he stood by Thomas's bed. "Will's eyes were as big as saucers while he was talking about how to make cross-country a better sport."

Thomas chuckled. "What did he come up with?"

"Well, he said each runner ought to dribble a ball."

"For three miles? Up and down hills?"

"Yeah, and get this: when you hit the finish line, you have to dunk the ball in an eight-foot goal, unless you get tackled."

"There's tackling?" Thomas said, laughing harder.

"Absolutely! And if you steal someone else's ball, you get double points."

Thomas shook his head. "That is one creative kid. Cross-country full contact."

"You should have seen the look on his face when I suggested you could tackle a person, steal their ball, and double dunk on them. Blew his mind."

Thomas threw back his head and howled. "And what did you say?"

John looked out the window as the sun streamed into the room. "I told him I liked it. But that I couldn't make any changes this year. He calls it Tackle Ball Extreme."

Thomas smiled. "Well, they do change the rules from time to time."

John sat by Thomas's bed. "There's a few schools trying to get earbuds allowed for runners."

"During races?"

"Yeah, but it won't happen."

John studied the man. Thomas was tethered to a monitor. He hadn't moved from that bed since they'd first met. And he hadn't complained about his situation. John asked questions, received coaching tips, but today he wanted to thank Thomas and share something deeper than a story about his family.

"So I've started implementing your running tips. She's running intervals now."

"Good. You should see some improvement."

John took a deep breath. "I also want to thank you for what you said. I think I'm more of a hypocrite than I'd like to admit."

Thomas turned his head slightly. "John, that's true of me, too. Three years ago, God had to let me lose my sight before I could see."

"You've only been a Christian three years?"

"Yeah, I tend to learn things the hard way." Thomas thought a moment and as he spoke, he seemed to relive the past. "When I was much younger, I *found* myself in athletics. Then in my job and friends. And it turned into drugs and women. I hurt a lot of people, John."

John could almost weigh the man's remorse in a balance. Getting the words out seemed painful, but at the same time, healing. Truth will do that to a person. As Thomas shared his past, John looked away as if Thomas cared about eye contact. Then John consciously chose to watch the face of this man as he revealed his heart.

"It all caught up to me," Thomas said. "And that's when I turned to God. Sick and broken. Now He's all I've got. He's everything to me."

John recalled something Thomas had said the first day they talked. "You said you grew up here."

"I did. I left Franklin fifteen years ago running from all my responsibilities. I had a child with my girlfriend. But we got hooked on meth. And it took her life. I left the child with her grandmother. Then I ran. I just ran."

John didn't miss the irony. Thomas was a top-notch runner, and when he couldn't face the pain he'd caused, he did what he knew best. "Was it a boy or a girl?"

Thomas smiled, his face lighting. "A little girl. She was born on Valentine's Day."

Fifteen years . . . Something sparked in John's mind, the math of Thomas's past. He was glad Thomas couldn't see the look on his face. As the story continued to unfold, John couldn't get past the startling detail about the birth date of Thomas's daughter.

When he finished, John thanked Thomas for sharing his story and told him he was an inspiration. Then he drove home in a daze, calling Amy before he arrived and asking if they could talk. "I have something I need to share."

He told her the story when he arrived home and Amy looked as shocked as he had been.

"Wait, you think this man who's been helping you coach . . ."

John nodded.

"She said that her father passed away."

"Maybe that's what she was told."

"So you don't think he did," Amy said.

John shook his head.

"That poor girl," Amy said. "What are you going to do?"

"Good question."

CHAPTER 21

✦ ✦ ✦

Hannah rode with the Harrisons to the next race and they seemed quiet, like maybe they'd had a fight. It could have been something with their sons that had them worried. She noticed little changes like that, the way they didn't make eye contact. Then she wondered if her grandmother had called and told them about her "problem." Maybe Principal Brooks had told them about why she was kicked out of Franklin High.

Hannah's mouth felt like cotton and she took a sip from her water bottle. She lived with the fear of someone discovering she stole things, a dark cloud that hung over her every day. It would have been enough to keep her from ever stealing again, if logic had anything to do with it. Who would want to live with that guilt?

When her grandmother had asked why she took things, Hannah told the truth. She really didn't know why. If she did, she would stop. It was just that every time she saw something of value, like the headphones on the bench or the watch on the bleachers, some inner switch flipped. It seemed each item she saw had a little sign only she could see, a voice whispering, "Take me! You need me!" She had to reach out and make them her own. Was it adrenaline that made her do it? Something else in her brain?

In science class, Mrs. Harrison had talked about all the chemicals and hormones in the human body and how intricately people were designed. But sometimes things got out of balance. Could her problem be too much of a hormone? Maybe her asthma robbed her of something, disrupted some vital brain chemistry, and that was why she stole. Hannah had all kinds of theories and possibilities but no way to know.

Another theory was that her parents had done this to her. One day she asked her grandmother about her mother. "When she was a kid, did she ever do anything that made you mad?"

Just the mention of her mom sent her grandmother into some other world. She'd shake her head and scowl. Hannah never brought up her father anymore. That door was closed and locked tight. So she was left to guess and come up with ideas on her own.

Mrs. Harrison had also talked about patterns of behavior and patterns of thinking that became paths in the mind. She said it was like water running through a channel and carving out a creek or a river. You do something over and over and it becomes a hard-to-break habit.

The truth was, Hannah wanted to blame her problem on anything but herself. She wanted to feel she couldn't control her actions, that she couldn't say no. If there was something in her brain going wrong, she didn't have to feel guilty. But that was just it—she did. Even now, riding in the back of the Harrisons' car, the weight of all those things in the blue box pushed down on her. It was like running with a backpack filled with rocks, and the longer she carried it, the heavier it became. She knew she needed to take that backpack off and pull all the rocks out, but she had no idea how. She'd carried it for so long.

She hadn't needed the things she stole. It wasn't like she was starving and grabbed a sandwich from someone's lunch. She could explain that. She took things like the bracelet with shiny pendants from a younger girl at the Y. The girl wore it every day that summer, and the first time Hannah saw it hanging out of a zippered backpack pouch, she grabbed it. Later, the girl had gone from one person to another, tearfully asking if anyone had seen it.

"My daddy gave it to me," the girl said. "He's in the Army over in Afghanistan."

That tore Hannah up. How would she have felt if someone had stolen something given by her father or mother? Hannah didn't have anything like that, except for the pictures she kept squirreled away in her closet. Could that be why she wanted what others had? Were those things filling up a space inside? There was something about the objects—the digital camera, the cute blue watch with the flowers. She never wore the watches, never used the camera, but having them made her feel something. Hannah knew where the owners of these items lived and that they weren't rich or spoiled, they couldn't go out and replace the stolen items. So why did she keep them and not return them? Why didn't she give back that girl's bracelet if it meant so much?

Deep inside, Hannah knew she could resist the urge to steal. It had happened many times. Something would be sitting on a table, a teacher's purse would be open and Hannah would see a wallet. But because there were others in the room who would see her, she held back. She knew she could choose a better way. She simply didn't, and that's what bothered her and made her feel guilty.

When they arrived at the meet, Hannah stretched and prepared for the race. Other runners paired off with team members or coaches, but Hannah stretched alone. Somehow she felt she didn't deserve to have others around.

"How are you feeling?" Coach Harrison said.

Hannah shrugged. "Okay."

"I have big hopes for you today. All the interval training we've done in practice—I'll bet this will be your fastest time yet. What do you think?"

Hannah looked at the ground. "I'll do my best, Coach."

"And that's all I'm asking."

When the gun sounded, Hannah bolted, watching the girls in front of her running in a pack, teammates pacing each other. For the first half mile, she was shoulder to shoulder with several runners, fighting for position. Then she felt a burst of speed. When she ran alone in practice, she gauged her success by her own pace and looking at a watch. During a race, she could step to the side and fly past others. Each time she did, it felt like she was progressing. And in some ways she seemed to take something of value from those she passed. She had been in their position and she didn't like it. To be the one moving ahead felt good.

She tried hard to focus on the race, but she couldn't get the face of her grandmother out of her head. She saw her holding Coach Harrison's watch. Saw her toss it on her bed. She blinked and tried to forget the look her grandmother had given before she left the room. It was sheer disappointment in her grandmother's eyes. She heard venom in her voice as she yelled her name.

"Girl, you're going to fool around and get your behind locked up."

Hannah imagined herself in an orange prison jumpsuit instead of a cross-country uniform. She saw razor wire and iron bars and the stern face of her dejected grandmother visiting a drab lunchroom, sitting across from her, shaking her head.

"And there's nothing I can do about it."

Running cross-country was hard enough when you could corral your thoughts. It was harder when they had free range to your soul. She tried pushing the memories away, tried outrunning them, but every time she took a breath, they condemned, accused, pointed a finger, passed her and looked back in frustration. The face of Headphone Guy flashed in her mind.

"If I see her again, she's gonna pay!"

Hannah ran faster as if he were chasing her. Could she use these negative thoughts for something good?

As she passed a runner on her left, something went wrong. She looked at the others ahead and her vision blurred. She heard a weird sound and realized it wasn't from the woods. It was from her. It was the familiar dry wheeze. Each step became like lifting bags of sand. She couldn't look ahead anymore, so she looked down and tried to breathe, just focus on that simple thing, breathing. But her lungs wouldn't obey. They were protesting.

Hannah hated asthma. She hated giving in to it and slowing down. She wanted to pretend it wasn't there, but it was back now, with a vengeance, stealing her breath.

Runners passed one by one until all of them were ahead of her. She didn't care. When you can't breathe, you focus all your energy and thoughts on that one thing. She slowed, bending to try any position to retrieve her breath. She stumbled toward a tree and put a hand out. Steadying herself, she remembered the inhaler.

She pulled it from its carrier and lifted it to her mouth, the canister heavy as a dumbbell. She inhaled a puff and waited. Her legs gave way and she fell, her back scraping rough tree bark. Sweat dripped from her nose. Trees blurred. She thought of taking another puff, but even her thoughts had weight now. Everything was too heavy. She dropped the inhaler and it fell somewhere in the leaves.

Where was she? Maybe halfway? No one would hear her if she yelled. And she couldn't yell anyway. How would she get back? What would Coach Harrison think if she didn't finish? His words weighed on her. He thought her time would be better. She wanted to finish in the top twenty. Maybe surprise everyone and get into the top ten. But now, sitting on the prickly pine needles, her back itching, she knew there was no finishing this race. And what was the point?

She felt a gust of wind in the trees and looked up, the world swaying above and underneath her. Such a peaceful place. Such a storm inside. She heard voices in the distance. It sounded like echoes from some faraway land.

"There she is!"

"Hannah!"

She didn't realize it was the Harrisons until they reached her, grabbing her arms and helping her up. Mrs. Harrison found her inhaler on the ground and Hannah took another puff. She wasn't getting the medicine.

"Do you need to go to the hospital?" Mrs. Harrison said.

Hannah shook her head. Her grandmother would kill her. "Replacement cartridge."

"Did you bring one?" Mrs. Harrison said.

Hannah nodded. "Backpack." *Wheeze.* "Front pouch." *Wheeze.* "In a cool pack."

Coach Harrison took off through the woods. He looked scared but determined. He disappeared into the trees and

Mrs. Harrison helped her walk, but they only made it about fifty yards. A few minutes later a runner with a Tucker High jersey found them. She had her hair in a blonde braid and wore braces. She handed the cartridge to Hannah.

"Coach Harrison said I would get this to you faster than he could," the girl said.

"Thank you," Mrs. Harrison said, looking through the trees.

The girl studied Hannah. "I passed you on the course and heard you breathing hard, but I didn't know you had asthma. I'm sorry. I should have stopped."

"It's okay," Hannah said, plugging in the new vial and taking a puff. Immediately she felt the difference. "Thank you for bringing this."

"Oh, no problem. Like I said, if I'd have known, I would have stopped."

When Coach Harrison returned, his blue coach's shirt was soaked with sweat. He kept looking at Hannah, obviously distraught. He walked with them to the starting line, where coaches and parents waited. Hannah didn't want to be seen. She didn't want their pity. She stared at the ground until they made it to the car and she waited inside while they took down the tent and packed up.

I hate asthma.

Was this God's way of punishing her? Had all her stealing piled up enough for Him to zap her during the race? Perhaps that was how life worked. If you did more good than bad, God would leave you alone. But when something tipped the scales, He acted. Maybe that was why her mother and father had died. They did one too many bad things and God punished them.

Her grandmother asked, but Hannah didn't tell her much about the race, only that she had to stop halfway through. She rested on Sunday, staying in bed all morning, then tried to study for a test but couldn't concentrate.

Hannah returned to school Monday with a better attitude. She had decided not to let that one failure derail her running career. It was just one race. She needed to put it behind her and move on. Besides, nobody at school knew about it except the Harrisons.

Two girls from her algebra class sat at a lunch table, and to her surprise they asked Hannah to join them. Leslie was tall, had long brown hair, and had played on the girls' basketball team the year before. Grace was African American and a whiz at algebra. She knew every answer when the teacher called on her. Hannah wanted to ask for help on a homework assignment, but she was new to the class and kept her questions to herself and tried to figure it out on her own.

"Leslie was telling me about a retreat she went on this weekend," Grace said.

"Where'd you go?" Hannah said.

"It was at a camp our church owns. Hiking trails and a lake. The cabins are pretty rustic, but it was fun."

"What did you do?" Hannah said. "I've never been to a campground."

"You should come to our youth group," Leslie said. "We

do Bible studies and play games. Best part of the weekend was the campfire. We sang and roasted marshmallows and ate s'mores."

Hannah had heard of s'mores, but she had no idea how to roast a marshmallow, and she didn't want to ask and look stupid. Her heart fluttered a little and she felt somehow her world was changing. Maybe she would try the youth group, if her grandmother let her. Maybe she didn't have to be on the outside looking in at everyone in the school.

She heard a familiar voice and looked up as Robert stopped in front of her. He spoke with a sneer. "So, Hannah, I heard you didn't even finish the race. What's up with that?" He said it loud enough for Leslie and Grace to hear.

Hannah looked at her food. To her surprise, Grace spoke up.

"Go away, Robert."

No one had ever stuck up for her like that and goose bumps rose on her arms. Hannah studied her food and hoped Robert would be gone when she looked up. Instead, he inched closer, staring as if he were waiting to see the look on her face when he zinged her again.

"I mean, giving up is even worse than coming in last."

Something rose up in Hannah and she grabbed the first thing she could find, a cup of red soda, and threw it at him. It splashed on his striped shirt. *Good luck getting that out,* she thought.

Suddenly Robert was receiving something he hadn't planned. He obviously didn't have a lot of experience with anyone responding to his taunts. The lunchroom quieted as he dropped his tray on the table. His mouth fell open in horror.

"Are you kidding me? You're such a loser!"

If Robert had gone away, none of this would have happened. If Robert had kept his mouth shut, there would be no stain on his brightly colored shirt. But Robert had finally hit the nerve of Hannah's anger and she wasn't through teaching him a lesson.

She rose from the table and in one motion tossed the contents of her entire tray at him. He recoiled, but not quickly enough. The tray slammed against his chest and food splattered to the floor. Students gasped at the scene and stared, suddenly quiet and riveted to the two, as if this were a reality show.

Robert had potato on his neck and chin and the lasagna had left a tomato-sauce stain on his shirt. If there had been judges watching the toss, Hannah thought she would have received a perfect 10 for accuracy.

Hannah looked for something else to toss his way when Mrs. Charles, the lunchroom monitor, swept in. "Robert, stop it! Now you go get cleaned up and come to the office."

Robert turned and walked without speaking, dripping as he trudged away. Hannah felt vindicated. Mrs. Charles had obviously seen how mean he had been and that he'd deserved to wear Hannah's lunch. She looked toward the two girls at her table. Leslie and Grace looked horrified. Hannah couldn't tell whether she'd just lost her only chance at new friends.

"And you," Mrs. Charles said, looking straight at Hannah, "come with me now."

It was the same look her grandmother had given and her voice was filled with disappointment and judgment. Hannah made the long walk through the lunchroom with people whispering and tittering around her.

She passed Ethan Harrison, the coach's son. He would tell his dad and even if she wasn't expelled, it felt like her cross-country career was over.

Mrs. Charles led Hannah to the principal's office, a long walk down a hall of shame, past staring students. Hannah sat in a chair and waited in the outer office while an assistant contacted Mrs. Brooks and alerted her there was a "DS" and she was needed. Hannah had been reduced to an acronym.

Waiting was always hardest. If she could have walked in and explained everything, just tossed the story out there, surely Mrs. Brooks would have understood. But the longer she waited, the more she stewed, and the more she felt everyone was against her.

She'd overheard one of the kids in the lunchroom saying Principal Brooks was tough. Hannah was inclined to agree. She had a nice smile, but you could tell she was in control, like a general overseeing an army. She'd been kind to Hannah, had remembered her name. But now Hannah was sure she was about to become an example.

Hannah heard heels striking tile and Mrs. Brooks arrived. She looked at Mrs. Charles, then glanced down and her mouth dropped open. "Hannah, what are you doing here?"

Mrs. Charles was more than ready to answer. They stepped inside Mrs. Brooks's office and closed the door, leaving Hannah straining to hear. The noise in the office and the thickness of the door made that impossible.

Finally the door opened. "Come on, let's go," Mrs. Brooks said when Mrs. Charles left, motioning Hannah inside with a tilt of her head.

Two chairs sat in front of Mrs. Brooks's desk and Hannah chose the one closest to the window. Mrs. Brooks closed the door and slowly sat at her desk. Her office was decorated with pictures of the Brooks family and her desk was busy but organized. A Brookshire coffee mug sat next to the biggest calendar Hannah had ever seen. There were sticky notes on the woman's computer monitor and a picture of her and a man Hannah guessed was her husband. The man had his arm around her, and Mrs. Brooks leaned against his shoulder. They looked happy. In love. A real family, like the magazine ad Hannah kept on her nightstand.

"What did Robert say to you?" Mrs. Brooks said. "Mrs. Charles didn't hear it."

"It doesn't matter."

Mrs. Brooks tipped her head. "Hannah, if it didn't matter, I wouldn't have asked. Mrs. Charles saw you toss your drink and heard him say something. That's evidently when you decided he needed to wear your lunch."

Hannah looked up and saw the woman staring at her with . . . not a smile but something close to it.

"What did he say?"

Hannah told her.

She pursed her lips. "My guess is, knowing Robert, this is not the first time he's done something like this to you. Am I right?"

Hannah nodded. "He's been doing this since the first day."

"And you didn't tell anybody because . . . ?"

"I thought if I ignored him, he'd go away."

"And how's that working out for you?"

"Not too good."

"So you held it in and it built up and today you exploded."

Hannah sat up, her adrenaline kicking in. "I didn't start it."

"I know you didn't start it. But you don't fight wrong by doing something wrong yourself."

Hannah stared out the window, waiting for the bad news. Waiting for the word *expulsion*.

Mrs. Brooks kept silent until Hannah's eyes wandered back to hers. "Hannah, you cannot control what other people say. You can only choose the way you respond."

She looked out the window again. There was a nice view of the trees in front. She remembered the trees she was under when the Harrisons found her, gasping for breath, two days earlier. It was the same feeling she had now.

She gritted her teeth and said something she wasn't expecting. "I hate asthma."

There it was. The truth about her life. Her life was asthma. She'd been controlled by it. She would always be held back by it. It was with her every morning when she awoke and every night when she went to sleep.

She waited for the yelling, like she'd heard from her grandmother. She waited for stern words and an angry look. That didn't come. Instead, Mrs. Brooks pushed back from her desk and moved to the chair next to Hannah. She looked her straight in the eyes.

"I am sorry that you have to deal with that. I really am. But your life is worth so much more than this."

It sounded like something the principal of a Christian school would say. Hannah looked at her and said, "To who?"

"To me. To us. To your grandmother. Hannah, even more than that, to God."

Hannah had been wondering when Mrs. Brooks would pull out the God card. But she'd been expecting it to be played against her. Mrs. Brooks seemed to be offering it to her.

"He created you," Mrs. Brooks said like she believed it. "He loves you. Do you believe that?"

Hannah felt trapped. If she said what she really thought, maybe she'd get kicked out of school. If you didn't believe God loved you, would they do that? She wanted to say, *If God loved me so much, why did He give me asthma? Why did He let my mother and father die? Doesn't seem like He cares a whole lot.*

Instead, she said something that felt as close to the truth as she could get. "I don't know."

Mrs. Brooks looked at Hannah and her face showed pain, like Hannah's words had touched some deep nerve. There was a commotion in the outer office and Hannah heard Robert's voice. "She ruined my new shirt. There's supposed to be a zero-tolerance policy. If she's not expelled, my dad's going to come here and you'll answer to him."

Mrs. Brooks rose primly, opened the door, then closed it behind her. Hannah heard the woman speaking in low tones and Robert saying, "But . . ." every now and then. A few moments later Mrs. Brooks returned to the room and Robert was gone.

"Is he right about the zero-tolerance policy?"

"I'm the principal, Hannah. It's my job to be fair and to enforce the policies. What you did was wrong. Do you admit that?"

"Yes, ma'am."

"I'll talk with Robert. He's upset about what you did, but given the information you've shared, I'm sure he'll want me to be fair with him rather than follow the policy to the letter. Everybody wants justice until *they* do something wrong. And then they want mercy."

"So I'm not expelled?"

"No."

"Can I still be on the cross-country team?"

She nodded. "I don't see this changing that." She paused a moment. "Mrs. Charles said you didn't have a whole lot to eat. I brought an extra sandwich in my lunch. Would you like that? Or I could get you Robert's shirt."

Mrs. Brooks raised an eyebrow and Hannah almost saw her smile. It made Hannah think she might want to become a principal someday.

CHAPTER 22

✦ ✦ ✦

John heard about Hannah's confrontation with Robert from Bonnie Reese, who worked in the lunchroom. Bonnie hadn't seen everything, but she had cleaned up the food and red soda after the incident. He talked with Olivia Brooks, who advised him to simply move forward without making a big deal of it. Hannah needed stability and encouragement and grace.

"There's a lot going on inside that girl," Olivia said.

John nodded. He wanted to tell her what he'd discovered about Thomas Hill but hesitated.

That afternoon at practice, Amy helped Hannah stretch and Will sat on the bench working on rules for Tackle

Ball Extreme, complete with pictures and diagrams. He'd decided to include a paintball section in each run.

John studied Hannah's times. There was no doubt she was stronger. She shaved a few seconds off her time each practice.

"Hannah, you've been doing intervals for a while. You want to see if you can break twenty-one minutes?"

Before Hannah could respond, someone said, "I can break twenty-one minutes."

John turned and saw Ethan walk up—swagger was more like it. "What are you doing here?"

"I went to work, and they're closed," Ethan said. "Roger told me he's moving Race2Escape to Fairview."

John shook his head. Was there no end to the bad news? However, there was something different about Ethan's response, something in the way he spoke.

"So who am I racing?" Ethan said.

"You want to run?" John said.

Ethan glanced at Hannah, who continued stretching. "I want to see if Hannah can catch me."

Hannah looked up and smiled.

"Oh, I want to see this," Will said, laughing.

John could see the disaster ahead for his son because he had experienced it. "You haven't been running. You think you can handle three miles?"

"Oh, please," Ethan said, lifting a foot behind him to stretch.

"He is your son," Amy said.

John stared at Ethan. There were some things you could tell your kids about life and others they needed to experience themselves. And somehow he thought this was a lesson Ethan needed to *feel*.

Ethan and Hannah lined up, Will pretended he was firing the gun, and they were off. Ethan shot ahead as if running from one baseline to another for a layup. He glanced over his shoulder to see how far ahead he was after a hundred yards, his cheeks flushing and sweat already staining his shirt.

When they were almost out of sight, Will pointed to a knoll above the field. "Up there," he said. He led John and Amy to the perch. From this vantage point they could see the two runners at different stages of the course.

Ethan was fast, no question, and had a sizable lead, but Hannah's steady pace was like clockwork. She ignored Ethan's speed and seemed to run with new confidence.

"Do you think he can stay ahead of her?" Will said.

"Wait till the switchback and we'll see," John said.

The two disappeared into the woods. The course wound back toward them and at the one-mile mark a runner appeared through the trees.

"Go, Hannah!" John yelled, pumping a fist in the air.

Will laughed. "Ethan was so far ahead."

"Not anymore," Amy said.

Two minutes later, Ethan huffed and puffed out of the woods, holding his side and lumbering like Frankenstein's monster.

"Oh, we can't let him keep going like that," Amy said.

"Hey, he said he wanted to see if Hannah could catch him. We have to let him face reality."

They returned to the field and Will and Amy packed up their things. Hannah came over the ridge, arms and legs in perfect position. Her feet struck the ground and she gained momentum as she came down the hill and crossed the finish line.

"How'd that feel?" John said, following her as she walked the length of the field.

"A lot better than during that last race," Hannah said. "What was my time?"

"20:56."

Her mouth dropped open. "Seriously? I broke twenty-one minutes!"

John nodded. "Hannah, something happened out there with Ethan sprinting ahead. You didn't chase him. You were consistent the whole way, and coming down the hill at the end, it's like you could have run another three miles."

She smiled. "When I passed him, his legs were cramping up and he grabbed at his side. I almost stopped to help him." She smiled. "Almost."

"We might want to take the cart out there and get him," Amy said.

"No, let's wait," John said. He glanced at his empty wrist.

When Ethan finally crossed the finish line, John was

sitting alone on the bleachers. Ethan's shirt was drenched and he moved like a zombie.

"You okay?" John said.

Ethan got enough breath to answer. "No." He stretched out on his back. "That was crazy hard."

John relaxed, taking in the sight.

"You said this wasn't a sport," Ethan said, pointing at his father.

John laughed and sat up. "Yeah, I was wrong. Mom, Will, and Hannah wanted to see you finish, but they got tired of waiting. They went home. I need to get a ride with you."

He stood and patted his son on the shoulder.

"If you'll drive," Ethan said.

"All right," John said, pausing to stretch in front of his son. "Boy, I'm tired."

John chuckled all the way to the car and as they drove home, Ethan mentioned he was in the lunchroom when Hannah had tossed food at Robert. "Makes me want to bop that kid and teach him a lesson."

"Maybe we should get him out here to run against Hannah," John said.

"I wouldn't wish that on anybody, not even Robert." He lurched forward and grabbed his leg.

"You might want to drink some water. Like a couple of gallons. Or your legs are going to do that all night."

"Sounds like you're talking from experience," Ethan said.

John smiled. "So why did you decide to do that today?"

"I don't know—I feel bad for her. I thought maybe I could encourage her somehow, you know, push her for a couple of miles and then let her pass me."

John laughed, then turned serious. "Hannah's going through some things no kid her age ought to go through."

"Like what?"

"I can't go into detail. Trust me. I think she's trying to figure out who she really is."

"Kind of like the rest of us," Ethan said.

John thought about what Thomas had said to him at the hospital—the question he asked. John knew he needed to bring that up with Hannah at some point, when she was ready.

"Ethan, I have a question."

"I'm not going out for the team."

John laughed. "No, not that kind of question. Who are you?"

Ethan scowled at him. "What do you mean?"

"What's the first thing that comes to mind when I ask you that? Who are you?"

The conversation lasted all the way home, and when they pulled in the driveway, John turned off the ignition and explained where he'd heard it. "I'm just learning this now, Ethan. If you can get this and really live the truth of it, there's no holding you back."

John and Amy asked to meet with Olivia Brooks the next day. Olivia came to Amy's science classroom and heard the story of John's chance meeting with a man named Thomas Hill.

Olivia's mouth dropped open. "You met T-bone? That's what people called him back when."

"You knew him?"

Olivia ignored the question. "What did he say to you?"

John told her and didn't hold anything back. When he finished, she looked out the window as the sun streamed in, casting shadows about the room. Olivia turned and faced them.

"And you think Barbara told her he was dead on purpose."

"That's what I'm wondering," John said. "I mean, if his influence led to her daughter's death, and then he abandoned Hannah, it makes sense that she wouldn't want anything to do with him."

With precise, clipped speech, Olivia said, "Well, I'd say that your assessment is correct."

"Why do you say that?"

"Because I knew her daughter," Olivia said.

"You knew Hannah's mother?" Amy said.

There was deep pain on Olivia's face. "We were friends, up until a year before she died. When this charming older guy came around, we warned her to be careful. She didn't listen. The next thing we knew, she was pregnant. And she cut off contact with all of us. Then, after she gave birth, she became an addict."

John felt the air go out of the room. The weight of the

story was too much. His mind raced with thoughts of what Hannah did and didn't know and how to help her cross the bridge between them.

"I didn't even know she was dead until after the funeral," Olivia said. "I went to go see Barbara, but I just saw bitterness. I reconnected with her this year and saw more of the same."

A switch clicked. Hannah's grandmother certainly couldn't afford the tuition for the school. "We wondered how Hannah was able to come here. You're paying for it."

Olivia's face said it all. She nodded.

"Thomas Hill is not the same man, but he is sick," John said. "If he and Hannah were to meet, it needs to happen sooner rather than later."

"Barbara may not be telling Hannah the truth," Amy said. "But she still is her guardian. How can we go around her?"

Olivia stared at the floor. It seemed to John she was weighing her words carefully as if this were some kind of court proceeding. He couldn't imagine the burden she felt as a friend of the family, someone who cared deeply.

"In my official capacity as the principal of this school, I can't advise you to go around Barbara. But I can tell you that if you include her, Hannah may never meet her father."

The words hung between them and Olivia walked resolutely out of the room. John's mind spun. If Amy hadn't volunteered him for the hospital visit, he would never have met Thomas. If all the negative things hadn't happened in town, he wouldn't have met Hannah, wouldn't have been assigned to coach her. His marriage had grown deeper because of all the seemingly bad things. There was more going on than he could understand, something bigger at work in their lives, bringing them together.

His thoughts turned to Hannah. Something was happening with her, too. He looked at Amy. "If it was you, would you want to meet your dad?"

Amy considered for a moment and he knew what a complicated question that was for her. Amy's relationship with her own father had been a struggle, issues she had to work through, disappointments and questions. Without a word she nodded. It was clear for both of them they had been placed in this position, between father and daughter, for a reason. But what in the world should they do now?

"Yeah," John said. "We need to pray."

Amy put her hand in his. "Father, we are overwhelmed at what we've learned from Olivia. And my heart is breaking for this girl who has lived with the belief that her dad has been dead all these years. But in Your mercy, You reached out to him and You have given him a new heart. And we're grateful for that. We thank You for that. But we don't know what to do. We don't know what's best. So I'm asking for wisdom. You say in Your Word that if anyone lacks wisdom, let him ask of God, and You will give wisdom generously. So we ask for that today, Lord."

John squeezed Amy's hand and continued the prayer.

"Lord, we need wisdom with how to tell Hannah. We need wisdom with how and when to tell Thomas. He's been through so much, Lord. And we need wisdom with how to be sensitive to Barbara. It's clear her heart has been broken by the loss of her daughter and all the pain she's lived with for the past fifteen years. Soften her heart, Lord. Help us to show her the kind of love that can only come from You. Help her see Thomas has changed and it's been a work You've done inside him."

"And I pray You would preserve him, Father," Amy said, "that You would restore his health so that he could spend time with his daughter and pour his life into hers. I don't know if Hannah knows You. I don't think she has a relationship with You. So would You draw her to Yourself through this—to her earthly father and her heavenly Father? And use us in any way You want. Make us sensitive to what's really happening here. Keep us from hurting anyone. You know we want to do what You've prepared for us and nothing more. Show us the way forward, I pray, in the name of Jesus. Amen."

The bell rang. John stood and wiped a tear from Amy's face. He felt it too. They were good tears, good emotion. The struggle was a sign of life, a sign that God was at work. And he was deliberately choosing to believe it.

CHAPTER 23

✦ ✦ ✦

John and Amy walked hand in hand past the fourth-floor nurses' station. Franklin General was becoming more of a home away from home for John. He used to avoid it at all costs, thinking only sick people were there. Now he saw it differently. Life was a hospital, everyone needing varying levels of care and compassion. Most didn't know how much they needed until their condition became acute.

When they reached Thomas's room, John looked at Amy and she nodded, telling him without words she was ready to walk together into whatever lay ahead. Praise music flowed from the room and John knocked lightly on the open door.

"Thomas?"

Thomas clicked Pause on the CD remote and his face lit. "John!"

"How are you?"

"Put me in, Coach. I'm tired of sitting on the bench." He smiled broadly, unable to contain his joy that a friend had arrived for a visit.

John stood at the foot of the bed. "First, I need to introduce you to my number one teammate. I brought Amy with me."

"Oh, my goodness," Thomas said, stretching out a hand. "I can honestly say I did not see that coming."

Amy chuckled. "Hi, Thomas. It's nice to meet you."

"The honor is all mine," he said warmly.

John studied Thomas, who looked straight ahead. He could see the wheels turning inside his friend's mind, sensing something was different.

"Well, the coach brought his wife. This must be an important day."

"It is an important day," Amy said.

John had rehearsed what he was about to say a dozen times and still his heart fluttered. *Give me the right words, Lord,* he prayed.

"We have something that we'd like to talk to you about," John said.

"Okay, shoot."

"You know that I have one runner that I'm coaching."

"Yeah."

"Well, that runner is fifteen years old. She lives with her

grandmother." He let the detail sink in. "She was born on Valentine's Day."

John couldn't take his eyes off Thomas's face. There was a solemn resignation to it as he listened, as if hearing a new diagnosis from a physician who had x-rayed his soul. Thomas's eyes wandered, shifting left to right, trying to view unseen things. When he didn't speak, John gently told him the whole truth.

"Her name is Hannah Scott."

Thomas reeled from the revelation. He and John had, without knowing it, been coaching Thomas's daughter. Every training tip, every pointer he had given to help John's "team" run faster had been for his own daughter.

Amy moved around the side of the bed and put a hand on the man's shoulder. "Are you okay?" she said gently.

Thomas's voice trembled. "Your runner is my daughter?"

The words were more than a question. They showed the heart of a man struggling with his past choices, his present condition, and all the years between.

Thomas shifted in the bed. "Tell me about her," he said softly.

"She's beautiful," Amy said. "She's quiet. She's observant. She's athletic."

As Amy spoke, Thomas couldn't hold back the emotion. His face tightened, his eyes filled with tears, and John thought they were treading on holy ground. Had Thomas prayed to hear from his daughter? How long? Was it even something he thought possible?

"We wondered," John said slowly, "if you would want to meet?"

Thomas struggled through the emotion, a vein showing in his forehead. "Does she know about me?"

"No, we haven't told her anything yet," Amy said. "We don't even know how she would respond. We wanted to talk to you first."

Thomas broke. Tears ran down his cheeks into his gray beard. He rolled his head from side to side. "I've had a conversation in my mind with her a thousand times. I've wanted to talk to her. But what daughter would want a dad like me?"

John wanted to reach out, say something, do anything to help with his friend's pain. But it was the comforting voice of his wife he knew Thomas needed to hear.

"Thomas, she needs a father. You still have so much to offer her."

Thomas choked on the emotion. "She'd be disappointed."

"No, that's not true."

Tears continued and Thomas did nothing to hold them back.

"Thomas," John said, "would you be willing to pray about it? If she's willing to meet, would you want to?"

Thomas calmed himself as if searching for something lost on a dark path.

A verse flashed in John's mind. *"Ask, and it will be given to you; seek, and you will find; knock, and it will be opened to you."*

Then came the soft voice of surrender, the door of a heart opening to the work of God.

"Yes. We can pray about it."

With that, Thomas reached out both hands. John drew closer on one side of the bed and Amy on the other, and the three of them prayed through their tears. They thanked God for bringing them together. They thanked God for preserving Thomas.

"Lord, You know how long I've prayed for my daughter. And how much shame and guilt I feel. I know You've forgiven me, but I don't know if Hannah can do that. Or Barbara. Oh, Father, she has gone through so much pain. Thank You she's raised Hannah. Now, would You give me the faith to believe that You're in this? I don't want to live the rest of my life in fear. I want to live by faith, not by sight. But I need You to help me. Lord, I'm so afraid."

CHAPTER 24

✦ ✦ ✦

Hannah felt confident at her next race. The Harrisons picked her up early and Mrs. Harrison walked the entire course with her. There was a hilly section that felt challenging and two muddy, swampy areas. It was helpful to know what was ahead instead of being surprised as she ran with the pack.

Hannah stretched, then sat on a bench with the Harrisons before the start. She had come in under twenty-one minutes in her last two practices and hoped she could keep that pace.

Coach Harrison asked how she was feeling and Hannah said she was okay.

"Well, at the coaches' meeting they said this course shows

who the real runners are. So we'll see if these new drills have helped. Got your inhaler?"

"It's on my hip," Hannah said.

Coach Harrison paused and looked her in the eyes. "Hannah, I want to pray for you. Can I do that?"

He'd never said that before a race, so it felt strange. And yet his voice was comforting and reassuring. She nodded and noticed Mrs. Harrison closing her eyes and bowing her head. They both acted as if talking to God was something real.

"Lord, we thank You for the chance to be here today. Thank You for Hannah. And, God, I ask that You would protect her today and help her to do her best. And I ask this in Jesus' name, amen."

As he prayed, Hannah looked up, glancing at them. When Coach Harrison finished, she felt a warm sensation inside.

"You ready?" Coach said.

"I think so."

She stretched some more as she moved to the starting line. When she lined up, she noticed Gina Mimms to her right again. She chased Gina in her dreams. And most of the time it felt like a nightmare. Hannah tried to shake the butterflies, but they were always present at the start of a race. Instead of chasing them away, she jumped in place. Maybe the butterflies could help her.

Someone yelled her name from the sidelines and Hannah scanned the crowd. It was Ethan Harrison. She had teased him in the lunchroom the day before about how long it took him to finish the race with her. Now he smiled and pointed at her. "You got this!" he yelled. And a group from Brookshire clapped and yelled encouragement.

All that fuss for one runner, Hannah thought. She glanced at the parents and coaches and saw the Harrisons staring at Ethan and the others. It was great having a cheering section, but she secretly wished her grandmother would come to a race. She couldn't because of her work, of course. Hannah knew that. Still, it would be nice to have a family member cheering.

Hannah took a deep breath, stepped to the line, and when the gun sounded, she ran hard. She heard her name yelled and as she passed the crowd, she settled into her rhythm.

Protect her. Help her do her best. That's what Coach Harrison had prayed. Could God do that? Was God interested in her? Didn't He have more important things to do than watch a fifteen-year-old run?

The first incline was tough, but Hannah paced herself well and she attacked it. There were runners ahead, but after a mile she glanced back and saw there were more behind than in front.

Stay focused, she thought. *I want to make the top ten.*

Her legs felt heavy in the muddy sections and she slid once but managed to keep her balance. When she reached a paved path by a lake, a breeze hit her and it felt like someone had turned on a fan at just the right time.

Something strange happened after the second mile. Instead of other runners passing her, she was the one passing them. She was tired, her legs fatigued, but the training had worked. She had more stamina, more power, and her pace actually increased.

She had become so focused on her stride and technique that she wasn't concerned about her breathing. She had her inhaler at her side but she didn't need it.

Coming down the final hill, she looked ahead and saw Gina Mimms. Hannah was always trailing her. But at least she could *see* her this time. That was progress. And that caused her to lengthen her stride and kick toward the finish.

The crowd cheered when runners came into view and by the time Hannah was a hundred yards from the finish line, people screamed and clapped. She heard Coach Harrison as she passed him.

"Come on, Hannah! Fight, Hannah! You got it!"

The last few yards before the finish line, she was spent. Instead of catching up to the runner in front of her, a girl behind pulled ahead. Hannah crossed the line and clapped as other runners finished.

She grabbed some water as the Harrisons joined her. "You did so good. That was amazing," Mrs. Harrison said.

"Nice job," Coach said. "Did you even need your inhaler?"

"No. What place did I come in?"

"You were eleventh," Coach said tentatively.

Hannah shook her head and pulled away but Coach Harrison wasn't having it. "Don't you be upset. You just ran your best race."

"That's right. That's nothing to be ashamed of," Mrs. Harrison said. "That was fantastic."

Their words were encouraging, but Hannah couldn't shake the fact that she had run out of gas at the end. "I thought I'd at least made top ten."

"You keep running like that and you will," Coach said. He waved at someone. "I think you've got a couple of friends who want to say hello."

Ethan and a group from Brookshire surrounded her, clapping and encouraging her. Grace was there, wrapping her in a hug, sweaty as she was, and Ethan gave her a high five. It was one thing for kids who weren't athletes to compliment her, but someone like Ethan knew what it took to compete. Was he just doing that because his dad was the coach? His excitement seemed genuine.

They packed up and the crowd dispersed. Coach Harrison drew her aside by the lake and sat on a cooler while she sat on a bench. "Every competitive athlete I've ever known has had this thing deep inside that wants to win. And when you don't do as well as you'd like, it feels awful. But what you've done in a short amount of time has been amazing. You know that, right?"

She nodded. "I think the training has made me faster."

"Hannah, can you tell before a race whether you might have an attack?"

"Sometimes. Today I felt good."

She remembered Coach's prayer. *Protect her.* Had that happened?

Mrs. Harrison sat beside her and Hannah wondered why they weren't heading to the car.

"You're a good runner, Hannah," Coach said.

"Ethan said he'd pick up Will," Mrs. Harrison said. "So we've got time."

The two of them looked at each other and nodded, like there was a secret code between them.

Coach Harrison leaned forward. "So I want to ask you a question and I want you to think about it, okay? Who is Hannah Scott?"

He stared at her like she was supposed to know the answer. Like this was a pop quiz in Hannah Scott 101. The longer he looked, the more nervous she became. Finally she said the only thing that came to her mind.

"I don't know."

He nodded as if he anticipated the answer. "Do you believe God loves you?"

She shrugged.

"He does, more than you know."

Something rose up inside. Normally she'd sit and listen to people talk about God and His love. This time she responded.

"Why did He take my parents?"

Coach dipped his head as if she'd played a card that beat all the others on the table. He paused, then said, "I think it's easy sometimes to blame God for decisions that we make. Or other people make. What do you know about your dad?"

"He was a runner," Hannah said. "He got into drugs. And it killed him."

"Your grandmother told you that."

She nodded.

"Do you know his name?"

She hadn't spoken his name in a long time. Nobody wanted to hear it, especially her grandmother. "Thomas Hill," she said. It felt good to say it, to just put it out there.

Coach Harrison looked at his wife and there was the code again. A look. A nod. What was it with these people?

Coach paused like he was trying to get up enough speed for a long jump. "Hannah, I went to the hospital recently and I met a man there. He's not doing very well. Diabetes has taken his eyesight. We've gotten to know each other. He used to be a runner years ago. And got on drugs. He had a daughter. A baby girl. And he left her with a relative when he left town fifteen years ago."

Hannah winced. She heard the words Coach said but she felt like she was someplace else. She saw the look of concern on his face, but her arms felt tingly. Was he saying what she thought he was saying?

Coach Harrison looked up, into her eyes. "His name is Thomas Hill."

She sat back. All she could say was "What?"

"Hannah, you were told your father died, and I believe

that was to protect you. I don't want to go around your grandmother, but I don't know how much time you have."

Her breath was short now. Her heart beat fast. This couldn't be true. But what reason would her coach have for lying to her?

"My father's alive?" she said.

"He wants to meet you," Coach said. "But only if you want to."

Mrs. Harrison leaned down and spoke softly. "Hannah, you don't have to do anything that you don't want to do."

Hannah had a million questions. The one that came to her was "Why did he leave?"

Coach looked pained. "He regrets it. He regrets it with his whole heart."

"But my grandmother told me . . ."

Mrs. Harrison put a hand on her shoulder. "Sometimes people who love us and want the best for us don't make all the right decisions. Your grandmother was just doing what she thought was the best for you."

Hannah stared at the ground, then looked back at her coach. "It's really him? Are you sure?"

Coach Harrison nodded and Hannah saw something in his eyes, something that made her feel he really cared.

"How long has he been at the hospital?"

Coach Harrison said he hadn't been back long and that he'd come from Fairview. "They sent him here so he could get dialysis."

"What's dialysis?" Hannah said.

The coach looked at his wife. It was like handing a baton to a runner in a relay race. She immediately picked it up.

"When a person's kidneys slow down or stop working, a machine is used to do what healthy kidneys do. Your dad needs that, so they sent him here."

Coach leaned forward. "Your dad has such a positive outlook. He's funny. He's taught me about running. But he's also challenged me about how I live."

"And dialysis is what's keeping him alive?"

Coach Harrison nodded.

Hannah shook her head. "I don't understand. How did you find him? Did you go looking for him?"

Coach explained he met Thomas by accident. "But looking back, I don't think any of this was chance. I think God was part of this."

They settled into silence and headed for the car, and when they reached Hannah's house, she got out quickly without saying anything and ran inside. As she closed the door, she waved to the Harrisons. She knew she should have said something, should have thanked them, but so much had stirred inside she couldn't.

She put her things on the couch and ran to her room, her footsteps echoing in the empty house. She showered and dressed, then crept into her grandmother's room. Her grandmother was at work but her room was off-limits, so Hannah couldn't leave any evidence she'd been here.

She opened the closet and saw her grandmother's uniforms. But it wasn't clothes she wanted. High on the top shelf was a small green box. It had been her mother's. As far as Hannah knew, her grandmother hadn't touched the pictures inside. She also hadn't told Hannah about them. Hannah had found them when she was ten, leading her grandmother to institute a rule about "not rooting around in my room."

"You keep out of my things and I'll keep out of yours," her grandmother said sternly, putting the box high in the closet.

Hannah pulled it down, then sat on the edge of her grandmother's bed and took off the top. Inside were old pictures, some faded with age, and she leafed through them until she found the one she wanted.

A young man with a #77 on his shirt was in midstride on a cross-country course. His legs looked strong and his form perfect. He leaned forward, his momentum propelling him, his arm muscles showing. His eyes drew Hannah. He was running past a tree and looked straight into the camera. Was it Hannah's mother who had taken the picture? A reporter for a local newspaper? She didn't know. All she knew was that this was her father. And the few times she had seen the picture, she had thought he was dead. That made it a sad photo. His eyes were ghostly. He was simply a memory she didn't share, a name she couldn't say around her grandmother.

Every time she asked about him, her grandmother got angry. So Hannah stopped asking. She didn't like upsetting her grandmother.

Now, with the Harrisons' news, the picture changed.

Her father was alive and at a hospital about the length of a cross-country race from her house. He could have died there and she would never have known. And it struck her that the picture hadn't changed. *She* had changed with the truth that her father was alive.

She thought about Coach Harrison's words and what Mrs. Brooks said. Were they right? Was God real? Did He care about her? When anyone brought up her parents, Hannah blamed God for letting them die. But could God have made a way for her to see her father?

She put the top on the box and placed it back on the shelf in the closet exactly how she had found it. She closed the doors and left the room, then returned to smooth out the bedspread. Back in her room, she pulled out a book to study, but she couldn't stop looking at the picture.

CHAPTER 25

✦ ✦ ✦

Barbara Scott checked her watch every few minutes of her shift at the hotel, imagining what Hannah was going through at that moment. She knew when Hannah was being picked up. She knew when the race started. She knew Hannah would finish about twenty minutes later, depending on how well she ran and if she had one of her asthma attacks. That concerned Barbara the most.

It had been several days after the last meet that Barbara found out why Hannah hadn't finished the race. She wanted to call a halt to the whole thing. No sense dying over a sporting event. She'd picked up the phone to call Coach Harrison, but Hannah stopped her.

"Grandma, you can't take this away. I feel like I was made to run."

"If you were made to run, God wouldn't have given you those lungs."

"I can't change that. But I'm not going to let asthma keep me from doing something I was made to do."

"Baby girl, where's this coming from?"

Hannah looked bewildered. "What do you mean?"

"The words you're saying. This focus on running."

She shook her head. "I don't know, Grandma. It's just in here, I guess."

She had pointed to her heart and Barbara put down the phone. Hannah was just as feisty as her mother. When she got it in her mind to do something, nothing could stand in her way. Hannah was like Janet and Janet had been like Barbara. Some things ran deep in the DNA.

Barbara chuckled as she finished vacuuming and changing the sheets in room 327 at the Franklin City Inn. People left tips at the restaurant but most didn't see the need to tip the hotel cleaning staff. Every now and then she'd find cash left on a dresser or nightstand, but it was mostly abandoned loose change. She and the others who cleaned had a jar in the laundry room they filled with nickels, dimes, and quarters and when it filled, they all guessed how much was there. The closest guess got the whole amount. It was something fun they looked forward to every few weeks. Just a jar filled with what people didn't want to carry.

She checked her clipboard and sighed. Room 332 was

the only one left to clean. She'd passed the Do Not Disturb sign two hours earlier, and checkout time had come and gone. She radioed the front desk and was told the guest hadn't checked out. She knocked on the door.

"Housekeeping," she said in a loud voice.

No answer. She didn't want to intrude, but she had a job to do. She checked her watch again. The race was about to start. She wanted to clean the room, drive to the race, and surprise Hannah at the finish line. That dream was dying as she stared at Do Not Disturb. If she couldn't get to the race, she could be home and have lunch ready. When Hannah arrived, they could spend some time talking about her day. Hannah loved mac and cheese and burgers. Barbara would have it on the table, steaming, when she walked in the door. And though it weighed on Barbara, she wouldn't bring up Hannah's "problem." Not today.

She used her key card and the door clicked. She opened it a few inches, again saying, "Housekeeping."

No response.

Her heart beat a little faster. She had once discovered a woman passed out in the bathroom and called 911. The staff had called her a hero. The lady who was led away by paramedics yelled at her. Barbara knew the woman wasn't in her right mind.

She expected the door to catch on the inside lock, but it didn't. The room was as dark as midnight, the drapes drawn. She stepped inside and said, "Hello?"

No answer.

She flicked on the light switch to her left and gasped. The room wasn't just a mess—it looked like an F5 tornado had touched down and had stayed two nights and called the front desk for a late checkout. She surveyed the damage. At least the walls were intact.

She turned on the light in the bathroom and calculated how long it would take her to clean it all. She went to the phone and called the front desk. The manager would want pictures.

Two hours later she jumped in the car and drove toward the river. She was relieved and at the same time frustrated when she saw Hannah's things. How many times had she told that girl not to drop her stuff on the couch?

She called for her and Hannah answered from her room. Barbara found her on her bed with her nose in a big textbook, two notebooks nearby. She didn't have her earbuds in, which was unusual. Maybe that was progress.

"Hey, baby girl, how'd your race go today?"

"I finished eleventh," Hannah said as if apologizing.

She finished. That meant no asthma attack.

"Well, you're improving," Barbara said. "I really wish I could have been there, but I thought about you all day at work."

Hannah stared at her. Out of the blue, she spoke the words that took Barbara's breath away.

"Did you ever see my father run?"

Stay calm. Don't overreact.

Barbara gripped the strap of her purse over her shoulder. "One time, at a city race." She let go of the strap and took a breath. "He was in his thirties."

There. She'd answered the question. She hadn't yelled or even raised her voice. Hannah probably just wondered where her athletic ability came from. She was at that age where questions popped up when she was alone and thinking. When she wasn't listening to music, perhaps. If only Barbara had gotten home earlier so Hannah wouldn't have had time to think of her father.

"And how did he die?" Hannah said, interrupting Barbara's thoughts.

She studied her granddaughter's face, then turned aside. Here she was again. She thought she was through with all these questions. She thought Hannah had moved on. Firmly, with as much kindness as she could muster, she faced her granddaughter.

"Baby, I already told you this. Those drugs got ahold of him. You don't even need to worry about that. The best thing you need to do is to get on with your life. He would want that."

Barbara felt good about the answer. In the last fifteen years she had told herself that story so many times she almost believed it was true. The drugs had to have gotten T-bone. She hadn't heard anything from him since that day when the world stopped spinning.

She quickly changed the conversation. "So have you eaten? Because I can whip us up something. I'm starving."

Hannah didn't seem ready to leave the history question she'd raised but she nodded slightly and said, "Okay."

Barbara forced a smile and walked to the kitchen. She boiled the water and put the pan on the burner and removed the meat from the refrigerator. As she worked, she couldn't harness her mind, couldn't stop the images stuck there from fifteen years ago. She cut an onion for the burgers and it stung her eyes. She thought of the trashed hotel room. It was a lot like her life. But there had been no one to clean it up, to vacuum the floor and make the bed.

Barbara knew why Hannah asked questions about her mother. She brought her up so many times because she was curious. And in a strange way, it was healing for Barbara to talk about Janet. Just speaking her name and laughing about some of the silly things that had happened made her life real instead of it being a dream.

But why did Hannah bring up her father? What triggered her heart to go down that overgrown path?

When she had lunch on the table, she called Hannah and the girl's face lit up at the sight of her favorite meal.

After they began, Barbara said, "So why did you bring up your father to me?"

"I don't know."

"Were you wondering about where you get your running ability?"

Hannah shrugged. "I guess so."

"Well, I know it's hard not getting the answers you

want. But I'm glad you don't have to go through the pain that comes with finding them. Do you understand?"

"Yes, Grandma."

CHAPTER 26

✦ ✦ ✦

John Harrison hadn't prayed about anything as hard as he prayed for Hannah and Thomas. The two were constantly on his mind, as well as Hannah's grandmother, Barbara. How she would react to the news that Thomas was in Franklin and wanted to see Hannah was anyone's guess.

Amy called Mark Latimer and said they had a difficult situation at school and requested prayer. She didn't go into detail.

"You don't need to tell me specifics," Pastor Mark said. "God knows what's going on. I'll put out the request right now."

John told Ethan and Will that he'd appreciate them

praying for Hannah too. Will prayed at the dinner table that night before the meal and asked God to "help Hannah with her asthma and everything else happening to her."

Ethan looked at John after Will's prayer. "When will you be able to tell us?"

"Soon, I hope."

John called Thomas Saturday evening and told him about the conversation with Hannah. Thomas wanted to know every detail of her reaction.

"She sounds like she's confused," Thomas said. "I wouldn't blame her if she didn't want to see me after the way I treated her. The way I abandoned her."

"I think we have to give her the time she needs. I don't remember processing anything remotely like this when I was fifteen."

"You and me both," Thomas said. "But at the same time . . ."

John heard the beep of the monitor in the background as Thomas searched for words.

"My fear is that by the time she wants to see me, I might not be here."

"Well, Amy and I are praying. There are folks from our church and Bible study lifting you up."

Thomas fell silent, and that made John want to be bold with his words. "Thomas, I want to pray for you right now. Would that be okay?"

"Yeah," Thomas said weakly.

John thanked God for the friendship they had developed. He prayed for healing for Thomas—for his body and for his heart. He asked God to show up in a mighty way and give Thomas hope, no matter what Hannah decided.

"Yes, Lord," Thomas whispered into the phone.

When John finished, Thomas thanked him. "I do feel encouraged. I think the best place to put all of this is in God's hands and leave it there. Life is one surrender after another, isn't it, John?"

"It sure is. But knowing that doesn't make it easy to wait."

"No, it doesn't."

John closed his eyes and he could see the man's face, his head against the hospital pillow. He'd carry that image of Thomas for a long time. He was a man seemingly helpless but who had decided to trust God for everything.

"You know, once I hit bottom and God grabbed my heart, I started praying for Hannah," Thomas said. "But every time I did, I felt so ashamed. Guilty. It almost stopped me from praying at all. I know that voice I was hearing wasn't God's because He's not the accuser. And when I realized that, I changed my prayer. I stopped asking Him to bring her into my life, and I started praying that God would draw her to Himself. I prayed He would do for her what He did for me. I prayed the same thing for Barbara. So my greatest hope has been that Hannah would come to know the love of God I've experienced."

"I've been praying the same thing, Thomas. It feels like more is going on here than we can understand."

"I hope you're right about that," Thomas said. "But you can be sure this is not going to make God's enemies happy."

"All the more reason to pray," John said.

The next practice, John found Hannah warming up on the field. Amy had to take Will to a dentist appointment, so the two were alone. He wanted to ask about her father but gave her space. This had to be Hannah's decision.

After running intervals, Hannah asked if she could hit the course and run a full race.

"Are you sure you're up for it?"

Hannah nodded. "I think it'll help."

Help with what? John thought.

He started the timer and watched her run up the hill and into the trees. With basketball, he was engaged with every aspect of practice. He was privy to everything that happened on the court. With cross-country, Hannah spent a lot of time out of sight. Today, he decided the best thing he could do was pray.

He sat on the bleachers, elbows on knees, head down. Anyone passing would think he was studying his clipboard, but he was deep in prayer for Hannah and her need for a relationship with God. And it struck him there was a parallel between Hannah's heavenly Father and her earthly one. Both of them wanted a relationship with her.

"Father, the most important thing for Hannah is that she would know You. So I pray You'd work in her heart, soften it, prepare her, so that she would reach out to You, receive Your forgiveness, and come to know You. Make me sensitive. Help me not to push too hard or hold back when I shouldn't. Use Amy in her life—You've already done that. Or bring someone else along who can help her understand Your love for her and who You created her to be. You've done that for me, Lord. And You've been so patient."

He heard footsteps and looked up to see Hannah flying down the hill.

"Thank You for her, Lord," he whispered.

He rose and waited at the finish line, ready with the stopwatch. Hannah looked like she was gaining momentum with each stride.

"Come on, finish strong," John said. "Good, good, good!"

She crossed the finish line and he clicked the watch and stared at the numbers. "20:45. Hannah, you're getting faster."

Her face glistened with sweat. She was spent but she wasn't laboring.

"How's your breathing?"

"Good," she said.

"I'll get you some water," John said, retreating to the bleachers. He grabbed a water bottle and heard her voice.

"I want to go."

John stopped and turned. Had he heard her correctly? He stared at her, waiting for an explanation and hoping it meant what he thought it meant.

"I want to go see him," she said.

John handed her the water bottle, thrilled but also cautious. "What about your grandmother?"

"She said he's dead."

John nodded. "You want to go tonight?"

"My grandmother will be home pretty soon."

"Of course. Tomorrow? We can skip practice for one day, I think."

Hannah paused a moment. "Do you think . . . ?"

"What is it, Hannah?"

"It's probably too much to ask."

"Go ahead."

"Do you think Mrs. Harrison would come with us?"

John smiled. "That'll make her happy that you suggested it. I think she'd love to be there."

It felt like he had just witnessed a breakthrough. It felt like winning a play-off game. And as he walked to his office, he paused at the door, closed his eyes, and thanked God for what had happened.

Then he called Amy.

Then he called Thomas.

Then he called his pastor and asked him to tell people to pray more than ever. Something good was happening and he wanted it to continue.

CHAPTER 27

✦ ✦ ✦

Hannah had butterflies all day. Before leaving for work, her grandmother asked if she had a test or any papers due or if there was "anything special" happening today.

Hannah wanted to say she was thinking of making a new friend, her father. She just shrugged.

In her wildest dreams, she never considered meeting her father. She had read a story in English class about an adopted boy who stared out the window wondering if any of the men walking by might be his dad. The story had stuck with her, but it always seemed like a fairy tale.

She chose her outfit carefully, going through her closet, picking a skirt and blouse, then putting them back. She had three dresses, but none of them seemed right. She settled on a shirt and nice sweatpants and looked in the mirror. It wasn't until she was walking to school and saw a woman with dark sunglasses and a cane that she remembered her father was blind. He wouldn't see what she wore. He never would. And that was okay. He didn't have to see her. In fact, that took some of the pressure off. She just wanted to look at him, to hear his voice, to see if what Coach Harrison said was true.

Mrs. Harrison complimented Hannah on her outfit in first period and winked. After class she said, "You ready for today?"

"I think so. I'm kind of nervous."

The woman smiled. "I'd be worried if you weren't nervous."

That put Hannah at ease for about fifteen minutes. She couldn't eat at lunch. She couldn't concentrate in her classes. All she could think about was what her father might look like and what he might say. And how her grandmother would react if she found out. That was part of the stomach churn—her grandmother had lied to her all these years. Or perhaps she really believed her father had died. Could she have gotten incorrect information? No, her grandmother knew details about everything.

Hannah found the Harrisons after school and they drove to Franklin General. Hannah didn't like hospitals. She associated them with the pain she felt the last time she'd been there and the look on her grandmother's face when she opened the bills. There were so many. They came in the mail and her grandmother asked to work out a payment plan. And then came something called collections, which Hannah only vaguely understood. It was a mess and Hannah vowed she'd never be admitted to the hospital again.

They rode the elevator to the fourth floor. Hannah walked behind the two, clutching her inhaler. For a hospital, it was eerily quiet. She heard every footstep they took. The Harrisons looked at each other on the drive over and in the hallway, not saying anything. Did couples get that way after being married a few years?

When they neared her father's room, she felt like she would be sick, but with the Harrisons there, she couldn't turn around. She had to go through with this.

Part of her fear was that her father's condition might alarm her. If he was close to death, he might look weird. Like a skeleton. Then she remembered he wouldn't see her reaction to him. She wasn't glad he was blind, but once again it took away a little of her fear.

"It's right here," Coach Harrison said, slowing as they reached room 402. The door was slightly open and Hannah glanced in and saw the bed, then studied the floor tiles.

"I'll tell you what, let me step in there for just a second, okay?" Coach said. Hannah had never heard him talk so softly.

When he went inside, Mrs. Harrison turned and put a hand on her arm. "Hannah, are you okay?"

"I'm okay." She felt the tightness in her lungs.

She took a puff from her inhaler, then slipped it into the pocket of her sweats.

"Listen, if you want more time, we don't have to do this now."

Relief. She could get on the elevator and leave. No, she couldn't, not when she was this close. "I want to. I'm okay."

Coach Harrison walked into the hall. "Okay, guys, you ready?"

When Hannah stepped into the room, it was like walking into another reality. She heard the *beep, beep* of a machine by the bed. There was that weird, antiseptic smell, alcohol and cleaning solution. And there was her father. He lay propped up in bed, staring straight ahead, like he was studying the wall on the opposite side of the room.

Her dad had a gray-and-black beard and mustache. She didn't expect that. His hair was salt-and-pepper. The only picture she had in her mind was the one of him running, with #77 on his shirt, and this man didn't look like that at all. His arms lay at his sides and he didn't move, except for the rise and fall of his chest as he breathed. The light from the window showed only half of his face. He wore a hospital gown and she remembered how uncomfortable those were.

"Well, Thomas, we're here," Coach Harrison said. "Um, you've met Amy."

"Hello, Amy."

That voice. That was her father's voice. Deep. Rich. But also strained. He seemed to be holding back. Coach

Harrison said he had a good sense of humor. Why didn't he smile?

"Hi, Thomas," Mrs. Harrison said, stepping forward to squeeze the man's hand. "It's nice to see you again."

He turned his head when she touched him. "I tried to pick out a better outfit, but I couldn't tell if anything matched."

Her father smiled and chuckled, but it felt forced. Was he as nervous as Hannah?

Mrs. Harrison laughed. "Well, you look just fine."

"And Hannah is here," Coach Harrison said.

The formal introduction. The moment she'd waited for. The moment he had waited for, probably. She looked at her coach. Her mouth felt dry, her lungs tight. Coach Harrison didn't speak again and she knew it was her turn.

She had no words.

She had practiced what she would say all day. She'd imagined this meeting as she went to sleep the night before. Now she couldn't think of a thing to say. She looked at her father. He was wearing something on the index finger of his left hand that was hooked to a machine by the bed.

"Hello, Hannah," he said.

Everyone in the room waited for her. All she could say was "Hello."

Beep, beep.

"Coach tells me you're his number one runner," her father said.

Something dripped from a plastic bag by the bed and she followed the rubber tube to her father's arm.

"I guess," she said softly.

Coach Harrison said something Hannah didn't hear. Something encouraging, she thought, judging by his tone.

"I hope you keep at it," her father said.

He wasn't a skeleton. His arms seemed strong. And she wanted to ask why he hadn't come back for her. Why had he stayed away all these years? But she couldn't. Not yet. She didn't want to hurt his feelings. But there was so much stirring inside.

"Thomas, I understand you were third in the state," Mrs. Harrison said, breaking the awkward silence.

Her father laughed. "Yes, I was, back in the day."

That was a phrase her grandmother sometimes used. *Back in the day.* That meant a long time ago. And a long time ago her mother was alive and the two of them knew each other, and she wanted to ask him a thousand questions about her and what had really happened. Had he ever thought of finding his daughter, ever wondered how she was doing in the last fifteen years?

Quickly the voice of her grandmother intruded. Scolding her for asking questions. Fear shot through her and Hannah wondered if any minute her grandmother would walk through the door and yell.

"Hannah! What do you think you're doing?"

Her father smiled nervously. "So, Hannah, how's Coach doing?"

Coach Harrison, Amy Harrison, and Hannah Scott talk strategy before a cross-country meet.

John and Amy watch for Hannah at the finish line.

Brookshire runner Hannah Scott competes against all odds in the state championship cross-country meet.

Olivia Brooks cheers for Brookshire at the state championship.

Principal Brooks shows her support for Hannah.

Barbara Scott and her granddaughter, Hannah, make amends after years of struggling to understand each other.

Overcomer was filmed at Brookstone School in Columbus, Georgia.

OVERCOMER

BEHIND-THE-SCENES PHOTOS FROM THE MOVIE

∧ Alex Kendrick's real-life son Caleb Kendrick plays his on-screen son Will Harrison.

❮ The Harrison family from the *Overcomer* movie: Ethan (Jack Sterner), Amy (Shari Rigby), John (Alex Kendrick), and Will (Caleb Kendrick).

Brothers Stephen (producer/writer) and Alex Kendrick (director/writer) record a behind-the-scenes interview on the set of *Overcomer*.

Director Alex Kendrick discusses a scene with actor Cameron Arnett (Thomas Hill).

Director Alex Kendrick gives notes to actors Priscilla Shirer (Principal Brooks) and Aryn Wright-Thompson (Hannah).

For some reason she didn't understand, Hannah now imagined her mother, what she would look like if she were alive. She would stand by his bed, perhaps hold his hand. She would say things the Harrisons said. She and her father would look at each other with knowing glances, the secret code.

She tried to breathe but it was hard. The walls seemed like they were getting closer as her lungs tightened.

"He's doing okay," Hannah managed to say.

"Oh, just okay," Coach said dryly. He was trying to lighten the mood, break the ice.

That was it. She felt underwater with ice above her and she couldn't get to the surface to breathe.

A nurse walked through the door with a stethoscope around her neck and a file under her arm. She smiled. "Excuse me. I need to get his vitals if I could, please."

"Hello, Rose," her father said, full-voiced. "You come to join the party?" He seemed comfortable with the nurse. More than with Hannah.

As the two bantered, Hannah turned to Mrs. Harrison and whispered, "I need to leave."

"Okay," Mrs. Harrison said.

Hannah slipped out of the room. In the hallway she felt like she could breathe. She clenched her fists, working feeling back into her hands, and she noticed a doctor and a couple of nurses down the hall. Everyone was busy, everyone had a job, everyone knew where they were supposed to be and what they were supposed to do and here she was, outside the room of her dying father with no idea what to feel, how to act, or what to say.

"Hannah, are you all right?" Mrs. Harrison said, turning her around to face her.

Hannah nodded, expecting to be told she should say good-bye to her dad, that she couldn't just walk away. Instead, Mrs. Harrison looked her in the eyes and said, "Let's go sit in the car, okay? John will be down in a few minutes."

And just like that they turned and she felt Mrs. Harrison's arm around her, pulling her close as they walked to the elevator.

CHAPTER 28

✦ ✦ ✦

John watched Amy follow Hannah into the hallway. When the nurse left, Thomas turned his eyes toward the foot of his bed and said, "So, Hannah, you probably have a lot of questions for me . . ."

"Thomas, Hannah stepped out," John said gently. "I think she needed to leave."

"Oh." His face fell. "Do you think I said something wrong?"

"I think it was a lot for her to take in, you know?"

"Yeah. I expect so." He folded his hands in his lap. "Maybe this was a mistake, John. Maybe it was better to let her think I was gone."

"I've always heard the truth will set you free."

"I've heard that too. But at the same time, the truth can hurt people you care about. You have to factor that into the equation."

John looked at his watch—that wasn't there. He couldn't believe how many times he looked for that thing. "I think I'd better go find them and take Hannah home."

"Sure. Go ahead. I understand. And tell Hannah that . . ."

John watched Thomas's eyes. There was a mist in them.

"Tell her I understand. Tell her she doesn't need to come back if she doesn't want to. And . . ."

"I'll tell her, Thomas."

"Just take care of her. That's all I need to know. That she's cared for. I appreciate what you tried to do."

John put a hand on Thomas's shoulder. "Keep praying."

They drove in silence toward Hannah's little house by the river. Every time he looked in the rearview, he saw her staring out the window. John told Hannah what Thomas had said, but he wanted to say more, to ask what Hannah was thinking. He glanced at Amy and she seemed to be in a similar place—unsure whether to speak or stay quiet.

When they pulled up to the curb outside Hannah's house, the girl opened the side door and was to the front steps before he and Amy could get out.

"Hannah, would you like me to stay with you until your grandma gets home?" Amy said.

Hannah looked back and shook her head. "It's okay." Then, with eyes focused on Amy, lasered in and mature beyond their years, she said, "I need some time to think."

"Okay, you have our number," Amy said. "Please call us if you need anything."

Hannah thanked her and walked inside. John wanted to apologize. He wanted to ask Hannah to give Thomas another chance.

Amy paused by the car. "Please tell me we did the right thing."

He wanted to respond immediately, to say they had, but he wasn't sure. He got in the car and sat, his hands on the steering wheel. "Here's what I know. There's no part of me that wants to do the wrong thing. We only wanted to help. That's what I'm hoping God will honor."

That night, while he was in bed and the house was quiet and all he could hear was the soft breathing of his wife, John stared into the darkness of the room and wondered about Thomas. He closed his eyes. Was this what his friend saw? Was blindness pitch-darkness? Was it a shade of gray or blue or crimson?

He got out of bed and quietly walked downstairs and sat on the couch in the dark. What do you do when your life doesn't match your expectations? How do you respond when events take you in a direction you hadn't planned? What happens when your efforts lead to doubt and more questions than answers?

John had written the script he wanted to see unfold

before him in that hospital room. He wanted to introduce Hannah to her father, then see them embrace and laugh and connect. He wanted a greeting card moment, a picture or video he could take that would go viral because it plucked all the heartstrings. He and Amy would steal away to the cafeteria, and hours later they would retrieve Hannah from her father's bedside. When Barbara realized the bond between father and daughter, she would be on board and they would smile and celebrate the reunion. Everything roses and daffodils.

John heard a creak in the house. Some unexplainable noise. Had he done this for Thomas and Hannah, or had he done it for himself? Had he acted in a way that made sense to him without taking into account the hurt that might come?

John was a born fixer. Something breaks in the house or the car, you fix it. If your team's defense breaks, you shore it up in practice. If the lawn mower quits, you put on a new head gasket or take it to somebody who can.

But this wasn't a lawn mower or a loose defense. These were hearts and souls, and sitting in the dark, he realized he had as little control over what happened with Hannah and Thomas as he did over the team, his son's future, the town, and everything that hadn't gone as planned.

Pastor Mark had said something in one of his recent sermons. He was in a series in 1 Corinthians and he said in any relationship struggle you could ask a single question: "What does love look like here?"

"Many throw that word around like it's simple," Pastor Mark said. "Loving others can be soft and tender. But it can also be bold with hard truth. Taking the risk to love means you might miss the mark. You might have to apologize. If you go there, you're in what I call 'God territory.' It's a place where He's working in others and in you as well."

What did love look like with Hannah and Thomas? And what about Barbara? And what could he learn from the painful process they were going through? He opened his hands in front of him and prayed. There was a peace in the middle of this storm. When he returned to bed, Amy's soft breathing was the sound that lulled him to surrender to both God and sleep.

Part 3

THE ANSWER

CHAPTER 29

✦ ✦ ✦

Hannah felt in a daze after meeting her father. She found the photo of him running and returned it to the box in her grandmother's closet. Then she sat on her bed holding the magazine ad she'd nearly worn out. She wanted her dad to be like the guy in the picture, smiling and holding her on his shoulders. She wanted to "create lifelong memories," just like the ad said. Tears came and she ripped the picture in half and then tore it again. How could someone trapped in a hospital bed give her anything?

She hadn't asked any of the questions she had planned. He hadn't apologized. There was no pleading for her to forgive him. But she hadn't really given him a chance. She felt bad about leaving so abruptly, but she'd been so confused in his room, by his bed. So many expectations from everyone there.

When her grandmother arrived, Hannah pretended to study and said she wasn't hungry. Finally she dried her eyes and asked how her grandmother's day had gone.

She raised an eyebrow. "What's gotten into you? Asking about work? You never do that."

"I just wondered, that's all."

Her grandmother told a funny story about what a customer had said at the restaurant and Hannah chuckled. But it was short-lived. All she could think about was her father. She wanted to tell her grandmother what he looked like and how sick he was. She wanted to ask why she'd said he had died when he hadn't. But she couldn't say that. She had to keep all those thoughts locked up. And that made her feel more alone than if her grandmother left for a year.

In her sleep, she heard the *beep, beep* of the heart monitor and dreamed she was running down a hospital corridor that never ended. Fluorescent lights flashed and flickered above her and each room she passed housed a stranger. She couldn't find her father.

The next day, she had a science test in first period. She stared at the words and the multiple choices, but all she could see was her father's face against that blue pillowcase. She looked up at Mrs. Harrison during the test and saw her teacher staring back at her. Tests were super important. But there was something bigger looming over her life.

She spotted Robert in the hallway after school and

managed to avoid him by darting into the girls' locker room. She dressed for cross-country and went out a side door to the field and sat on the bleachers. Coach Harrison walked down the hill and she wondered if he'd had second thoughts about introducing her to her father.

"How we doing today?" he said.

"I don't really feel like running."

He stared at her and she noticed the light spot on his arm where his watch used to be. Guilt washed over her.

"So maybe we take the day off," he said.

He sat on the bleachers a few feet from her and studied his stopwatch. After a while he lifted his hat and turned slightly toward her. "Hannah, I'm sorry that taking you to the hospital caused you pain. I know that must have been difficult."

It was the silence between them and Coach Harrison's ability to sit and not say anything that prodded her to respond. Finally she let go of something inside. "I want to go see him again."

Coach Harrison looked at her, clearly surprised. "Are you sure?"

She nodded. "But this time, could we talk alone?"

"Of course."

"I didn't say anything I wanted to say."

Coach Harrison gave a quiet laugh. "Neither did he."

"Could we go now?" Hannah said.

"Let me get Amy. We'll take you up to his room and leave the two of you to talk."

Thirty minutes later, Hannah sat in her father's hospital

room. Her dad's face lit up when he heard footsteps. When the Harrisons mentioned they had brought Hannah for another visit, he smiled broadly.

Once they were alone, her father's face grew serious and with a halting voice he said, "Thank you for coming back. I was worried I said the wrong thing."

Hannah shook her head. "No, you didn't."

"I know you must have a lot of questions. You can say anything, ask anything you want. I promise to be honest."

Tears came to her eyes and she could only think of two words. "What happened?"

There it was. Two words held the weight of the past. Hannah studied her father's face as he thought.

"You know how people like to think that they're a good person? I thought I was. But I wasn't, Hannah."

Just the sound of her name touched something inside, resonated in her heart. The look on his face was sincere— like he wasn't putting on any mask or trying to say something she wanted to hear.

"I lived selfish all my life," he continued. "I lived it for me. I hurt so many people. Your mother. Your grandmother. You. And so many others."

Each word was like a weight her father lifted with his breath. She watched his face through the blur of tears. She didn't say anything. She didn't have to because he was pouring out all his life, all his regret before her.

"I left because I was a fool. And I wouldn't listen to anyone. Especially God. I ran from everything that mattered.

But because God loves me, He let me be broken. And I needed to be broken." Her father leaned forward slightly in his bed as he talked about God, and big tears formed in his eyes. "He finally got my attention and I gave Him my heart because that's the only thing I got left."

Hannah had wondered if a blind man could cry. When the first tear ran down her father's cheek, something broke inside her own heart. He struggled for the next words and she watched, feeling as if there was something trapped that was rising to the surface at last.

"So I'm sorry, Hannah. I'm sorry I wasn't there for you. If I could take it all back, I would. I know I don't deserve it, but I pray that one day you will forgive me."

His eyes wandered. She was so quiet he probably didn't even know if she was still there. Finally she managed to say two more words that were stuck in her own heart.

"It's hard."

He lay back on his pillow. Just those two words were enough for him. "I understand," he whispered. "I understand."

She felt as if she had received a gift she desperately wanted. She had heard her father ask for her forgiveness. He had owned his actions and was sorry about the pain he caused. And something else he said touched a nerve. He said all of this was motivated by God's love. It was the same thing she heard from Mrs. Brooks, Mrs. Harrison, and Coach. The same thing she heard in Bible class. The teacher had said the Bible was one long story of God's love reaching out to those who don't deserve it but who desperately need it.

"I don't know if I can forgive," Hannah said before she left. "I want to. But I'm not sure how. Or what that means."

"You don't know how much it means to me that you would even think about these things, Hannah. I'm so grateful you came today."

She touched his shoulder before she left and he placed his hand over hers.

"Thank you for coming back."

On the ride home, the Harrisons didn't ask what had happened. They let her ride in silence, and as she stared out the window, somehow things looked different. The greens of the landscape appeared deeper and the reds darker. She could not have explained it if someone had asked, but if they had, she would have described the advertisement she had ripped apart. She felt like that little girl on her father's shoulders.

Somehow, she felt like she had begun a new race. But she wasn't sure how far she would have to run to finish.

The next day before practice, Hannah sat on a chair in a study room at Brookshire, a place with desks and comfortable chairs. The students called it the Lighthouse because a wall of windows allowed sunshine access to every inch of the room.

As she laced her running shoes and prepared to head down the hill, Mrs. Brooks walked inside. She wore a bright-pink dress and Hannah thought she looked like a walking advertisement for successful educators.

"Hey, Hannah, how far do you run in practice?"

"Three miles. Sometimes five."

The woman seemed impressed. Then she got a concerned look. "Are the Harrisons coming?"

Hannah explained that they had tutoring on Wednesdays so they couldn't be at practice. But she was allowed to run if she wanted.

Mrs. Brooks put her purse on a chair and pushed a stool close to Hannah and sat, looking into Hannah's eyes.

"I know you've had a lot on your mind lately. I've just been wondering how you're doing."

Something about the woman's face, her tone of voice, allowed Hannah to let down her guard.

"I met my dad."

"That's a big deal," Mrs. Brooks said. "How'd that go?"

"He said he was sorry he left."

"How did it make you feel?"

"I still wonder," she said, butterflies in her stomach. "I wonder why he didn't want me."

Mrs. Brooks's face wrinkled with concern. "Do you believe he's sorry?"

Hannah shrugged. "I guess."

Mrs. Brooks leaned forward. "Do you know you have another Father who has always loved you?"

"You mean God?"

She smiled. "Yeah, I do. And listen, He's not like your dad. He's a perfect Father. And He wants you to know Him."

Hannah sat forward. She didn't want to be mean, but all the talk about God and love and a relationship with Him didn't feel real. It felt like something people talked about in order to escape their questions.

"How do you know God?" Hannah said.

"God went to great lengths to express His love for you. You've heard in Bible class how Jesus died on the cross, but do you understand why?"

Hannah shook her head. "No. Not really."

"You were created to know Him. And to worship Him. But we reject Him when we do wrong. When we sin, that's the thing that separates us from Him."

Hannah thought of the box she had at home. A box full of the sins she had committed.

"So He sent His Son to pay the price to get you back. And it was a painful price. But then He rose from the dead and He made a way for you to get right with God . . . if you trust Him. If you believe. That's faith. But He doesn't force it on you. He just offers it to you because He loves you."

As Mrs. Brooks spoke, her voice became softer and it almost felt like a mother talking to her daughter. Would her own mother have talked this way? Face-to-face? Looking her in the eyes?

"We've all sinned, Hannah. We've all lied or stolen . . ."

Hannah's heart jumped when Mrs. Brooks said *stolen*.

"But when we give our heart to Jesus," Mrs. Brooks continued, "He starts cleaning it. He takes better care of it than we ever could . . . if we'll trust Him. Is that something that you'd like to do?"

Hannah felt the sting of tears again, but they were

different somehow. She wanted to say yes, but she didn't know what would happen or what Mrs. Brooks might ask her to do. Somewhere in her heart she knew this was what she needed. It was like in a race: you just put one foot in front of the other and repeated the process.

Her father had been changed on the inside. Somehow God had reached inside and helped him turn around and become a new person. And after seeing him, after hearing his heart, she knew she was ready to step toward God, even though she still had questions. She did believe He was there and that He cared like Mrs. Brooks said, and Mrs. Harrison and Coach, too.

"Yes," Hannah said. "But I don't know what to pray."

"Would it be okay if I led you through it?" Mrs. Brooks said.

Hannah nodded, her vision blurry. Mrs. Brooks held out a hand and Hannah reached out to her. Mrs. Brooks closed her eyes tightly and began to pray and Hannah repeated what she said.

"Lord Jesus, I am a sinner. And I need a Savior. I believe You are that Savior. So today, I place faith in Christ alone to forgive my sins. Come live in me. In Jesus' name, amen."

When she finished, Hannah looked into Mrs. Brooks's smiling face.

"Hannah, that was beautiful. You know that the Bible says when you ask Christ to come live in you, you are a brand-new creature. You are brand-new."

Hannah smiled and nodded. Could that really be true?

Was this just something that happened in your head, or had God really taken away all the bad things she had done? She thought about the box in her nightstand. She thought about the backpack of her life and how heavy it seemed with all the mistakes she had made and the bad breaks she had been given. Maybe that was what God had done. He had reached inside and had taken all of those rocks away so she didn't have to carry them any longer. She couldn't stand up under the weight of that backpack and she couldn't pull all the rocks out herself. So God had done that as only He could do.

"I want you to do me a favor," Mrs. Brooks said. "There's a book of the Bible in the New Testament—it's called Ephesians. I want you to read the first two chapters and just write down everything that it says you are as a believer in Christ. Can you do that?"

"Yes, ma'am."

"Do you have a Bible at home?"

"I think my grandmother does."

Mrs. Brooks told her to wait and left the room. She returned with a Bible and opened the cover. She wrote something inside and handed it to her.

"Now when you go home, before you read those chapters, I want you to pray a simple prayer. Just say, 'Father, open my eyes to see the truth in Your Word about me and about You.'"

"Yes, ma'am."

"I'm so proud of you. And I believe God has good things in store for you. I'm going to be praying."

CHAPTER 30

✦ ✦ ✦

Hannah had read parts of the Bible and she'd heard pastors speak, but it didn't make a lot of sense. She'd heard the stories of David and Goliath and Noah's Flood. The pastors talked about Jesus, and she'd heard His name yelled by kids at the Y when they were mad. She'd even read the Sermon on the Mount somewhere.

"Blessed are the . . ." She couldn't remember any more and didn't know what *blessed* meant.

There was something special about Jesus, no question about it, but she didn't know what it was. However, the discussion with Mrs. Brooks had turned on a switch inside her. Instead of Him being just a person in history, someone who taught lessons about loving people and doing good things, she now saw Him as someone who came to run a race for God—to live a perfect life so that when He finished, He could offer Himself for her and take her punishment. He could change her heart and forgive her sin. And He fully followed His Father with every step.

To Hannah, being a Christian had always been about doing the right things, not doing the wrong things, and knowing the answers to life's test questions. Now, she realized that being a Christian was simply agreeing with God about her sin and receiving His forgiveness. And that meant starting a new race, just following Jesus. Period. It wasn't about doing more good than bad. It was about having a relationship with God and being "in Christ." That's what Mrs. Brooks had said, and whatever it meant, she had to find out.

Instead of heading to the cross-country course, Hannah went home. She couldn't wait to begin the assignment Mrs. Brooks had given her. She started out walking but found herself jogging the mile. Her backpack bounced behind her as she picked up her pace, and it felt lighter somehow. That made her smile.

Things began to make sense. Christmas, for example. It wasn't about candy canes and lights. It was about God becoming human. Jesus was God, but He was born a helpless baby. Why? So He could run a perfect race and give Himself for her. For her father.

Easter wasn't bunnies and bonnets, but a celebration of

that man giving up His life for her and then rising from the dead. If that was true, if Jesus really did come back from the dead like Christians believed, it changed everything. And if it was true, that same power could change her from the inside out.

She was flying now, bounding up the stairs and running inside. She pulled out the Bible and a notebook and tossed her backpack on the couch. She sat at the kitchen table and opened the Bible's cover and saw the date written in blue ink. Below it were words in flowing cursive:

To Hannah, on your spiritual birthday. I thank God for you. I pray you will understand who you are in Christ, and that God will give you a spirit of wisdom and open the eyes of your heart to see the hope, the inheritance, and the power you have in Him. God bless you, Hannah.

Love in Christ, Olivia Brooks

She read the inscription again and wondered where those words had come from. She looked at the table of contents and found the page where Ephesians began.

What was the prayer she was supposed to pray? She closed her eyes tightly and bowed her head. "Father, open my eyes to the truth about me and about You that I'm going to read. Amen."

That wasn't exactly what Mrs. Brooks had said, but it was close. She began reading words written by a man named Paul. It was a letter to people who lived a long time ago. As she read, it felt like a letter written straight to her heart.

> Blessed be the God and Father of our Lord Jesus Christ, who has blessed us in Christ with every spiritual blessing in the heavenly places, even as he chose us in him before the foundation of the world, that we should be holy and blameless before him.

She pulled the notebook closer and at the top wrote, *In Christ.* Underneath it she wrote, *I am blessed.* She didn't understand all that meant, but if she was "in Christ," it meant she was blessed with "every spiritual blessing."

Then she wrote, *I am chosen.* Jesus chose her before the foundation of the world. She stared at the word. Could that really be true? Had God seen her and planned for her to respond to Him even before she knew about Him? Had He been drawing her to Himself all her life? If so, that meant He cared more than she could understand. He was thinking of her. And if this was true for her, it was also true for her father. God had drawn him the same way. And if God was really in control, if He really did care this much, He was using everything that happened in her life for a purpose.

Asthma.

Maybe asthma wasn't God's punishment. Maybe it was something He had allowed to help her see she needed Him more than she could understand.

She read the next verses.

In love he predestined us for adoption to himself as
sons through Jesus Christ, according to the purpose
of his will, to the praise of his glorious grace, with
which he has blessed us in the Beloved.

She wrote, *I am adopted* in her notebook and looked
at the word. She was God's child because He had adopted
her. But why? If God knew all the bad things she had done,
why would He want to adopt her? And then she noticed
two little words: *in love*. It was because of His love.

Hannah smiled. God wanted good things for her, so He
had blessed her and chosen her and adopted her. Her heart
felt full.

In him we have redemption through his blood, the
forgiveness of our trespasses, according to the riches
of his grace, which he lavished upon us.

She knew *redemption* came from *redeemed*. That one she
would have to look up later. It sounded kind of complicated. But she wrote, *I am redeemed*. She moved on to the
next word. It was totally understandable.

I am forgiven.

She took her time writing that and then stared at the
word. Writing it was one thing. Believing it was another.
Was it true?

She thought of the blue box. It was full. Was God able to forgive those things she'd done? She thought of her father. He'd gotten into drugs and had been responsible for her mother's death. He'd abandoned his own daughter. That was in his blue box.

If a person who was "in Christ" was really forgiven, then all those things weren't held against them by God. He had forgiven them. He had cleaned out the blue box of their lives by the power of His love. And forgiveness wasn't just looking the other way or calling things good that weren't. It was a choice God made to give His only Son.

She suddenly sensed a freedom she had never experienced. It felt like a puff of the inhaler to her soul. She could breathe again.

Her dad's face flashed in her mind. Just because he was forgiven by God didn't change the truth about his bad choices. No, there was something deeper going on.

What if she lived this way? What if she really believed and acted as if she were adopted by God and chosen by Him? What if she lived forgiven instead of living guilty? What if she lived loved by the holy God who made everything? What kind of change would that make in her life?

She picked up in the middle of the long sentence. This guy Paul wrote really long sentences.

. . . in all wisdom and insight making known to us
the mystery of his will, according to his purpose,
which he set forth in Christ as a plan for the fullness

of time, to unite all things in him, things in heaven
and things on earth.

In him we have obtained an inheritance, having
been predestined according to the purpose of him
who works all things according to the counsel of his
will, so that we who were the first to hope in Christ
might be to the praise of his glory.

In him you also, when you heard the word of
truth, the gospel of your salvation, and believed in
him, were sealed with the promised Holy Spirit, who
is the guarantee of our inheritance until we acquire
possession of it, to the praise of his glory.

She wrote, *I am sealed.*

She'd never read the Bible this way, as if it were speaking
to her, as if it applied directly to her life. It was always just
a bunch of words or wise sayings. Now, even though there
were parts she didn't understand, she read on until she
reached some words that almost jumped off the page.

But God, being rich in mercy, because of the great
love with which he loved us, even when we were
dead in our trespasses, made us alive together
with Christ. . . . For by grace you have been saved
through faith. And this is not your own doing; it is
the gift of God, not a result of works, so that no one
may boast. For we are his workmanship, created in

Christ Jesus for good works, which God prepared beforehand, that we should walk in them.

I am loved.
I am saved.
I am God's child.

She put down her number 2 pencil, sat back, and looked at the list of truths. She couldn't wait to show Mrs. Brooks. She felt something strange inside. It wasn't white light and angels singing. It was what Mrs. Brooks had encouraged her to pray. She was seeing the truth about herself and God. And she felt as if God was right there helping her understand and see things she couldn't see on her own.

As she studied the list, she knew these things were now true of her, not because she was a good person or had earned points with God, but because she was in Christ. She had asked Him to forgive her and change her. So when God looked at her life, He didn't see everything bad she had done. He saw Jesus' life and everything He had done for her. She didn't understand how all of that worked, but she knew it was true.

Hannah set aside her Bible and notebook. She had to get outside, into the sunlight. She left the house and jogged toward the river and along the winding, paved pathway. There was a lightness to her steps, a freedom to run, a step-by-step release that was simply her response to what God had done and was doing. She ran fast, taking longer strides, using her arms to propel her farther and faster, the wind and sun on her face. She came to the bend in the river where the water gushed and streamed over the rocks, and she stopped and smiled. The water was deep and powerful, like the grace and mercy of God. The water was His love for her and the sound of it spoke like a whisper to her heart. She wasn't alone. She wasn't abandoned. She wasn't guilty. God had plans for her, good things for her to do in the power only He could offer. Good things He had prepared for her to walk in. Good things to run in.

I can run for God's glory, she thought. *I can let His power be at work in me with every step, every breath.*

She didn't care who saw her. She didn't care what anybody thought about the girl by the river who was lifting her hands high, her arms spread wide. She looked at the heavens and said, "Thank You."

CHAPTER 31

✦ ✦ ✦

Troy Finkle caught John in the school hallway, as he was prone to do. John liked to help other staff members where he was needed, but judging more drama monologues was about as exciting as a root canal. Troy insisted.

John sighed. "Troy, you don't need me."

"Yes, I do. You're a judge! And I even have a part for you in the spring play. You don't even have to audition."

"Good, because I'm not doing it."

"Too late, I've already given you the part. We'll talk details soon. Now, come to drama class sixth period."

Two hours later, John found himself sitting at the judges' table, listening to one lifeless monologue after another. He tried to focus on the performances, but again, all the students seemed to miss the heart of the material they delivered. When the last one had finished, John handed Troy his notes as the kids waited for the bell.

Something caught his eye in the wings to the left of the stage. Hannah stood by a curtain, staring at him. She glanced at the students on the risers and took a breath. There was something about the way she looked at John. What was going on? Was she having an asthma attack?

"Hannah, are you okay?"

She nodded. "Ask me who I am."

Had he heard her correctly? John looked at the other students, then back at Hannah, puzzled. It took a moment for her words to register. It was the question Thomas had asked him at the hospital, the question he passed on to Hannah at practice one day, the one she hadn't been able to answer.

"Ask me who I am," Hannah said again, a little louder.

The other students continued talking.

It dawned on John that she had an answer to the question. He called to her across the room. "Who is Hannah Scott?"

Hannah took a step forward, breathed in deeply, and with a confidence John had never seen in her, she put her shoulders back and looked him squarely in the eyes.

"I am created by God," she said. "He designed me. So I'm not a mistake. His Son died for me just so I could be forgiven."

Her voice carried through the auditorium. She used her hands when she spoke, emphasizing each syllable. And he thought he saw something glisten in her eyes.

"He picked me to be His own, so I'm chosen. He redeemed me, so I am wanted."

The students hushed and turned their attention toward her. She took a few steps forward, and now there was no mistaking it. There were tears in her eyes and flowing down her cheeks, and there was no shame, no holding back.

"He showed me grace, just so I could be saved."

The room was quiet, captivated by Hannah's authenticity.

"He has a future for me because He loves me. So I don't wonder anymore, Coach Harrison. I am a child of God. I just wanted you to know."

John sat stunned. He and Amy and the boys had prayed for Hannah and Barbara and Thomas, but what he saw here was beyond anything he could have asked. Somehow, God had broken through into the girl's life. There was power in her words. She'd been changed.

Hannah turned and walked toward the open door behind her. John rose and followed her. Behind him he heard Troy's voice.

"Did you see that? That's what I'm talking about! That was fire! John, why is she not in my class?"

John kept walking. He couldn't answer Troy's question because he had to catch Hannah. He rushed into the hall and called for her.

"What happened to you?" John said, beaming.

"I talked to Mrs. Brooks yesterday. And prayed. And then I read, um . . . in Ephesians?"

"Yeah," John said, nodding.

"And it was like God was talking directly to me."

"This is amazing. What you said in there was amazing."

"I want to know more," she said. "I want to read more."

"You can." John's heart beat faster as if Ethan had just hit that shot at the buzzer in the championship game. No, better than that. This was much better. He wanted to jump up and down and pump his fist in the air, but he controlled himself. "I want Amy to hear this. Can we go see her?"

As they walked, Hannah told him more. She was a quiet girl who kept things inside, but now a dam had broken and a cascade of words flowed.

"Coach, I've read the Bible before, but this time it was like the words jumped off the page."

"That's God's Holy Spirit helping you, Hannah. He's at work inside. He's the one making you hungry to know more, to read more."

She nodded. "And it's not just understanding the words. It's like God was whispering these things, that I'm forgiven, that I'm chosen, I'm adopted."

They walked the hall together and John couldn't remember a happier moment. With all the success he'd had as a player and coach, there was something about the change he saw in this girl that arrested him. No win on the court could compare with this feeling.

Amy looked up as the bell rang and her students filed out of class. She saw Hannah, then glanced at John, then back at Hannah.

Later, John heard that every teacher in the classes up and down the hall came out of their rooms to see who had shouted so loudly. Several traced it to the science classroom and peered inside to see Amy embracing Hannah, both of them crying, and Coach Harrison with both hands over his face, wiping away tears of joy.

CHAPTER 32

✦ ✦ ✦

When Hannah got home from practice, she put her things on the kitchen table, then remembered what her grandmother had said so often. "You can run five miles lickety-split, but you can't put your backpack on the hook?"

Hannah smiled and promptly hung up her backpack. Then she fell on her bed with a sense that things had changed. Hope had somehow burrowed deep within her, and the feeling didn't come from changed circumstances but a change inside. She still had tons of questions about life, but now she didn't feel alone.

She had found her father—or, better put, God had helped her father find her. She'd received love from her heavenly Father, who had pursued her. Now, lying on the pillow, her heart finally at rest, she turned and opened her nightstand drawer, pushing the shirt away to reveal the blue box. She took off the top, then sat up and pulled the box to her lap and pawed through all the things she had stolen. The iPod. Coach Harrison's watch. Jewelry. Her sin was in this box and all the evidence stared back at her like witnesses at a trial.

Who are you to call yourself a Christian after all the bad things you've done?

It wasn't a voice, just thoughts. And she wanted to silence them by sealing the top and tossing everything into the trash. But she knew that wouldn't solve things. Even if she tossed the box into the sea and let it sink to the bottom, she'd know it was there. And God would know.

God *did* know.

Hannah thought of her list. She was loved by Him. She was saved. She'd been chosen before the foundation of the world. Redeemed. She was *forgiven*.

But at the same time, she was guilty. The box was evidence of who she was.

And then it clicked.

This box *wasn't* who she was. The box was evidence of her sin. It held the evidence of *what she had done*. But this was not *who she was* any longer. Only God had the right to tell her who she was, and He'd said all of those things about her in the Bible.

So what did a forgiven person do with a blue box? How did a forgiven person act after receiving love?

Her father had abandoned her, and he'd let shame and guilt keep him away for fifteen years. How she wished he had come looking for her years earlier. No doubt he felt the same way. But God had changed him, just like He had changed Hannah. God had given him another chance.

She looked at the box again. The expensive headphones caught her eye first. They were right where she had put them. And even though it frightened her to think of it, she knew what she had to do.

The next day, walking home from school, her heart beating wildly, she took a detour toward Webb Park. At the knoll, she heard a bouncing basketball and voices of boys in competition.

She stopped behind a tree and studied the players. Three of them had run after her that day. Including the one who had promised to find her and make her pay. Headphone Guy.

Everything in Hannah told her to turn and run. Everything but the quiet voice that said she needed to do what was right. The voice that said she wasn't defined by her sin any longer.

She unzipped her backpack and took out the headphones, then walked down the hill toward the court, holding them by her side as she slowed her pace. She passed the basket. The boys kept playing. She stopped at the edge of the court and waited.

Headphone Guy dribbled the ball and finally saw her. "Hold up, hold up." He looked straight at her and dropped the ball and it bounced away.

Hannah had played the scenario out in her mind. She had a whole speech ready. She'd apologize first. Then she'd tell him that God had forgiven her and that she was returning the headphones.

"And I'd like you to forgive me. I'm sorry."

That's what she wanted to say, what she wanted to happen. And in her dream, she would tell the kid what she had read in the Bible and how much better she felt inside knowing God had loved her enough to die for her. And the kid would be so overjoyed at getting his headphones back that he would smile and ask questions about what she was talking about. And she would pray with him like Mrs. Brooks had done and she would tell him to read Ephesians and the other kids around would listen and they would want to pray.

She stood there, holding the headphones out, and watched the boy walk toward her. There was anger on his face.

"I don't believe this," he said to his friends. Then the venom came. "You're the little thief who took my headphones."

Thief.

There it was again. The accusation. But that wasn't who she was. She'd been forgiven. She wasn't a thief. She wanted to protest—but instead she just held out the headphones as the others gathered. She tried to say something, but the words wouldn't come.

He snatched the headphones from her in anger and inspected them. Finally Hannah gathered her courage.

"I'm sorry." Her voice was soft and reserved, but she had said it. It wasn't the speech she had rehearsed, it wasn't some eloquent sermon, but it was all she could give.

Instead of smiling, Headphone Guy's face contorted. Sweat dripped from his nose and his muscles tightened, and when he spoke, it felt like he was spitting.

"Who do you think you are? You just take whatever you want?" Veins popped in his neck and he moved closer, his eyes boring a hole in her.

"I'm sorry," she said again.

That was it. Her words unleashed a response she didn't expect. He drew back like he was going to punch her, then violently pushed her and she fell hard.

Someone shouted. A woman's voice. "Hey, get away from her!"

Hannah was on her back, the woman over her now, trying to help her up, but Headphone Guy moved forward, hovering like a linebacker taunting a sacked quarterback.

"See what happens when you take something from me!"

The woman stood her ground and pointed a finger at him. "That's enough!" She helped Hannah to her feet.

So much for asking forgiveness. Was this what happened when you tried to do the right thing? Was this what following Jesus looked like?

"What's your name?" the woman said gently.

Hannah couldn't breathe. Couldn't think. She'd felt so good about returning the headphones and now, so defeated.

"I need to go," she said, turning and running for the woods.

"Hey, wait a minute!" the woman called after her.

"Yeah, that's what I thought!" Headphone Guy yelled. "You'd better run. Thief!"

The word echoed in her soul. She ran until she felt safe enough to stop, far from the sound of the voices. She sat by a tree. How would she be able to prove that she was no longer the same person? How could she get others to understand the change that had happened inside?

In the front pouch of her backpack were other items she needed to return. No one had told her she had to—it was just something she felt God wanted her to "walk in," like it said in Ephesians. She'd written that verse in her journal. She believed God had prepared good things for her to do ahead of time, things He had for her to accomplish. One of those things was taking back all she had stolen.

She pulled out her English notebook. She'd written a bunch of essays this year, but these notes would be even harder to compose. For each item, she turned to a blank page and wrote something to the owner.

Hello,

My name is Hannah and I took this from you in the locker room at the Y. I'm sorry. I've asked God to forgive me, but I know I need to make this right with you. I apologize. I hope you can forgive me. It's because God loved me that I'm returning this to you.

Sincerely,
Hannah

She knocked on doors, and when no one answered, she left the items and the notes. At one house, she knocked and heard feet clambering inside on hardwood.

"Who is it?" a voice called. It sounded like the girl from the Y, another latchkey kid like Hannah. She'd seen her walk to this house from the Y's after-school program.

"My name's Hannah. I have something I need to give you."

The door opened just enough for the girl to see. She looked up at Hannah, then her eyes traveled to the bracelet Hannah held.

"You found it!"

The door unlatched and the girl opened it wide and grabbed the bracelet. "I've been looking everywhere. Where was it?"

"It was at the Y and I—"

"Oh, thank you!" the girl said, interrupting. "I thought it was gone forever." She clutched it to her chest like it was a long-lost friend. "How did you know it was mine?"

Hannah paused. She could make something up, fudge

the truth. But she looked into the girl's face and knew she couldn't tell her anything but what had really happened.

"I took it."

The girl squinted, the front door wide-open behind her. "What do you mean?"

"It was sticking out of your backpack one day. Nobody was looking."

Her mouth formed an O. "You mean you stole it?"

Hannah nodded.

"You shouldn't have done that. That's mean. My mom says that . . ." The girl paused.

"I know. Your mom is right. Stealing is wrong. And I've asked God to forgive me. And I want to ask you to forgive me too. You don't have to."

The girl looked like she might cry. "My daddy gave it to me right before he got deployed, and I thought it was my fault I lost it." She studied Hannah again. "So nobody made you bring it back?"

Hannah shook her head.

"That's awesome," the girl said. Then her face turned sour. "I took some money from my mom's wallet once. I never told her."

"I bet she'd forgive you if you did," Hannah said. "And you might feel better about it."

"Yeah. Maybe." She looked at the driveway. "Well, I'm not supposed to open the door for anybody. I need to go. Thanks for bringing this back."

She closed the door quickly and Hannah walked home.

She sat on the porch and watched cars and people pass. The word *thief* echoed in her head. She pulled out the page she had shown to Mrs. Brooks, the one with all the things the passage in Ephesians told her she was in Christ.

She scanned the list and realized she had a choice about what to believe. She could believe what others thought—or even her own feelings—or she could believe what God said. She could trust His words were really true.

Mrs. Brooks had said that trusting God and believing what He said was faith. And what Hannah had just done, returning items and asking forgiveness, was walking out what she believed. Every step she took to return the things she stole, every word of apology she wrote, was her choosing to believe in and trust God.

She recalled her father's words and the emotion he showed on her last visit. Suddenly she knew she had to see him. She couldn't wait one minute to go and tell him what he had longed to hear. She couldn't have him thinking she hadn't forgiven him.

She jumped on her bike and rode to Franklin General. When she reached the front entrance, she realized she had forgotten to bring her bike lock. It would be ironic if somebody stole her bike after she'd returned so many things.

She got a visitor's pass and rode the elevator to the fourth floor, excited to walk in on her father and tell him. She found his room and pushed the door open, ready to burst in and give him a hug.

His bed sat empty.

The noisy machines, the tubes and bags of dripping liquid—all of it was gone.

She'd missed her chance. She would never be able to tell her father about the forgiveness she wanted to offer him.

Tears came to her eyes. Her mother had died at this hospital. Now her father had done the same. There was so much more she wanted to say to him and now . . .

"Hey, are you looking for Thomas Hill?"

Hannah turned and saw a dark-haired nurse with a clipboard.

She turned away, not wanting the nurse to see her tears. "Yes."

"Are you a relative?" the nurse said.

"I'm his daughter." As she said it, Hannah realized she had spoken the truth about herself. And the truth felt good. Thomas Hill was her father, and she was glad.

The nurse put a hand on Hannah's shoulder. "Well, he's just been moved to ICU, sweetie. You want me to take you?"

A flood of relief washed over her. She felt like she could breathe again. She followed the nurse and asked what *ICU* stood for. It sounded ominous. When they reached her father's new room, Hannah looked through the window and asked the nurse if he was okay.

"His EKG showed signs of a heart attack during dialysis. But he's stable now. You can go in."

Hannah slowly walked inside and stood by her father's bed, studying his face. The same beeps were here, but there were more machines. The window shades were drawn. Her father turned his head at the sound of her sneakers.

"Are you okay?" she said softly.

He smiled, immediately recognizing her voice. "Hannah."

She loved that he knew it was her. She loved that he spoke her name.

"They said you had signs of a heart attack."

He chuckled to himself. "I just needed a little excitement. Sometimes I get a little bored, and so I decided to shake things up a little bit."

"Well, maybe you shouldn't do that again," Hannah said.

"I admit I don't want to," her father said. He caught his breath and said, "So how are you doing?"

"Well, I want to tell you something. Two things, really."

"Okay."

"I made the decision to follow Jesus."

That brought a huge smile to his face and it seemed he couldn't keep still. His legs moved beneath the covers and his whole body reacted to the news.

"I've been learning a lot," she said. "And reading a lot. And one thing I've learned is, if Jesus can forgive me for all the things I've done, then I can forgive other people."

The smile left his face and he became somber.

"So I wanted you to know that I forgive you. And I want to spend more time with you, if that's okay."

Tears came to her father's eyes. She reached for his hand on the bed. It was wrapped with tape that held a tube and needle in place. When she touched him, he opened his hand and grasped hers tightly and squeezed.

"Yes," he said, and his face lit again. "I love that so much. Thank you, Hannah." His eyes filled and his voice was pained. "I wish I could be there for you."

"It's okay. I don't mind coming here."

Hannah pulled up a chair and held her father's hand as they talked. She asked the questions she couldn't ask before. Her father told her things about her mother she'd never heard. He even said he had a nickname when he was younger.

"Why did they call you T-bone?"

He smiled. "For some reason I thought eating meat before a race would make me faster. So just before every race I ate a steak. Some of my teammates heard about it and the name kind of stuck."

The conversation was easy and it only felt like they'd been talking five minutes when Hannah noticed the sun was going down. She told her father she needed to leave but would come back the next day.

"I'll be looking forward to it," he said.

When she walked through the front exit, she looked at the bike rack. There was her old bicycle waiting and ready for the ride home. It felt like an answer to prayer.

CHAPTER 33

✦ ✦ ✦

John and Amy ate lunch together as often as they could, and today they had things to talk about over sandwiches in John's classroom.

Their conversation turned to Thomas, and John gave her the latest update. He was still in ICU, but doctors were encouraged by his response to medication.

"Any idea how much damage was done to his heart?" Amy said.

"They don't think it was extensive."

"So no surgery."

John shook his head. "There's no way he's strong enough for surgery. With his kidneys not functioning and now his heart, it's a miracle he's still with us."

"It's almost like he's hanging on for a reason."

"More like God has kept him alive for a purpose. You should hear his prayers, Amy. He's only been a believer three years, but the depth of his relationship with God . . . He's not letting his circumstances dictate his faith, you know?"

Amy nodded. "Which is where we all are. The town, the school, your team—Ethan's college prospects. We have to believe that God is going to use all of this. That He's at work in spite of . . ."

Her voice trailed and John looked up from his lunch. She was looking past him at the door, which he had closed. It was open now and Hannah walked in and stood by his desk, a serious look on her face. It almost seemed like she was about to cry.

Before he could ask what was up, or even say hello, he recognized what she was holding. With both hands out as if presenting an offering, she held his wristwatch. It had been missing for so long. She placed it on a book on his desk and he stared at it, trying to put the pieces together.

He looked up at her and saw hurt and pain in her eyes.

"I'm sorry, Coach," Hannah said. "That day when you ran with Will and me, I saw this on the bleachers. I took it."

John glanced down at the watch, then turned to Amy.

"If you need to report this, I understand," Hannah said. "But I had to give it back."

John stood. He didn't say a word. He didn't have to. The feelings inside were overwhelming. He touched

Hannah's shoulder and smiled. Then he gave her a hug and thought about Jesus' parable, when the father embraced his son who had squandered his inheritance. The father had waited, watched the horizon for so long, and when his son returned, he was ready to forgive. That's what this felt like. Hannah had not only given her heart to God, she was following through with her commitment.

Amy stood and hugged Hannah. When she pulled back, she said, "I'm so proud of you."

Hannah grinned. She turned to John and said, "Every time you looked at your wrist, I felt guilty."

"It takes a lot of courage to admit your mistakes, Hannah. You could have kept it."

"I was reading the book of James, and there's a lot I don't understand, but it said, 'Confess your sins to one another.' This is the last thing of all the things I took."

"So there were more items?"

"A lot more. And I knew I needed to give them back. All of them."

John pulled up a chair and asked her to sit. "What else was there?"

She listed a few items.

"And how did it go when you returned them?" John said.

"Pretty good. Some not so good. Some people weren't home, so I left a note. I knew I couldn't just leave a note for you. I needed to tell you face-to-face."

John smiled. "Not everybody will hug you when you apologize. Not everybody will forgive."

"I know."

"So why did you take all those things?"

"I don't know, Coach. I didn't need your watch. I had an iPod my grandmother gave me. But when I saw those things, something inside made me want them."

Amy leaned forward. "I've worked with a counselor at our church. She told me that sometimes when people feel empty, they do things to fill that space."

"Like drugs?" Hannah said.

"Sure. It can be a lot of things. But it sounds like for you, taking those things added something valuable to your life. You were trying to fill an emptiness that could never be filled with things. Does that make sense?"

Hannah nodded like she'd never have come up with that explanation. "I don't want to do that anymore, Mrs. Harrison."

"That's clear," John said. "You've returned everything. You've confessed it to God and asked His forgiveness. Anytime you bring sin into the light, God will help you. It's painful, though. I'm glad you're reading James—that's such a practical book."

"My dad suggested it. He said it's really helped him."

John sat up straight. "You've been to see your father?"

"Most days after practice, I ride my bike over and sit with him. I'm going over today after school to do homework and talk. I never knew talking could be that much fun."

John glanced at Amy and she looked shocked by the news.

"I've forgiven him," Hannah said. "I told him that and I think it helped."

"I'll bet it did," Amy said. "For both of you."

Hannah smiled. "I thought I was doing it for him, so he wouldn't feel guilty. But it actually made me feel so much better."

"Forgiveness will do that," John said. "It's a gift you give others that comes right back to your own heart."

"So you know your dad's health took a turn," Amy said.

Hannah nodded. "He's hoping to go back to his regular room today. I think he's going to be okay."

John shook his head in amazement. "So you opened your heart to your heavenly Father, and you got your earthly one back too. You've taken some huge steps, Hannah."

"Yeah," she said, her face beaming. "I think everything's going to work out fine now."

CHAPTER 34

✦ ✦ ✦

Hannah read a section from her biology book to her father and he listened with interest. He admitted he hadn't been the best student in school, but he said he was proud of her for taking her studies seriously.

She read him a poem she had written for English class. It was titled "Meeting My Dad for the First Time."

Meeting my dad for the first time
Was like meeting a stranger.
Gray hair, gray beard, and eyes that can't see.
A big smile. A nervous laugh.
I didn't say what I wanted and neither did he.

So we tried again.
I forgave him for leaving.
It feels like he came back from the dead.

"Wow," her father said when she finished. The words seemed to take his breath away. "That's heavy, Hannah. And really good."

"Yeah."

"What grade did you get?"

"I didn't turn it in."

"Why not?"

"I don't know. I don't think I'm ready for everybody to know . . ."

"Ah, you mean you're not ready for your grandmother to know."

She nodded.

"Hey, you have to talk. I don't know if you're nodding or shaking your head."

Hannah laughed. "Yes, you're right about my grandmother. She doesn't see all of my schoolwork, but there's a parent-teacher conference coming up, and you never know. I don't want the poem getting back to her before . . ."

"You probably need to tell her about coming here, don't you think?"

Hannah nodded, then said, "Yeah."

There was silence between them and Hannah studied his face, trying to gauge if now was a good time or not. He'd said she could ask him anything.

"Can you tell me something about my mother?"

His eyes wandered. "Sure. What else do you want to know?"

"Tell me again what she was like."

He closed his eyes and took a deep breath. "She was like a cool breeze on a hot day. Now that sounds like poetry, but it's true. She lit up the room when she walked in. She had a laugh—oh, she could laugh and it would melt your heart. And smart? Unlike me, she'd know exactly what that biology book was saying. Prettiest thing I ever saw. It was like there was a light inside that streamed out of her. I could go on and on about your mother. There aren't enough words. What else do you want to know?"

"Did you want to get married?"

"She did. When she found out you were on the way, she suggested we elope. I was different back then, Hannah. I only thought of myself. So I made excuses. Told her it was too soon, not the right time, I needed a steady job, that kind of thing. Truth is, I didn't want the responsibility of being a husband and father. I wanted to have fun."

"Is that why you took drugs?"

His face clouded, the past sneaking up through her words.

"You said I could ask anything, right?" she said.

He smiled sadly. "Absolutely. So the drugs. I hope this is never something you experience firsthand. The drugs took away all the problems I had, but only for a little while. They made me feel good when I felt bad.

"I heard a preacher on the radio who described my problem. He was talking about sin but I changed *sin* to *drugs*. It goes: 'Drugs will take you farther than you want to go, keep you longer than you want to stay, and cost you more than you want to pay.' That's what happened to me. Unfortunately your mother paid the biggest price. I had no idea how many people my decisions would hurt. But every day I wake up and wish I could go back and take a different path."

"But you can't."

"No, I can't change the past. And God, in His kindness, has forgiven me. But I've promised Him that I will use every breath I have left to praise Him and tell others about His grace."

Hannah closed her book and put it in her backpack. "It's getting late. I need to go."

"Hannah, these visits mean so much. I look forward to every day now. I know I can't make up for the time I lost, but having you here is a dream come true."

She hugged him. "I'll be back tomorrow, okay?"

"I look forward to it."

She unlocked her bike and rode home thinking about the forgiveness the Harrisons had offered her. What she had dreaded doing had drawn them closer together. The time with her dad, asking hard questions, had been the same. She felt like she was floating home as she pedaled over the hill and put her bike inside the gate.

She had enough time to get inside before her grandmother got home. She walked in and locked the door behind her.

"Where've you been?"

Hannah jumped and turned to see her grandmother sitting in the living room, glaring at her.

"You scared me," Hannah said.

"I wasn't feeling well, so I came home early. You weren't here. Mrs. Cole didn't know where you were. You want to tell me?"

Hannah was frozen by the door, unable to move, unable to look her grandmother in the face for more than a second or two.

"Hannah, I want the truth."

Hannah hung her backpack on the hook. She wanted to talk with her grandmother about how God had forgiven her, about the blue box and her father. Sometimes the people closest to you are the most difficult to tell such things to.

She sat on the floor in front of her grandmother without a clue where to begin.

"I met him."

"You met who?"

"My father. Thomas Hill."

Her grandmother's mouth dropped open. "What are you talking about, girl?"

"He's alive, Grandma. He's not dead. That's where I was today."

Her eyes flashed fire. "Did he come looking for you?"

"No, Coach Harrison was over at the hospital and—"

"Coach Harrison?"

"Yes, he met my dad and found out I was his daughter. He's really sick, Grandma. He's blind now and he has to have dialysis because his kidneys—"

"Back up," she said, interrupting. "I don't understand. Are you saying your coach introduced you?"

Hannah hoped the more she explained, the more her grandmother would listen and accept the story. But the look on her face made Hannah suspect things weren't going to get better.

CHAPTER 35

✦ ✦ ✦

Barbara had stewed all afternoon waiting for Hannah to
arrive. She'd asked Mrs. Cole, their neighbor, where she
thought Hannah might have gone on her bicycle. The
woman didn't know and said Hannah had taken off on
her bike after school each day that week.

The sick feeling she'd had at work felt like the flu. But
this was worse. Hannah wasn't just taking things that didn't
belong to her; she was sneaking around and who knew
what trouble she was into. Barbara's mind raced with all
the possibilities. She turned the chair toward the door and
planted herself. She'd wait as long as it took.

When Hannah arrived, Barbara opened the floodgates

of her anger and the girl sat on the floor like she used to do as a toddler, playing with her dolls and horses. This time, however, she wasn't playing make-believe—she was telling a story that Barbara had never imagined she'd hear. Barbara had spent fifteen years making sure Thomas had no access to Hannah. He'd taken Janet from her, the dearest person in the world. Barbara would never let him near Hannah. That was the vow she had made.

And yet, here he was, sweet-talking her, answering questions, no doubt telling Hannah how awful Barbara had been. Hannah had gotten partway through the story when Barbara heard the magic words. How had Thomas made contact? He'd used the coach at her school. That sent her over the edge. She'd trusted that place. She'd trusted that coach.

She got her purse and car keys and pointed a finger at Hannah. "You are not to go out of this house—do you hear me?"

"Grandma, why are you so mad? I don't understand—"

"Of course you don't understand. You're too young to know what I've been through. I will not go through this again, you hear? I ought to run over that bike of yours!"

"Grandma, no!"

"You set foot out of this house while I'm gone, and you'll see what I'll do."

"Where are you going?"

"Never mind where I'm going. You get in that room and you stay there. You understand me?"

"Yes, Grandma."

Barbara got in the car and was ready to speed away before she realized she had no idea where to go. She stormed back into the house, slamming the door behind her, and opened the Brookshire directory she'd stashed in a kitchen drawer.

Barbara found the number and address. She recognized the street. It was about fifteen minutes away. She slammed the house door, slammed the car door, and noticed Mrs. Cole on her front porch with a worried look.

Ten minutes later, after ignoring the "Drive like your kids live here" signs, she parked on the tree-lined street in front of the Harrisons' home, a nice two-story that had all the marks of privilege. Big yard. Concrete driveway with a basketball hoop. They probably had a pool in the back.

She had her speech ready. It was locked tightly somewhere in her heart. She flew across the lawn and up the front steps and rapped hard on the door. Coach Harrison opened it and recognized her.

"Mrs. Scott," he said, looking shocked to see her.

"I need to speak to you," she said. It was all she could do not to unleash on him right there on the front porch. Better to get inside and let them both hear so she didn't have to repeat it.

"Come on in," he said.

His wife joined him in the living room and offered Barbara something to drink. They asked if she wanted to sit. She stood instead, trying to control the volcano bubbling inside, glancing at the nice furniture and nice pictures on the wall and the nice life they led. Everything neat and tidy.

"This won't take long," she said, planting her feet on the shiny hardwood. "I come home early from work, expecting to find Hannah there. And two hours later she walks in having ridden her bike to the hospital, where she has been visiting the one person I vowed she'd never meet."

Amy kept her eyes on the floor, like a scared pup seeing a rolled-up newspaper. Coach Harrison at least looked her in the eyes. As her anger seethed, Barbara felt she was doing a good job restraining herself.

"Then I find out you two connected them!"

"Mrs. Scott," Coach Harrison said with a conciliatory tone. She'd heard that tone before. Some clerk at a store telling her to settle down when she'd been overcharged.

"I am not finished," she snapped, raising a finger. That shut him up. She stared at him, then glared at his wife with fire in her eyes.

"She's been going there while I'm at work and not telling me. I didn't know he was back in Franklin. And I don't care what shape he's in!"

The emotion came and she fought it. A vision of Janet flashed in her mind, that happy-go-lucky girl with all the hope in the world. Barbara remembered the sheet that covered her, the way the man pulled it back so she could see her face and identify her. She choked back tears.

"He's caused me more pain than anyone in my life." She

let the words linger between them. And then she launched another salvo. "You had no right to interfere. It was not your place. I am the one that raised her! I am the one that provided for her! Not him!"

Amy nodded and Barbara thought she could at least understand, a mother's heart would understand her pain. A mother's heart should have put a stop to Hannah walking into that hospital.

"She will not see him anymore. And if you take her there, I have a right to bring action against the school and against you."

Both of them stood unable to speak, looking like their house had burned to the ground. And Barbara felt glad. "Now I've said what I came to say." She turned and walked out, slamming the front door.

CHAPTER 36

✦ ✦ ✦

John stood, shell-shocked not only at what Barbara had said
but how she said it. There was such anger and bitterness in
her voice that it lingered in the room after she stormed out.
As much as he wanted to be angry at Barbara for not listening to their side of the story, he couldn't. His heart broke
for this woman and all she had been through and all that
led to the release of her tirade.

"What just happened?" Amy said breathlessly.

John went to the window and watched Barbara drive
away. "I wonder what she said to Hannah. What is that girl
going through?"

He closed his eyes. He wanted to fix things, wanted to

explain. He wanted to call Olivia and tell her what had happened. There were a thousand things he could do, but only one seemed right. There was only one place they could go with trouble bigger than both of them.

Kneeling on the living room floor, John put his elbows on the ottoman. Amy knelt beside him and clasped hands with him, and at first, neither of them spoke.

John was unable to hold back a groan. "I'm sorry, Lord. Please forgive me if I've jumped ahead of You. You know I only wanted to help them. Please, don't let this hurt Hannah or the school."

Amy held his hands tightly and said, "Yes, Lord Jesus. Thank You."

"Lord, I don't know what to do. I need You to show us. Lord, please don't let this hurt Hannah. Please take care of her. And I ask that You would take care of Barbara and help her to find healing. Lord, we need You. We need wisdom. Lord, if You have to remove me from this situation, then do it. But show us what You want us to do. We want to honor You, Lord. Please help us. Please, Lord, help us. In Jesus' name."

Amy picked up the prayer. "Father, when I heard Barbara's words, I heard a hurt mother and grandmother. She has a broken heart, Lord, and she's carried it for so long. I know she cares for Hannah and wants the best for her."

"Yes, Lord," John prayed.

"Would You somehow use Hannah's relationship with her father to draw Barbara to You? You've done something miraculous in Thomas's heart. You've drawn Hannah to Yourself. She's now Your child. Now, Lord Jesus, mend Barbara's broken heart. Show her how much You love her and care for her and want to show her Your compassion. I pray in Jesus' name, amen."

"Amen," John said.

The two knelt on the floor, eyes closed, hearts drawn together in the pain they felt from Barbara's words. Then John heard a voice from somewhere in the house. Amy heard it too. They walked down the hall by the kitchen.

Amy pointed to the stairs. They crept to the top landing and saw Ethan's door open. He and Will were kneeling by Ethan's bed. It was Will's voice they had heard.

". . . and she's got asthma, and a lot of bad stuff has happened. But she's decided to follow You now. So I pray You would encourage her and help her see that no matter how bad it looks, You're with her and You have a future for her."

Amy put a hand over her mouth and closed her eyes. John could barely hold back the tears. The boys had heard the commotion and had turned to prayer. They too knew God was the only One who could help them. They needed His power.

They crept downstairs again and Amy grabbed the phone. "I want to update the Bible study. Nothing specific, I just want to encourage them to keep praying."

It was then John remembered what Larry, from their Bible study group, had said. He had reminded John of a prayer he had prayed months earlier. He had asked God to bring people and circumstances that would help grow their faith and stretch them to depend on God like never before.

John saw their struggle in a new light. He had wanted everything to get better. He wanted a fix for the problem. But what if God was working in the middle of the mess with Barbara? In the middle of the misunderstanding and hurtful words?

"I'll call Pastor Mark and ask him to pray too," John said.

CHAPTER 37

✦ ✦ ✦

"What did you say to them?"

Barbara put her purse on the kitchen table, still trying to calm her racing heart, and turned to look at Hannah, not believing what she heard. "Are you worried about their feelings? How about worrying about the one that has taken care of you for the last fifteen years?"

Barbara looked closer. Hannah had been crying. Tears streaked her face.

"Hannah, do you think I'm trying to hurt you? I'm trying to protect you!"

Hannah gave her a pained look, like she wanted to say something, wanted to defend her father.

"You don't know him like I do!" Barbara said. "Having

him in your life is pain. And I've had enough of that. You should have told me instead of deceiving me."

Tears ran like a flood down Hannah's face. She found her voice and said, "You told me he was dead!"

Barbara looked away. She had only said that to protect her. It was easier if Hannah thought he didn't exist. Easier for them to move on with their lives. And Barbara had *assumed* he was dead, given the way he had lived.

"I want to know my father," Hannah said. She said it with everything in her. She said it like it was the most important thing. Then she turned and walked into her room.

Barbara couldn't believe it. Tears came to her eyes. All the sacrifice and love she had given, and now to be treated this way. Life had never been more unfair. She'd learned her lesson with Janet's death. Keep everything locked tight. Keep everything safe because if you don't, it will be ripped from you. So she'd done that, and look where she was. Right back in the middle of the pain. Life was like a lazy Susan. No matter how many times you spun it around, you kept coming back to the same things inside.

Barbara surveyed the kitchen and the living room. Her eyes rested on a picture of her daughter. It was then she knew what she had to do.

Barbara parked the car and stared at the entrance to Franklin General. She'd been here only twice since Janet died. Once to see a friend who'd had surgery—one of the servers at the restaurant—and once when Hannah had an asthma attack. Both times the memories had risen like a flood. Anytime she came this direction, she took the long way around so she wouldn't even see the hospital.

There had been construction and a new parking lot and brickwork done out front, but no matter how much they changed it, unwelcome memories intruded. Now, here she was, about to face the man she had counted as dead because to her, he was.

She should have moved away. Should have gone to Texas. Her sister lived there and had said she and Hannah could stay with her. There were lots of jobs in Texas and taxes were low, her sister said. But Barbara's heart was in Franklin, and even if many of the memories were bad, there were good ones, too. She wanted to raise her granddaughter here. She didn't want to run away like *he* had run.

T-bone. Thomas Hill.

She shook her head. His name felt like a curse word.

Three times she put the key back in the ignition but she couldn't drive away. Finally she found the strength to get out. At the welcome desk she asked for the room number of a patient named Hill.

"First name?"

"Thomas." She closed her eyes and tried to get the bad taste out of her mouth.

The desk worker, an older woman with a kind face, pointed down the hall. "Take the elevator up to the fourth floor. Room 402. If you have any trouble, stop at the nurses' station."

"I'll find it," Barbara said.

She followed the directions and wound up in the middle of the hall outside room 402. The door was slightly open and she heard music inside. It sounded like the songs they played on the Christian station. Praise and worship and God is good all the time.

That sent her over the edge. Thomas had gotten religion. And religion was supposed to change everything. She was supposed to jump up and down and be thankful that he had walked some aisle or repeated some prayer. She didn't understand that. As if saying a prayer made everything better. Wiped the slate clean. All you had to do was tell God you were sorry and you got to move on as if nothing had happened. And all the people left in the wake of the tsunami you'd created were supposed to just get over it and move on with life.

She stepped closer and peeked inside. When she saw him, her first thought was *How the mighty have fallen.* Thomas had been so strong, so full of himself, muscles and speed and that swagger that made him look in control. He drew Janet in like a fly to a spider's web. And now he was trapped in a hospital bed hooked up to machines. Death warmed over.

Good, she thought. *Serves him right. He can rot right here.*

She pushed the door open all the way and crept in and stood at the foot of his bed, watching him mouth the words to the song on the CD. His eyes didn't register, so Hannah was right. He was stone blind. She didn't feel an ounce of pity. There was nothing he could go through that could compare with her pain. She felt it every night when her head hit the pillow and every morning when she awoke, that dull ache of pain and loss. But there were other moments when she'd see Janet in Hannah's eyes or some small thing that ambushed her and brought her to her knees.

Barbara controlled her breathing, but Thomas must have sensed her presence. He held out the remote and stopped the CD.

"Is someone there?"

Barbara stared down at him, rage seething inside. She remembered that day he brought Hannah back. The day her world fell apart. The day he ran. And without emotion, without venom, she spoke.

"I won't let you hurt her."

She said it evenly, stating the facts. She didn't want him to have the satisfaction of knowing that he had angered her. She didn't care for him any more than she would a bug on the sidewalk.

Thomas froze at her voice. His eyes tracked to the ceiling and a look of recognition came over his face.

"I wondered when you might come."

Immediately the anger rose. "Oh, I didn't want to come. But Hannah is so determined to learn more about you. And I have told her about what she might find."

Thomas listened and waited. When she finished, he spoke with resignation and remorse. "You've got every right to hate me. I can't defend the wrongs I've done. And I know I don't deserve your forgiveness."

Barbara focused on the machines, unable to look at his face. She wanted to scream. She wanted to pull every tube out of him and let him feel some of the pain she had felt. In this hospital, just a few floors below where she stood now, she had stared into the lifeless eyes of her only daughter. And Thomas was the reason that memory was imprinted forever. And there was no erasing that memory with a few words of regret.

Thomas turned his face toward her and there were tears in his eyes. With a trembling voice he said, "But I'm not the man you knew. I only want to love and to help Hannah."

Barbara wasn't moved. She didn't care about his tears, his feelings, or his newfound religion. "Help her? You want to help her? It's been fifteen years and now you want to help her?"

Barbara didn't want a back-and-forth yelling match. She wanted to tell him to stay away from Hannah and leave, just like she'd done at the Harrisons' place. But his words sparked something inside she couldn't hold back.

"How are you going to help her?" she said, a hand on one hip. "You can't even help yourself!"

Her words were like darts and she could tell they connected. His face contorted in pain. They had reached deep and hit the mark.

"You want to help Hannah?" she continued, and this was what she had come to say. This was the sword she hoped would pierce him. "Leave her alone."

She let the words sink in. But she had three more to say.

"Let her go."

She glared at him, remembering the look on his face when he'd stumbled to his car that long-ago day. He'd run so fast all his life and now she was asking him to keep running. It was the least he could do after the hurt he'd caused.

She turned to leave, her face set toward the elevator. She had said what she wanted to say. But just outside the door she heard it. Like the howl of a wounded animal. She stopped.

"You just gave her to me," Thomas said.

Barbara took a step back toward the room before she realized he wasn't talking to her.

Thomas was sobbing. "Give me the chance to love her, Lord. Don't You leave me here useless." He gritted his teeth and prayed harder. "Don't You leave me here useless."

Barbara's mouth dropped open as she studied his face. A nurse walked toward her. Barbara turned and quickly went to the elevator, her hand shaking as she reached for the button.

She had walked into the hospital with anger and bitterness. But her resolve was shaken by what she had heard. She didn't want to admit it, but Thomas looked different. Sounded different. There was no swagger to his voice, just contrition. There was no justifying his behavior or blaming Janet or anyone but himself. He had owned the pain he had caused, and that surprised her.

What was she supposed to do with all of that? She had held on to a desire that Thomas would get a double dose of what he had dished out, that God would punish him and make him pay. Now he was broken and bruised, but somehow, even in a hospital bed, he seemed more alive than she was. He had reached out to God, something she couldn't do. Something too hard after all the years of pushing Him away.

It was one thing to believe God could forgive a sinner. It was another thing to believe that the sinner could live forgiven.

The restaurant was slow the next day and Barbara felt like she was carrying a table full of dishes on her back. She couldn't get the sight of Thomas in that bed out of her mind any more than she could get the anger and bitterness and hurt to leave. And his wounded cries cut her heart to the quick. She wanted to keep hating him. As harsh as it sounded, she wanted him just to die and be out of her life and Hannah's too. That way the problem would end.

"Big, Tall, and Handsome just sat down," Tiffany said to her.

"And what would I do with somebody like that?" Barbara said.

"Get his food, I guess. He asked for your section."

Barbara stared at the back of the man's head. Nicely dressed. Alone. She didn't recognize him. "My section? Are you sure?"

"Is your name Barbara Scott?"

She moved a little, trying to see his face. Was he a customer from some previous visit?

"He's got a gold band on his ring finger," Tiffany said.

Barbara shook her head and chuckled. "Last thing in the world I need right now . . ." She didn't finish her sentence.

"I got him a cup of coffee and a menu," Tiffany said. "The rest is up to you."

Barbara grabbed a coffeepot and refilled a customer's mug at a nearby table, then walked slowly toward the man. He was African American, broad-shouldered, with neatly trimmed hair and a kind face. He had placed a Bible in the middle of the table in front of him but studied the menu at the moment.

"Are you ready to order?" Barbara said, smiling.

He looked up from the menu. "Well, is there something you would suggest? This is my first time here."

Barbara pointed out the special of the day and the man said that would be fine. He handed the menu back to her and said, "Thank you, Barbara."

She put the menu under her arm. "Do I know you?"

"I don't think so," he said, smiling.

"Well, if this is the first time you've been here, how do you know my name?"

"You mean other than the tag you're wearing?"

Barbara dipped her head. "You asked to sit in my section, right?"

He nodded. "A friend told me you worked here."

She glanced at his Bible. On the front she read, *Rev. Willy Parks.*

"You a pastor?"

He nodded.

"And who is this friend of yours?"

"Someone in the area I'm visiting. A member of the flock."

"Where's your church?"

He mentioned the name of the church and that it was located in Fairview.

"That's a long way to go for a visit."

"It is, but the drive helps me think. Clears my head and my soul. You'd be surprised how many sermons I've come up with driving from one place to another. Listening to people's stories. Listening to the pain."

"There's plenty of that to go around," Barbara said.

He chuckled. "I won't disagree with you there, Ms. Scott."

His familiar tone unnerved her. She thought of letting Tiffany take the table, but what would it hurt to hear him out? She turned and said, "I'll get your order started."

The man cleared his throat. "My parishioner is in the hospital here. Over at Franklin General."

Barbara stopped. Without looking at him, she said, "Is that so?"

"Mm-hmm. They had to move him here from Fairview. He's on dialysis."

Barbara's heart fluttered. She stared into his eyes. Of all the nerve, to track her down here.

Barbara gritted her teeth. "Did he send you here?"

The man sipped his coffee and put the mug down. "No, he didn't. In fact, he's been adamant that I not reach out to you or your granddaughter."

"Then why are you here?"

Another flash of teeth. "Well, first of all I'm hungry. Second, I have a long drive ahead of me, so I need the coffee to stay awake."

"Is there a third reason?"

The man's voice grew soft. "Barbara, would you sit with me a moment?"

"I'm working, Reverend."

He glanced at the dining room. "But you're not busy. It won't take long. I promise."

Flustered, she looked at the ticket. "I need to get this to the kitchen if you want food."

"All right," he said, taking another sip of coffee.

She put the order into the computer and paced in the prep area. When Tiffany spoke, it startled Barbara.

"What did he want?"

"He wants to talk with me. Wants me to sit down with him. He's a minister."

Tiffany seemed full of questions. Instead she said, "I'll take anybody who comes in next. Go ahead and talk with him."

"I don't want to. He has nothing to say that I want to hear."

"What's he want to talk about?"

"I don't know exactly." Barbara shook her head. "Come rescue me in five minutes, okay?"

"Whatever you say," Tiffany said.

Barbara freshened the man's coffee and reluctantly sat across from him. "I only have a couple of minutes."

"I appreciate you taking the time. I didn't plan this. I drove by and saw the restaurant name. Your granddaughter mentioned you worked here—"

"You spoke with Hannah?" she said, interrupting him.

"No, I'm sorry. Hannah told Thomas the name of this place. That's how he knew it. And he mentioned it to me along the way. He told me you visited him."

"I don't see how any of this is your business."

"It's not. And I may be stepping over a line here—"

"You most certainly are," Barbara said.

"—but I always try to be obedient."

Barbara furrowed her brow. "Obedient?"

"As I drove by, something clicked inside. I got the impression that . . ." He paused and folded strong hands on the table. "Do you believe the Lord speaks to people, Ms. Scott?"

"You're the reverend. You're asking me?"

He smiled. "I have a hard time with people saying the Lord told them this or that. My conversations are often one-sided. At least they seem that way."

He held out his mug and steam rose above it as she poured him another cup.

"As I drove by, I felt a strong urge to stop. To see if you were here. Maybe share something from the Word."

"I thought you were hungry and wanted coffee."

"I think it's all three. Thomas didn't put me up to this. He's resigned to having you hate him because of what he did."

"That's good," Barbara said, sitting back. "Go on."

"We were talking this morning. He said it was the guilt

that kept him away. The shame. He couldn't call. Didn't reach out. He was scared. And since meeting Hannah, he's grateful he doesn't have to be held back by the regret and guilt."

"Bully for him."

The man nodded as if expecting her sarcasm. "Do you know what he asked me to pray for today?"

"I couldn't care less." Barbara stood. "I need to check on your order."

She walked toward the kitchen. Tiffany was there.

"Why didn't you come get me?" Barbara said.

"It hasn't been five minutes yet."

"Seemed like five hours."

She toasted the man's English muffin and buttered it, and the kitchen finished his order. She walked it to his table and paused because the man had his head bowed. His lips moved and she watched. When he looked up, she put the plate in front of him.

"Just like manna," he said, rubbing his hands.

"Can I get you anything else?" she said.

"Ketchup?"

She retrieved a bottle and put it beside him and placed the check on the table. "There's no rush on this. I'm just putting it here."

"I understand, Barbara." He lowered his voice. "I understand more than you can know."

"What's that supposed to mean?"

"Six years ago I lost someone dear to me. Feels like yesterday."

Barbara put a hand on her hip. "Who?"

"My son." He lifted his fork and pointed toward the chair. She looked at it, looked at him, then sat.

"There's a lake down the road from our house. On my day off I used to take my son fishing. But being a pastor means you're important. People call at all hours. Sometimes you're not there when you said you would be."

The reverend got a far-off look, like he was watching something in the distance, something he didn't want to see.

"There was a teenage girl who had just gotten her license. She was driving to work. Her first day at her new job. Got distracted. The radio or her phone. Doesn't matter. By the time she realized she'd run off the road and corrected . . ." His voice trailed. "She thought it was a dog. Heard a thump. But she kept on going because she didn't want to be late. It was her first day and all."

Barbara stared at him.

"She didn't know. Didn't understand the hurt she'd caused. It took us a day to find him. Tangled in some bushes. He had his rod and reel and the tackle box with him."

Barbara swallowed hard. "You came here to tell me that? To say you forgave her and everything's okay?"

He stared at his food. "No. I came here to tell you I think God is on your trail, Barbara. And that He cares more than you know. The hardest thing for me was living every day thinking I could have done something different. If I'd said no to those people who called, I might be fishing with my son right now."

Barbara studied his face. "I'm sorry for your loss."

He nodded. "I'm not asking you to give Thomas another chance. I'm not even asking you to forgive him. I think the reason God stopped me here was something different."

"And what was that?"

"I think He brought me here to ask you to open your heart to the possibility that He's walking with you through all this. Just like He walked with me."

Barbara stared at his plate. She wanted to tell him his food was getting cold, that he ought to eat it. Instead she said, "What happened to her? The girl who hit your son."

"She moved away not long after the law got through with her. Her parents tell me she's struggling. She's having a hard time putting all of it behind her. I pray for her every day."

Barbara's eyes blurred and she felt her chin quiver. "Well, I'm glad for you. I'm glad you've been able to get to that place."

He leaned across the table. "I didn't get there on my own. I had to lay down the hurt and pain and regret. I poured it out day after day. And I told God He was the one who would have to lift it. That's when things changed."

"What do you mean?"

"I began to receive the love He wanted to pour out. He wanted me to live fully loved, fully forgiven. He wanted to guide me, instead of me being led around by hate or regret or anything but His kindness."

Barbara looked out the window. Clouds hovered over

the town, but in the distance there was the faintest gleam of sunlight reflecting on edges of the sky.

"For years I'd have this dream. My son's walking up that road with his fishing pole on his shoulder. Now I have a bigger dream. A bigger hope. Now I see a young girl walking home, out from under the weight of the past. I'm believing God that one day I'm going to look out and see her sitting in my church."

"And what will you do if that happens?"

"Not *if*, but *when*," he said, smiling. "I'll stop whatever I'm preaching and I'll march down those steps and hug her the way I would embrace my son. That's what I'll do."

Barbara nodded. "I believe you, Reverend."

He put a hand on hers. "I think that's what God wants to do with you today. He loves you like crazy, Barbara."

The pastor left a nice tip, as well as his card with a phone number and an e-mail address. There was a verse reference he wrote on the back along with the words *I'm praying for you.*

At home, Barbara glanced at the picture of Janet in the living room, that smiling face. Then she saw Hannah's backpack on the hook by the front door. Such a small thing. But big changes started with small ones, didn't they?

Perhaps people could change.

The pastor's story had moved her. She believed him when he said Thomas had not asked him to find her. She believed that somehow God had moved the man to reach out and try to give her hope. There was no way to explain what she'd seen in Thomas's face outside of God doing something miraculous. And as sick and broken as he was, she knew he was in better shape than she was. And in that moment, she felt a strong tug on her soul and she sat at the kitchen table. Thomas had run away and wound up running into the arms of a God who loved him in spite of all he'd done. How could a holy God embrace someone like that? Love like that didn't make sense.

She caught sight of her reflection in a mirror across the room. She hated the look on her face. She didn't want to be angry anymore. She didn't want to carry the weight of hate. But she'd carried it so long it was just part of her now. And she carried it because she had closed the door to God, thinking by doing that she could keep the hurt and the pain and the regret away.

She crossed her arms on the table. Quietly she began the conversation she had avoided for fifteen years.

"Hey, God, it's me. I haven't talked to You in a while because I've kind of been mad at You." The emotion came and she felt her chin quiver. "Ever since You took my baby. No parent wants to outlive their kid. Angry. Mad. I'm not like You, God. I don't know how You do it. I mean, everything they did to Your Son and You just forgive them. You just forgive them. I'm not there yet."

It was as honest as she could be. And in the process, she was being honest with herself. Tears came and she made no effort to stop them.

"My baby's gone and now he wants to take Hannah, too? I'm not handling this very well. God, I'm working two jobs, I'm trying to do everything I can do on my own, and it's not working."

She heard an echo of a whisper spoken long ago. *"Come to me, all you who are weary and burdened, and I will give you rest."*

Oh, how she wanted rest. She wanted to let go of the burden and the weariness she felt down to her bones. But how?

If God knew everything, she wasn't telling Him anything He didn't already perceive about her, but just saying the words made her feel something. The emotion rose, not anger this time, but something that sent a shiver of warmth through her. It was close to the feeling of surrender.

"So look, if You want me to do this forgiveness thing, You've got to help me!"

Her voice bubbled with struggle, just like she'd heard in Thomas's cry to God. She was praying the same prayer but from a different heart. *"Don't You leave me here useless."* The emotion overwhelmed her and she choked out, "Because I can't do this anymore. I need Your help, God."

For the first time in fifteen years, she felt heard. She felt like she had broken through the portals of heaven itself. But she knew deep inside God had been there, waiting, ready to listen as she brought her broken heart to Him.

"You've got to help me, okay? You've got to help me forgive."

Part 4

THE VOICE

CHAPTER 38

✦ ✦ ✦

As the cross-country season drew to a close, John watched Hannah grow stronger. She was running faster than ever and had a level of endurance she didn't have at the beginning of the season. Her grandmother still wouldn't allow Hannah to have contact with Thomas, but Hannah held out hope that might change. Barbara hadn't taken action against John or the school, for which he was grateful. It felt like they were in a holding pattern.

The week before the state championship race, John attended the annual dinner with the league's fourteen cross-country coaches and the association leaders. He ate rubber chicken, unspeakable peas, and enjoyed the banter between coaches about the depth of their teams, as well as the fresh lament over the changes in Franklin.

Mitch Singleton, who also coached basketball, made a remark about Brookshire's one-runner cross-country team. Other coaches stifled laughs and John took the ribbing in stride. But as he ate, he realized how much he had enjoyed the season and how much Hannah had improved. He wasn't ashamed of his one-runner team. In fact, he felt proud. He believed in Hannah. The other coaches had dozens of great kids, good runners, but he had one exceptional young lady with a huge heart who deserved to run alongside the top athletes in the state.

Gene Andrews, the association president, spoke at the lectern in front of the group and informed them what they already knew, that Sherwood College would host the state championship race and McBride Racing Events would time the event. The college would also provide medical personnel.

"At this time, Cindy Hatcher, our vice president, has an item to discuss with you."

Cindy was a no-nonsense official who cut straight to the chase. "So we have three rule changes in consideration this year. A few of our schools have requested that runners be allowed to wear earbuds during a race."

She explained there were two potential problems with the request. The runners needed to hear signals or warnings during the race. Plus, any live communication would give an unfair advantage. But the league had come up with a solution.

I can't wait to hear this, John thought.

"If the runner uses only one small earbud, and the content is prerecorded only, we will allow it, pending your vote. So for instance, if the runner wants to listen to music or recordings of their favorite motivational sayings, we're willing to try it."

John turned to Mitch and whispered, "This is ridiculous."

Another coach asked for clarification and Cindy responded that the player would have to be small enough to be strapped to the arm or waist, but no loose wires.

Another question came and John rolled his eyes. Who cared whether runners listened to anything? As if that was going to matter in a three-mile race. Everybody in the room knew who was going to win. Gina Mimms certainly didn't need music to motivate her.

Cindy asked for a yes or no vote and began going around the room. As the first few coaches responded, John suddenly sat straight in his chair, a flash of an idea coming to him—fully formed. He could see the whole thing, could hear the content of the recording they would make. He imagined Hannah's face when she heard the audio. As his mind spun, he could hardly contain himself.

When it was his turn to vote, he held up a hand and confidently said, "I vote yes."

Mitch stared at John like he was crazy. John whispered,

"Say yes." Then he leaned forward and a whole row of coaches stared at him. "Say yes," he said loudly.

It worked. They had enough votes for the motion to pass. On the way to his car, he called Ethan and began to set his plan in motion. They only had a couple of days to pull off the idea, but John was confident they could do it.

At home, with a map of the Sherwood course in front of him, John met with his family. "Gina Mimms won the state championship last year on this course with a time of nineteen minutes and forty-five seconds. So I need to know where she would be at any given point during the race."

"Why do you need to know that?" Ethan said.

"We're going to help Hannah," John said.

John called the head of building and grounds at the school and asked if he could borrow the golf cart. He and the boys took the cart to the Sherwood course. Will sat in the back and kept the stopwatch while Ethan used his tablet to record the route. It was a rough ride in certain parts, but when they crossed the finish line, they had perfectly timed the pace Hannah would need to keep up with Gina Mimms.

John dropped the boys at the house and raced toward Franklin General. He was just outside Thomas's room when Nurse Rose stopped him. "What is all this?"

"I need to do something with Thomas today," he said.

"And what is that?"

"Rose, Hannah is running a race this weekend. I think Thomas can help her."

"He's in no condition to do anything. You can't move him from—"

"No, I'm not going to move him at all." He explained his idea.

Rose relented. "I'm giving you one hour."

"Thank you, Rose."

Thomas was surprised by the activity and the equipment John had placed on his bed. "What is this again?"

"The state championship race is this Saturday. You've wanted to be there for Hannah, and now you're going to. I'll walk you through the course, and then you're going to coach her."

John hooked a lapel mic onto Thomas's hospital gown. He finished setting up the equipment just as Ethan had told him, fearful he'd get something wrong and not hit Record. He told Thomas what they had done in the golf cart, the pace they had driven and the pace Hannah needed in order to match or exceed Gina Mimms's time the year before.

"Does Hannah know anything about this?" Thomas said.

"Nothing. And I'm not telling her ahead of time."

"You're pretty sure about this plan, aren't you?"

"I know what it's going to mean for Hannah to hear her father's voice. She loves you so much."

"It's been hard knowing she's so close but can't come to see me." Thomas pursed his lips. "One time when you came in here, I said, 'Put me in, Coach.' I guess that's going to happen today."

John explained the signals he would give Thomas when they reached different stages of the race. He would give different taps on the arm for a hill and the straight, flat ground. He would give signals for the first mile, the half-way point, and the beginning of the final mile. There was a signal for when Hannah would near the finish line, assuming she kept up her pace.

"You ready?" John said.

"Let's do it," Thomas said.

CHAPTER 39

✦ ✦ ✦

Hannah practiced hard at the start of the week and did lighter workouts as she neared race day. She asked her grandmother if she would watch her run her final race. Her grandmother said she had to work. On Friday evening Hannah asked one more time.

"You know how much I want to be there," her grandmother said. "It's just that Mr. Odelle is hard-nosed about missing work. I can drive you to the race, but I have to leave before you run."

"That's fine," Hannah said.

"My boss said you know his son. His name's Bobby."

Bobby. She didn't know a Bobby. Then it clicked. "Wait, you work for Robert Odelle's dad?"

"Do you know Bobby?"

"Unfortunately," Hannah said.

"What's that supposed to mean?"

Hannah told her what had happened. She described what Robert had done and how she tried to not get angry at him. That led to an explosion in the lunchroom.

"Why didn't you tell me about this?"

"I should have. But something good came out of it. I had a long talk with Mrs. Brooks. She explained what it means to have a relationship with God."

"Is that so? What did she say?"

Her grandmother sounded interested. Hannah told her about praying with Mrs. Brooks and coming home and making a list from Ephesians.

"Do you still have that paper?"

Hannah got it from her backpack and showed her the list she had written and the notes she had taken since then.

"Look at all the places it says 'in Him' in these verses," Hannah said, pointing them out. "And it talks about God's will over and over."

Her grandmother studied the page. "This is really something, baby. Who taught you how to do this?"

Hannah shrugged. "I just asked God to help me. And after I read this through, I realized something about . . ."

"About what?"

"I don't think you want to hear it."

"Yes, I do. Tell me."

"It's about my father."

Her grandmother nodded, urging her on.

"I knew I needed to forgive him because God forgave me."

Her grandmother glanced away but Hannah continued.

"I took a lot of things, Grandma. A lot more than the stuff you found. I hid them from you. So when I received God's forgiveness, I knew what He wanted me to do. I needed to return them. So I did. And it wasn't easy, but I felt a lot better. And I figured, if God could forgive me for the bad things I've done, I could forgive my dad for not being there for me. I could choose not to hold that against him anymore."

Her grandmother wiped something from her face. "All this forgiving you're doing, what does that mean about Robert?"

"I don't know. I've been thinking about talking to him. Maybe I'll tell him what's happened to me."

"What if he makes fun of you?"

Hannah shrugged. "I can't control that. I only control how I act toward him."

Her grandmother nodded. "That makes a lot of sense, baby. I hope he listens. You've got something good to tell him if he does."

Hannah smiled. "Yes, Grandma."

That night she wrote her father a long letter. She included the conversation she'd had with her grandmother.

When I brought up the subject of forgiving you, she listened. I think she's coming around, but it's taking time. And I'm worried you don't have much time left. But I have to trust that God knows all this.

I wish I could hear your voice, but I think you'd tell me to listen to my grandmother and obey her. So that's what I'm going to do.

I love you, Daddy.

Later, she tossed and turned, trying to sleep. She thought about the course, going over the hills, flat stretches, and especially the long stretch to the finish line. Some old fears crept in, like the one about finishing last or not finishing at all. Then she remembered who she was in God's eyes. She pulled out the list and went to sleep thinking about who she really was.

The next day at the race, Hannah hugged her grandmother and thanked her for giving her a ride, then stretched and watched the other teams. She wondered what it would be like to run with teammates instead of feeling alone against the world. The dew hadn't burned off the grass and her shoes got wet as she walked across the lawn to find the Harrisons.

The stands at the Start/Finish line began to fill with parents and students. Hannah spotted her grandmother by a chain-link fence with her purse over her shoulder, waving good-bye. Hannah wished her father could be there, even if he couldn't see her run—just to look at him in the crowd would have been encouraging. Of course, in his condition, that was impossible. There was no way her dad would ever be at one of her races.

Mrs. Harrison helped her make final preparations. She pinned her number onto her jersey and Hannah didn't even glance at it. Mrs. Harrison made sure she had her inhaler. Coach approached and asked how she was doing.

"I feel like I'm going to throw up," she said.

"Yeah, I'll bet half the girls out here feel that way." He handed her a small device that kept her time electronically. "Here's your chip. Make sure you lace it up tight."

"You're going to do great today, Hannah," Mrs. Harrison said. "Don't be nervous. This is just another race, okay?"

Coach Harrison glared at his wife. "No, it's not—it's a huge race. I'm nervous."

"That's not helping, John," Mrs. Harrison said.

He apologized and also asked if she had her inhaler. Hannah showed him and Coach turned and scanned the grounds. "Check out the stands. You've got a cheering section today."

Hannah saw Ethan and Will, along with Grace and a few other students she'd gotten to know at Brookshire. She smiled as she realized that though she was the only runner on the team, she wasn't alone.

As she moved toward the starting line, Hannah noticed several runners with armbands connected to an earbud. She hadn't seen anything like that all year, but she put it out of her mind. She had enough to think about.

Coach Harrison approached her a few minutes before the start of the race. He carried something small.

"Okay, Hannah, I want you to do something for me."

He took her arm and slipped a band with a small mp3 player around it and strapped it tight.

"What is this?"

"There's only one track on it. As soon as the race starts, I want you to hit Play."

Mrs. Harrison strung the single earphone from the player to Hannah's ear.

"Is this music?" Hannah said.

"Nope," Coach said. For some reason he wasn't giving her a complete answer. "As soon as the gun fires, you hit Play and start running, okay? Trust me." He gave her a final look. "You can go to the starting line."

Hannah walked away, securing the earpiece. She lined up, shaking her arms and legs, trying to get the butterflies to leave.

"Runners, take your mark," the starter said over a loud-speaker.

Just as the gun sounded, Hannah hit Play.

CHAPTER 40

✦ ✦ ✦

"Hannah, this is your dad."

Hannah nearly stopped when she heard her father's voice. She couldn't believe it. It was really him.

"I'm going to coach you through this race," he said. "And be with you every step of the way. We're going to do this together. Just stay with me."

A big smile on her face, she ran with a pack of runners, except this time she had someone else with her. Her dad was there. And somehow hearing him had chased away the butterflies. But how had he recorded this? How had Coach Harrison worked it out? She didn't have to know. All she had to do was listen and trust her dad and run her race.

The crowd cheered and Hannah sprinted with the others toward the trees and the uphill-downhill course ahead. The dew had burned off and her legs felt good, like she could run all day and as fast as she wanted.

"Don't burn yourself out too early," her father said. It was like he was right beside her, watching her every stride. "Settle into an even pace. About 70 percent of your max speed. But we're going to need to save some energy for the end."

The smile in her father's voice buoyed her. She ran in single file now with runners a few yards ahead and some just steps behind.

"You don't win races with just your legs. Victory or defeat happens in your head first. This is a mental competition. So I want you to start thinking like a winner."

Hannah smiled and pushed the earphone in a bit. She wanted to hear every word.

"I'm your biggest fan," her father said. She could see him now, the look on his face, the light in his eyes, even though he couldn't see. "You're going to do great today."

Hannah didn't usually smile during races. She focused on technique and form and didn't allow herself to consider anything else, but hearing her dad's voice, the clear words he spoke only to her, pushed her and gave her a feeling she'd never experienced while running. Her hair blew in the breeze, her arms pumped, and her legs carried her toward the first hill she needed to climb.

"Now find a girl in front of you and speed up for a few seconds to pass her."

There were a lot of girls in front of her. She sped up and moved around one girl in a black uniform.

"Then find your pace again. We're going to take them out one at a time."

Another runner was just ahead of the girl in black. Hannah passed her as well and settled onto the path again.

"When your body tells you that you can't do it, don't listen to it. It'll tell you that you should quit. You tell your body that your mind is in charge today."

He was right. There were moments in every race when she wanted to give up or at least slow down. She wanted to give in to the thought she couldn't beat anyone. But with her father's clear, caring voice, that wouldn't happen in this race.

"Give God your best today, Hannah. And no matter what, I love you."

As she approached the first hill, Hannah was still smiling. She couldn't have explained the feeling if she tried. She was full of energy, full of hope, full of her father's love. And it was because for the first time she wasn't running alone.

"Right now, you're coming to your first hill," her father said. "A lot of girls are going to slow down, but not you. You're going to attack this hill. I want you to pump your arms hard. Your legs are going to speed up too. Pick out the next girl in front of you and pass her. You can do this, Hannah. I know you can. Get after it."

Hannah saw a girl in front of her in a red jersey. Hills always made her want to slow her pace, but she listened to her father's voice, sped up, and moved around the girl and pushed harder. Though her father couldn't see, he was guiding Hannah, helping her navigate the course.

"When you get to the other side, let gravity do the work. Take advantage of that free speed, then find your pace again."

Hannah flew down the hill and caught the breeze off the lake to her right. She would never forget this day or this run or this feeling.

"You're doing great, Hannah. Even if your legs start to hurt, don't slow down. That can make them hurt even more. Keep your pace and push through. You'll find a second wind."

Hannah came to a marker on the course, and as she neared it, her father said, "The first mile is done. You're doing it, Hannah."

His timing was perfect. How had he recorded these words at the exact pace of her race?

"Don't look back to see who's behind you. Don't worry about them. Focus on what's ahead. It's just like in life. You can't let the past slow you down. Press on to what's ahead."

She felt a tightness in her lungs and a familiar fear. She didn't want to give in to it, but she knew she needed a puff from her inhaler. Keeping her pace, Hannah reached for the device at her side and took a puff, then put it back in its holder. There was no way her father could have predicted this, no way he could have anticipated this moment in the race, but still, his words as she breathed deeply warmed her heart.

"When we give our life over to God, He helps us, He forgives us, He can turn the bad to good and carry us forward."

Hannah had labored with her breathing, but she was able to pass another runner. The course rose and fell and she kept moving, attacking the hills and using her momentum to increase her speed.

As Hannah neared the midpoint of the race, coaches lined the course and shouted encouragement to their runners. She looked for Coach Harrison and was surprised he wasn't there. And then she realized that was okay because her father was.

"Hannah, having you in my life is an answer to prayer," her father continued. "I asked God for it, but I knew I didn't deserve it. I begged Him to forgive me for not being there for you. One of the greatest blessings in my life has been getting to know my daughter. I praise God for you, Hannah. You don't know how proud I am of you. I wake up every morning with a smile on my face ready to pray for you."

Hannah passed the last coach and, like her father advised, focused on what was ahead. She saw the next runner about twenty yards farther and wondered how far ahead Gina Mimms was. She was somewhere up there. Could Hannah catch her?

"I've been praying that you would know that I love you. And that God loves you. He says, I know the plans that I have for you. Plans to prosper you and not to harm you. Plans to give you a hope and a future. I've been praying for your grandmother, too, that He would help her and draw her to Himself."

That was exactly what Hannah had been praying for her grandmother. And Coach Harrison and his family and the people at their church were praying the same thing. Again, she realized she wasn't alone.

She had just come to a long incline that wound through rocks and trees when she heard her father say, "Hannah, the second mile is behind you. One more to go."

With two-thirds of the race done, she came to a plateau where she could see clearly. The next runner ahead was about fifteen yards away. Beyond her, two more, and in front of them, Gina Mimms. Like everyone expected, Gina led the race with her powerful strides.

But something strange happened then. Instead of comparing herself with Gina, instead of believing there was no way she could win, Hannah focused on her father's words.

"Find your breathing rhythm because we have one more hill coming up. This is where you'll pass another girl. Remember, attack this hill. If someone is in front of you, fight past her." Her father gave a little laugh. "You can shake her hand after the race."

Coach Harrison had talked about being "in the zone," and Hannah was in it now. There were moments in races when she was so focused, so caught up in the running, it was as if all her thoughts and physical energy were gathered and used for one purpose. But she'd never had a race where every part of it felt like that—like she was fully engaged in the task. Of course, she'd never run to her father's voice.

"Big breath, Hannah. Now take the hill."

Hannah felt like she was flying as she pulled up to the girl to the right and passed her. She did attack the hill, shortening her stride but running faster. A race official was at the top of the hill pointing them left and Hannah saw Gina Mimms hit the top and turn. There were now two girls between her and Gina.

"Hannah, if you're like me, this is where your body hits the wall. But we're going to push through it. This is where you think like a winner. Most runners will slow down, but not you. You have half a mile to go and it belongs to you. If your legs are burning, let them burn. Your lungs may be tired, but they're not done yet. Other runners are feeling the same thing."

She felt the burn in her legs and in her lungs, but she also felt a power she had never experienced as she passed the next girl ahead of her.

"You've got to get yourself in position. Your last kick is coming. If anyone is in front of you, you've got to get around them. Don't let anyone block you."

Hannah heard her father in her left ear and in her right was the sound of girls running behind her, the girls she had passed who were desperately trying to keep up. She would not slow down. When the runner in green, in second place, moved to her left and slightly blocked her, Hannah pushed through, went around, and kept striding ahead.

She came to a clearing. They were close to the edge of the woods and she could see sunlight and the straightaway that led to the finish line. Hannah also saw the telltale strides of Gina Mimms in front of her and suddenly her lungs felt like they were closing. In any other race she would have slowed because of how powerful Gina looked and how fast she was going and how many titles she had won. But not this race. Instead of seeing Gina Mimms as unbeatable, Hannah saw how close she was. She wasn't about to slow down.

"You're near the finish line," her father said. "And we're going to finish strong. You're about to come out of the woods. If Coach Harrison is right, the lead runner is about thirty yards in front of you."

Hannah couldn't believe how close her father was to the truth. She was maybe twenty-five yards behind Gina now. She was close enough to hear the girl's footsteps.

"It's almost time to kick it in. This is where you pull all your reserves. This is where you leave it all on the course."

Hannah lengthened her stride. She pushed herself to run faster. Her lungs told her to slow down. She told her lungs that today, she was in charge. They would not control her. She was listening to her father. Her lungs needed to obey.

"Now, my daughter, it's time!"

Arms pumping, feet pounding.

"Hannah, track her down!"

In one defiant motion, she grabbed the inhaler and threw it aside and felt like she'd tossed off a weight holding her back.

Hannah sprinted through the trees, watching Gina Mimms pick up her pace as well. There was nothing left to do but run the race she'd been given. Her feet pounded the ground and she pushed herself forward like never before.

Gina ran from the shade of the woods into the sunlight and around a curve in the course, and Hannah lost sight of her. When Hannah came around the same corner, she heard the crowd in the distance. And there was Gina, still twenty-five yards ahead. But there was something strange about her strides. She seemed to be slowing. And then Hannah realized it wasn't that Gina had slowed—it was that Hannah was flying, gaining ground with each step.

"You can do this," her father said. "Give it everything. Catch her, Hannah. Extend your stride."

She was fifteen yards behind now, and Gina did something Hannah had never seen her do—she turned and looked behind her. And it was in that moment that Hannah put on a burst of speed that brought her to within ten yards of the lead.

"Pump your arms," her father said.

She did. She pulled five yards behind Gina.

"Keep your eyes on the finish line and fight for it."

She pulled even with Gina and didn't glance at her. She

was narrowed in on the spot near the bleachers where the crowd cheered and she saw the word *Finish*.

"I'm right here with you. You can do this. I can see you winning."

Gina picked up her pace and matched Hannah stride for stride.

"I can see you winning."

Hannah reached for the reserve she'd kept all through the race. She felt Gina by her side but didn't take her eyes off the finish line. She heard Coach Harrison somewhere on the sidelines yelling for her to fight. She heard wild cheers from the stands. The voices coalesced into a rich sound track and background that was overcome by the one voice she heard above them all.

"Do it, Hannah. Do it, my daughter. Do it, Hannah!"

She stared at the word *Finish*, but something strange happened. Her vision blurred and her lungs ached and though she told her body to obey, it wouldn't listen. She was there, the line was just ahead, and she leaned forward, but it was too far. She lost her balance and barely got her hands in front of her to brace herself before she fell and hit the ground.

CHAPTER 41

✦ ✦ ✦

As the race began, John Harrison paced like an expectant
father, looking at his watch, wondering where Hannah was
on the course and whether her father's words were helping.
There was a chance his efforts would backfire. Hearing her
dad in one ear could ignite Hannah's emotions and scatter her thoughts, rather than help her focus. But from the
moment he'd gotten the idea, John knew he had to make it
happen. It was a gift to both Hannah and Thomas.

John had always wanted to give his athletes something
they could cherish the rest of their lives. He'd thought that
meant a state championship, a scoring title, or a most valuable player award. But no matter what happened today,

he'd given Hannah something she would never forget—the sound of her father's voice as she ran her race.

There was a chance this would upset Barbara. She could use it to move forward with her threat to sue him or the school. But Barbara's cold attitude seemed to be thawing. For some reason she had allowed Hannah to write to her father.

John couldn't believe the Brookshire turnout. Ethan led the cheering section with other students, and they were engaged and listening for updates as the race continued.

Olivia Brooks approached him about eight minutes into the race. "Hey, John, are you not going with the other coaches to the midpoint?"

"I'm not coaching her today," he said matter-of-factly. "She's got a better coach."

It was clear Olivia didn't understand, but he didn't explain. He knew she would enjoy hearing the details later. She turned and walked to the stands.

The prevailing opinion was that no one would beat Gina Mimms. She was too fast, too strong, too consistent. And with each update by race officials there was a growing sense the race had been decided before it started. But John had a feeling Hannah might surprise people with her finish. She had gained speed with each practice, and with her father's voice in her ear, he hoped she would place in the top ten. That would be a fantastic finish for her year.

John had listened as Thomas recorded his words to Hannah, and it seemed like the man came alive when he quoted Scripture or told her he was praying for her. There was passion in his words. There was no script, no notes—he simply poured out everything from his heart. Several times John had to wipe tears from his eyes as he listened and studied the course on the iPad.

The section on the recording about Barbara and how Thomas was praying for her shocked John. This was the woman keeping him from Hannah, but Thomas displayed no anger or bitterness, only understanding. It sounded like Thomas really cared for Barbara and understood her actions.

The final kick, where Thomas encouraged Hannah to track down the lead runner, sent chills through John. Thomas strongly believed that Hannah could achieve more than she could imagine. His words made John believe too.

"We have another update," an official said through a loudspeaker. "With half a mile to go, it's Gina Mimms in first, Anna Grant in second, and Joy Taylor in third."

Amy put an arm on his shoulder. "Do you think she's in the top ten?"

"I think she can medal."

"Top three? Seriously?"

"Yeah. Maybe even top two."

Amy raised her eyebrows. "You have faith in her new coach."

John nodded and studied the woods. He'd heard Gina's coach say there were only four runners who had any shot of finishing close to her. Hannah wasn't on his radar. What would happen if Hannah caught up with the third-place runner?

He saw movement in the trees. The first runner appeared from the woods.

"There's Gina," he said to Amy. Everyone knew she would be the first one out, but there was something about seeing her that deflated him. He had such high hopes, maybe too high.

As soon as he mentioned Gina, there was more movement and another runner turned the corner. For a moment, John couldn't see who it was because Gina blocked his view. He craned his neck to see around her. He saw a blue jersey.

"Is that . . . ?"

He didn't dare say it out loud. It was too wonderful to believe.

"That's Hannah," Amy said.

His eyes widened and with every ounce of energy he pumped a fist at the ground and yelled, "Run, Hannah!"

Beside him, Amy jumped and shouted. The crowd at the finish line responded. They could see the race was on. The Brookshire contingent went wild, but John was focused on Hannah's strides. She looked like she had reserved her final burst of speed just like Thomas had coached her. She was finishing fast.

"Come on, Hannah! Run!"

Gina's coach shouted for her to sprint, and for a split

second the lead runner glanced behind her and spotted Hannah.

"Catch her, Hannah!" John yelled.

Hannah was five yards behind Gina now and closing.

"Come on! Catch her, Hannah!" Amy screamed, tears in her eyes, clapping, yelling.

"Fight!" John yelled. "Fight!"

And that's what Hannah did: with each stride, she fought and clawed at the air. John felt like he was running every step with her, willing her to go faster. When she pulled even with Gina Mimms about fifty yards from the finish line, Gina regained momentum and matched strides with Hannah. The two ran as one, arms pumping in unison, legs and feet pushing them forward.

John looked at the stopwatch. Hannah had never run this fast. The two passed him and he heard a familiar sound—a wheeze instead of deep gulps of air. He leaned out to see around those who had surged forward, but as Hannah and Gina neared the finish line, it was impossible from his position to tell who was in the lead.

And then came the audible gasp from the crowd.

"What happened?" Amy said.

"Dad, she fell!" Ethan shouted from the stands.

John rushed onto the course and sprinted toward the finish line. Gina Mimms stood a few yards ahead, hands on hips, sweating and fully spent, looking back at a figure on the ground. Hannah lay like a rag doll just past the finish line. She didn't move. He couldn't tell if she was breathing.

He knelt beside her and put a hand on her back, and Amy joined him. He heard the telltale sound of an asthma attack as Hannah struggled for air. He looked for her inhaler. It wasn't there.

"Hannah, come on," he said, rolling her onto her back. "Hannah? Breathe for me."

Like lightning, the medical staff were there with equipment, checking Hannah's pulse.

John lifted her to a sitting position. "She needs oxygen. You got oxygen?"

"Take some deep breaths," Amy said as the paramedics put a mask on her.

"We've got to move her. We've got runners coming," an official said.

John picked her up and carried her out of the way. He noticed the stands were quiet now, no cheering for other runners. Everyone was concerned about Hannah.

John gently placed her on a bench and she was able to sit up. She nodded to answer his questions, and he could tell she understood. She was just trying to breathe now. More runners crossed the finish line, gasping for air. Some fell to the ground. Others walked with hands over their heads, stretching.

Hannah's breathing evened and she spoke through the oxygen mask. "Who won?" She looked at John and then Amy.

"They're trying to figure that out," Amy said. "But no matter what happens, you ran a fantastic race."

"The way you kicked at the end, Hannah," John said. "That was amazing. I'll never forget that as long as I live."

"I knew I had a chance when she looked back," Hannah said. "She looked kinda scared."

"She had a good reason to be scared," John said. "You saved all your reserves for that final burst."

"What did you think when you started the recording?" Amy said.

Hannah beamed. "I couldn't believe it. How did you do that, Coach? How did you get my dad to see that course?"

"He didn't see the course, Hannah. He saw you. He knew you could run fast. And so did I. He's going to be so proud of the way you ran today."

Hannah nodded.

John stood and scanned the judging area. Each runner had an electronic chip that recorded their time. There shouldn't be a controversy. But the two main judges hovered around a computer. They pointed and replayed the images on the screen, searching for something.

The medics packed up, apparently confident Hannah was breathing well on her own. John and Amy thanked them for their help.

Then John noticed the head official approaching the Westlake coach, who stood with Gina and the others on her team. The man smiled, shaking the coach's hand. Gina Mimms stood with hands on hips, listening. The official shook her hand too, and John knew the outcome.

So close. Hannah had come so close.

"Hey, I'm very proud of you," John said, looking at Hannah. "You've never run better. You're amazing."

"I gave everything I had." Hannah looked like she was near tears, sensing she hadn't given enough to outrun the state champion.

Gene Andrews, the association president, made his way to them and knelt in front of Hannah. "Young lady, you doing okay?"

Hannah took a breath as if she was preparing herself for the bad news. "I'm okay."

"That was quite a finish. A little scary, too. I understand you've never won a race before."

Hannah shook her head. "No, sir."

John studied her, ready to hug her and tell her how great it was to be second in the state.

Andrews glanced down, then looked at Hannah with a smile on his face. "Well, you have now."

John put a hand on Andrews's shoulder. "What did you say?"

"We actually had to go back and look at the video because the computer had the identical time. It turns out you were leaning forward just an inch more than she was. Congratulations. You just won the state championship."

Hannah burst into tears and leaned back in Amy's arms. They were tears of joy, tears of victory. The emotion seemed the culmination of everything she had been through, the loneliness and fear, the hurdle of asthma, the guilt over things she had done. The girl who had been abandoned and had great loss, who ran alone with no team. She overcame it all listening to her father's voice.

John didn't know what to do, where to go, how to act. He threw both arms up and leaped in the air. He spun like a top and pumped his fist and yelled, "Yeah!"

The Brookshire crowd erupted.

"Hannah, you did it," Amy said, hugging the girl and crying along with her.

John raised both fists and walked toward the stands, looking at Ethan and Will and Olivia and the others in the stands. Some covered their faces with their hands, overcome with emotion. Others laughed and cheered, unable to contain their excitement.

John was a man looking for something he couldn't find, looking for someone to share what he felt inside. He ran back to Hannah and hugged her. "You did it, you did it, you did it!" He said it over and over. Then he pulled back. "Hannah, you're the state champion. You are number one in the state."

Emotion subsiding, she smiled and sat back on the bench, the audio player still strapped to her arm.

Ethan and Will and a horde of supporters ran to her and hoisted her high on their shoulders and began the chant: "Hannah, Hannah, Hannah!"

With her face turned toward the sky, John saw Hannah point and say, "Thank You, Lord."

CHAPTER 42

✦ ✦ ✦

Barbara intended to watch the start of Hannah's race and head to work. She stood by the concession stand and had a view of the starting line. Standing here, waiting, she realized how much she had missed.

All her life, Barbara felt on the outside looking in. It had happened as a child and then in her marriage. With Janet, she'd felt like life had spun out of control and all she could do was stand back and let it whirl by like a tornado. All she got from that was debris and Hannah.

Was there a different way to live? Through the chain-link fence, she saw the runners milling about. Hannah glanced her way, and Barbara gave a little wave, hoping that was okay. She didn't want to make her nervous. Barbara watched her stretch and then Mrs. Harrison pinned a number on her jersey.

Something strange happened at that moment and Barbara couldn't figure it out. It was like a different flavor put into some recipe that you noticed with your tongue but couldn't quite place. Hannah turned and Barbara saw her profile, and a picture flashed in her mind. She saw T-bone in the picture that Janet kept in the box. And then she realized Hannah was wearing #77, the same as her father all those years ago. Had the Harrisons worked that out, or was it happenstance? Or maybe it was God answering her prayers, opening another door for her to walk through.

The girls lined up, the gun fired, and off Hannah went, disappearing into the crowd of runners heading for the woods.

There. She'd done it. She'd risked being late to see the start of the race. As she walked to her car, she heard someone call out her name and Olivia Brooks ran to her in her bright-blue Brookshire T-shirt. The woman was all smiles. "Barbara, you made it!"

"Yeah, I wanted to at least see the start before I leave."

"Your granddaughter is really an inspiration to us. I hope you know that."

"Inspiration?"

"With all the challenges she's faced, she's made some really good decisions this year."

Barbara spoke softly. "And she wouldn't have had the

chance to make them if you hadn't stepped up. I wondered if you had given that scholarship. Did you?"

Olivia put a hand on Barbara's shoulder. "I loved Janet. And I was so sorry for what you went through. The Lord placed Hannah on my heart a long time ago and I promised God that if I ever got the chance to be part of her life, I would do it. This was just my small way of getting involved. And I'm so glad she's with us."

"Well, we're both grateful for what you've done."

"Are you staying to the end of the race?" Olivia said.

"No, I have to get to work. My boss is going to be upset the way it is."

"I understand."

Barbara walked to her car and put the key in the ignition. Only days earlier, seeing Olivia or anyone from the past would have devastated her, but hearing Janet's name and knowing Olivia cared for Hannah sparked something. She'd felt a change in the last few days. She had lived trying to avoid pain. In the process, she pushed God and church people away. She worked and provided and worked some more and fell into bed each night, only to get up the next day to do it all over again. And there was a comfort in the exhaustion.

But when she looked into the unseeing eyes of Thomas Hill and observed a changed man, the world tilted. She felt she was looking at that man in the Bible—what was his name? Lazarus. Old Lazarus had died and they wrapped him tight and put him in a tomb where it was all dark.

Just like Thomas. She'd considered T-bone as good as dead. But in the Bible story, here came Jesus, weeping for His friend Lazarus and calling his name. And out he came, old Lazarus wrapped up and tied up. The people around the tomb helped unwrap him and turn him loose.

Thomas had said he experienced the same thing. He was blind and his body was failing, but he had a hope for life that Barbara didn't have.

Reverend Parks had helped unwrap the cloth around her own heart. His story about his son, the loss he'd been through, and the way he said God had walked with him gave her hope.

Sitting in her car, the key in the ignition, a light flashed on the dashboard of her soul. All the pain she had tried to avoid, all the hate she held on to was there in front of her. Seeing Hannah run and hearing what Olivia said and remembering what Reverend Parks told her made Barbara think she didn't have to live outside of God's love any longer. Maybe the pain and struggle could lead her to something good, something unexpected.

Her phone buzzed in her purse. She looked at the number and shook her head. She wanted to ignore it, but she answered the call.

"I know I'm late. I'm in the car. I'm about fifteen minutes—"

"Whoa, hold up, Barbara," Doyle Odelle said. "Are you at the cross-country meet?"

"How did you know that?"

"Bobby told me about it. Your granddaughter is running. It's Hannah, right?"

Bobby was the kid who gave Hannah a rough time. "That's right. I wanted to see the start of the race."

"Well, why didn't you tell me?" Doyle said. "It's the state championship, right?"

"Yes, sir. It is. But if I leave now, I can make it there in—"

"If you leave now, you won't see her finish. We can handle the restaurant. Understand?"

She didn't know what to say. "Uh, well, yes sir. Thank you. But I don't get it. What did Bobby tell you?"

"Look, I know he and your granddaughter have had problems. My wife got a call from the principal. I finally got the truth out of him. Heard the whole story—not just his version. I feel badly about the way he's treated her. She deserves an apology."

"Well, that's good to hear."

"We can talk more later. I want you to stay till the end of the race. And I won't take no for an answer. And then you get here and tell us what happened, all right? It's not that busy here, but after the race things might pick up."

Barbara smiled. "I'll be there after the race, then."

"Good."

"And thank you, Mr. Odelle."

She couldn't believe what she had just heard. She took her keys from the ignition and walked back to the fence in front of the concession stand. She was watching from there ten minutes later when runners appeared at the edge of the woods. When she saw Hannah in second place and moving up fast, she screamed and yelled and pulled on the chain-link fence. There was a commotion at the finish line and Barbara couldn't see what happened. It was all she could do to keep from going forward to see what all the fuss was about.

CHAPTER 43

✦ ✦ ✦

Standing on the winner's podium felt like a dream for Hannah. The official shook her hand and placed the medal around her neck. Gina Mimms stayed stoic beside her, not saying a word, and Hannah thought the girl was probably so mad at losing she wanted to throw her second-place medal into the woods.

To Hannah's surprise, as she stepped from the podium, Gina turned and smiled and held out a hand. "Congratulations. You deserved the win."

"If I hadn't fallen at the end, I might not have."

Gina grasped the medal around Hannah's neck. "I think there's a lot more of these in your future. I'll tell my coaches at the university to watch out for you."

Hannah gave her a hug, then found the Harrisons. As they left the track, Coach pointed to Mrs. Brooks, who was standing next to Hannah's grandmother. Hannah went to her and embraced her grandmother in a warm hug.

"Grandma, you stayed."

"Yes, I'm late for work but it was worth it." She looked at Hannah and something seemed different in her face. The hardness, the bitterness, the edge her grandmother showed had been replaced by something tender and gentle. "I am so proud of you."

"Thanks," Hannah said. She held her grandmother's hands and looked her in the eyes. Like a runner gathering the energy and courage to pass someone on the track, she took a deep breath. "I want to go see my father."

No scolding. No accusation. No scowl or furrowed brow. Her grandmother nodded and without a word gave her blessing. Hannah felt like she had won Olympic gold.

Her grandmother drew her in for another hug and Hannah wanted to pinch herself to make sure it was real. But it was. The whole day had been real.

Her grandmother walked toward Coach Harrison. "Just get her home safe," she said.

It felt like a breakthrough. It felt like Hannah finally had a clear path to her father.

Hannah found Mrs. Brooks and hugged her. "Thank you for everything."

Mrs. Brooks didn't say a word. She just smiled and watched Hannah and the Harrisons walk away.

The Harrisons drove straight to the hospital. On the fourth floor Hannah pushed the door open and found her father waiting.

"I hear three sets of footsteps coming," Thomas said.

"Hey, Thomas, how are you?" Coach Harrison said.

"I've been on pins and needles all day. How is everybody?"

"We're good, Thomas," Mrs. Harrison said.

Hannah moved close to her father. "Hey, Daddy."

"And how is my daughter?" he said gently.

Hannah pulled the medal from her pocket and put it over her father's head so that he was wearing what she had earned. She fixed the medal over his heart and he placed his hand over it. His face broke into a wide grin.

"You won a medal."

"Thomas, that's not just any medal," Coach Harrison said. He didn't need to say any more.

Tears formed in her father's eyes. He struggled to get the words out. "You mean to tell me . . . my daughter won the race?"

Hannah sat close and leaned forward. "I had a really good coach."

Her father couldn't hold in the emotion any longer and he put his head back on the pillow. Hannah bent down to rest her head on his chest and he wrapped an arm around her, pulling her close and kissing the top of her head.

She heard Coach Harrison leave the room and then

Mrs. Harrison followed, and she and her father were alone. His chest heaved with emotion.

"Oh, Lord, You helped me. You saved me. You restored me. You saved my daughter. You've made her an overcomer. Only You could have done this, Lord. I don't deserve Your kindness and Your mercy. But You've given it to me and I bless Your name, Jesus."

Hannah listened to the beat of her father's heart, the sound of his breathing, his voice.

"Did you hear my directions during the race?"

She pulled back to answer him. "Yes. I heard every word. And you wouldn't believe how right you were so many times."

"You can thank Coach Harrison for that. Tell me what happened."

Hannah walked him through the race and described the sections where he had helped her the most. "It was like you could see what was happening right in front of me and all I had to do was listen and do what you said."

Her father laughed. "This race was one of the good things God prepared for you in advance, Hannah. And I got to be with you. I'm so glad. And God is going to be with you every step of your entire life. Do you know that?"

"Yes, Daddy. And guess what else happened?"

"I can hardly imagine anything better than I've already heard. But tell me."

"Grandma said I could come to see you. She was at the

race. She stayed through the whole thing even though she had to be at work."

Her father smiled and put his head back on the pillow. "I think the Lord is working on her just like He's working on us, Hannah."

"I think you're right."

CHAPTER 44

✦ ✦ ✦

John didn't so much leave the room as float from it. Seeing Hannah in her father's arms, hearing Thomas weep for joy and kiss his daughter was too much. He signaled Amy that he couldn't take it and walked into the hall, hat in his hand, unsure what to do with the emotions.

John knew the feeling of winning as player and coach. He had set goals for himself and his teams, but even when he reached them, there was always something hollow inside, a desire for something more, something lasting. Filling that empty space was a never-ending climb up one mountain that led to another.

Now, pacing the hallway, holding back his emotion, he felt something he'd never experienced. He had surrendered his hopes and dreams for the basketball season. He had placed that on an altar and had given God his future and his family. And along came this wisp of a girl—he remembered the first day he saw her and how lonely she looked on the bleachers.

What I would have missed if I hadn't coached Hannah Scott, he thought. *I wasn't placed here to help her. She was placed here to help me.*

Amy came out of Thomas's room, tears in her eyes, and drew close. John pointed to the room and tried to speak. He blew out air as if that would help make room for the words. Finally he tapped his chest.

"I'm full," he said, surrendering to the emotion.

They had been through so much in the last few months. Life had not gone the direction they had hoped. But he had seen a miracle today. And the miracle wasn't Hannah winning a race, as good as that felt. The miracle was watching Thomas, whose only hope was in the power of God. Thomas had fully trusted his heavenly Father to do what he was powerless to do. God had reconciled hearts and had drawn Hannah into a relationship with Himself.

Amy embraced him. They'd had deep questions about the future, and God had used Thomas, Hannah, Barbara, and the struggle in the town to bring them closer together. Wasn't it just like God to accomplish that by using something that seemed awful?

"Thank You, Lord," John prayed, holding Amy's head close to him. "Thank You for all You've done."

CHAPTER 45

✦ ✦ ✦

Hannah enjoyed extra attention at school because of the state championship win. Mrs. Brooks made an announcement over the intercom and teachers and classmates congratulated her, some who hadn't seemed to know she existed.

She saw Robert in the lunchroom and approached him with her tray. She had a speech ready. She wanted to tell him she was sorry for throwing food and soda at him. And she wanted to say she forgave him for being mean. Mrs. Harrison said forgiving others was a choice. You weren't saying what they did was okay. You were releasing them from your anger. But before she could open her mouth, Robert scooted back from the table and held up his hands.

"You're not ruining another shirt!" he yelled.

Hannah retreated to the other end of the lunchroom. Grace found her. "Don't waste your time on Robert."

"I just wanted to talk to him."

Grace frowned. "Some people can't be talked to."

Hannah looked back and saw Robert alone. She felt sorry for him.

"Hey, you were amazing at the race," Grace said. "You're a rock star."

Hannah smiled and shared the condensed version of finding her father and the way he had helped her win.

"Wait, you didn't know your dad was alive?"

Grace sat with mouth agape as Hannah told the whole story. By the time she finished, a group of girls had joined them.

"So you go to visit your dad every day?" Leslie said.

Hannah nodded. "I'm riding over after school today."

"What do you do at a hospital every day?" Grace said.

"We just talk. Sometimes he helps me with my homework. Sometimes he's tired and he goes to sleep while I'm there. Then the next day he'll have more energy. Those are the good days."

"He must be really glad he met Coach Harrison," Grace said.

"Yeah. If it weren't for that, I never would have met him, I don't think."

On Friday evening her father asked Hannah not to come to the hospital the next morning. They had often spent

Saturdays together listening to music, or Hannah would read to him. The nurses sometimes rolled a cot in and she took a nap on it next to her father.

"Coach Harrison has a little project for me, so why don't you come in the afternoon?"

"What are you and Coach Harrison doing?"

"You'll see. For now, it's our secret."

He was tired when she arrived in the afternoon that day and seemed kind of distant and emotional. He perked up when she suggested she read him his favorite psalm. She watched him mouth the words along with her as she read.

"Whoever dwells in the shelter of the Most High
    will rest in the shadow of the Almighty."

The next Tuesday afternoon, her grandmother surprised her. She was waiting inside the front door for Hannah when she got home. She was nicely dressed and was holding her car keys.

"Aren't you supposed to be at work?" Hannah said.

"I got a new job."

"A new job? Doing what?"

"I'm supposed to be your chauffeur. Now, if you'll kindly get in the car, Miss Scott, I'll take you to your destination." She paused. "Oh, but you'll have to get changed first. There's something in your room you need to try on."

Hannah ran to her room. On her bed lay a beautiful blue dress with pretty flowers all over it. She squealed and tried it on, then walked into the living room to show her grandmother. "It's perfect! But what's the occasion?"

"I'm just the driver here. Now get your shoes on and let's get in the car."

Her grandmother drove them to her restaurant, which Hannah thought was odd. They walked inside and the waitstaff, all her grandmother's friends, greeted Hannah and told her how pretty she looked.

"Right this way, Miss Scott," the owner said. When they reached the back room, he paused and shook her hand. "I'm Doyle, your grandmother's boss. She told me about your state championship."

Hannah nodded.

"Well, I hope you have a lovely evening, young lady. This is our banquet room and it's for you and your guests."

She walked inside and found a long table decorated with hearts and flowers and streamers. A silver sign above the table said, *Happy Birthday, Hannah.*

Mrs. Harrison hugged her and Coach Harrison smiled. Ethan and Will were dressed in coats and ties.

Mrs. Brooks introduced Hannah to her husband. "This is our state champion runner I was telling you about, Charles."

"It's an honor to meet you, Hannah," the man said. "I've heard a lot about you."

Mrs. Cole, their next-door neighbor, greeted her, as well as Shelly from the Brookshire office.

And then a woman with a familiar face approached,

and it took Hannah a moment to place the nurse. "Rose!" Hannah said. "I'm glad they remembered to invite you."

Rose gave her a quick hug. "I wouldn't miss it. I'm here to make this a party you'll never forget."

"But it's not my birthday," Hannah said. "My birthday is—"

Rose held up a hand and disappeared behind a curtain at the back of the room. Then she pushed a wheelchair into view. Hannah put a hand over her mouth.

"Daddy!"

"Happy birthday, my daughter!" He was laughing and smiling from ear to ear. "Are you surprised?"

"*Surprised* is not the word." Hannah turned to her grandmother and wiped her eyes. "You knew about this?"

"Somebody's been planning it for more than a week," her grandmother said. "And he didn't do this alone. Mrs. Harrison got everybody together."

"You chose the venue," Thomas said, winking at Barbara.

"I suppose I had a little to do with that."

"But I thought you couldn't leave the hospital," Hannah said.

"There are some things more important than a hospital," her father said.

Rose leaned down and whispered, "I'm going to take good care of him while he's here. Don't worry."

"But, Daddy, my birthday isn't until—"

"I know it's not Valentine's Day, Hannah," her father said. "But you have to remember, I've missed fifteen of your birthdays. I'm not going to miss another one. So I decided . . ."

Her grandmother finished his sentence. "We decided to have a party with some of your favorite people."

Rose wheeled her father to the front of the table and Hannah sat next to him. At first, her grandmother helped the servers, but then her boss entered the room.

"You're not on the clock now, Barbara. Sit down and let us do our jobs."

While they ate, Coach Harrison told the story of meeting her father "by chance" at the hospital. Her father picked up the story and told how surprised he was that without knowing it, he had given running tips to his own daughter. Everyone laughed.

Her father held up his glass of water. "A toast." Everyone joined him with their glasses of water or soda. "To Hannah Scott, first in the state, first in my heart. I'm grateful God brought you back into my life."

Rose checked her patient's vital signs every few minutes. He hadn't eaten much at the meal and seemed content just to take in the conversations.

When the table was cleared, more dishes arrived, and Thomas spoke up. "I have a special treat for your dessert." He signaled Rose, who stepped out of the room. "This is for my state champion daughter."

Rose brought a cake in the shape of a medal with *#1* on top and placed it before Hannah. Ethan took pictures of the cake and of Hannah blowing out the candles. It looked too good to eat. But they ate it anyway.

Hannah glanced at her grandmother several times through the evening. She was quiet but seemed to enjoy herself. There was laughter and a few tears around the table as the evening progressed.

"And now for the present," her father said. He pulled a small package from his pocket and handed it to her.

"What's this?"

"You have to open it to see," he said.

She unwrapped and opened a rectangular box, revealing a gold necklace. In the middle was a pendant in the shape of a cross. She looked at her father, then back at the necklace.

"Well, put it on and see how you like it," he said.

Her grandmother helped her and she put her hand over it and beamed. "Every time I wear this, I'm going to think of you."

He nodded. "And I want you to thank God that He brought us together in His time and through His grace. That's what the Cross is all about—God's amazing grace."

They were all lining up for a group picture when her father slumped in his wheelchair. Rose went to him quickly. He blinked and bobbed his head backward.

"I think it's just too much excitement," he said, slurring some of his words.

"We need to get him back to the hospital," Rose said. "I'm sorry."

The room quieted and Hannah watched Rose wheel her father to the van parked outside. Hannah wanted to go with him, but Rose said she could see him tomorrow. Coach Harrison and his boys helped Rose get her father into the van. While they did, Mrs. Harrison and Mrs. Brooks prayed.

"Maybe he shouldn't have come," Hannah said to her grandmother as they watched the van pull away.

"Your father wouldn't take no for an answer. He wanted to give you this party if it was the last thing he did. He had Olivia buy that dress for you."

Hannah turned to Mrs. Brooks. "Is that true?"

"I took my phone to the store and described all the dresses I thought you might like," Mrs. Brooks said. "When he heard about this one, the pink-and-white flowers on top of the blue, he said, 'That's the one for my Valentine. I don't care how much it costs.'"

Hannah and her grandmother drove home in silence, the rest of the cake in a cardboard container in the back-seat. When Hannah was in bed, her grandmother came into her room and sat.

"I just got a text from Rose. She says your father's resting. He's fine. Like he said, it was too much excitement."

Hannah opened her nightstand drawer and pulled out her blue box. It was now filled with pictures of her and her father that they'd taken in the past weeks.

"He's not going to get better, is he?" Hannah said.

Her grandmother stared at her hands. "I could make

something up to help you feel better, but you're old enough for the truth. Rose doesn't think he has much time left. That's partly why she worked it out so he could be at the dinner."

"Do you still hate him, Grandma?"

She looked at Hannah with sad eyes. "No, baby. I spent the last fifteen years hating him. I made a vow he would never come into your life. But that was before I saw what God can do on the inside of a person. I had no idea how He could change your father. I had no idea what He could do inside of me, either. Your father is a different person. And so am I."

Hannah stared at the photos and felt the emotion creeping up on her. "I don't want him to die. It doesn't seem fair that God would bring him to me and then just take him away. Does that make sense to you?"

"I don't have a good answer for that one, baby." She took one of the pictures from the stack and studied it. Hannah and her father mugging for the camera. "I keep wondering what would have happened if he hadn't been brought here from Fairview. Or if your coach hadn't stumbled into his room and struck up a conversation."

"Maybe instead of feeling bad about the little time I have, I can be thankful for the time we do have together."

"You need to feel whatever you feel. This is hard all the way around. But it's good, too. And you're right about it not making sense. I feel that too."

"Daddy says you don't have to understand everything God does in order to believe Him or trust Him."

"I think he's right. God wouldn't be God if we could understand everything, would He?"

Hannah put the lid on the box and placed it in the drawer. "I used to keep all the things I stole in there. You never found them."

"Did you really give all of them back?"

Hannah nodded and closed the drawer. Her grandmother smiled. "I never told you what happened that day, did I? The day your mother died."

"You've never told me anything about it."

"Thomas brought you to me. T-bone is what we called him. You were wrapped in a blanket. It was the last thing he did before he ran away. I was dealing with the hospital when he banged on the door. They had called about your mother being there. He put the blanket down in front of me on the floor and you pushed your tiny fist through the folds. I picked you up."

Tears came to her grandmother's eyes and she looked away for a moment, then continued. "Even then, he cared about you. Even though he was out of his mind with the drugs, you know. He could have left you at the hospital. For some reason he drove all the way over here."

"I think it's because he loved me."

"No doubt," her grandmother said. "I've never been able to think about that day without having it bring up all the pain of losing your mother. But when I thought about you and that blanket just now, it didn't stop me in my tracks."

"Maybe it's because you've forgiven him."

"I never thought I would. Never believed it possible."

"How did you do it?"

She handed the picture back to Hannah. "I think somehow forgiveness is a gift you have to open every day. First, you open it for yourself and receive it. Once you do that, you wrap it up and give it to somebody else."

Her grandmother rose and looked down at her. "I'm sorry for all the times I yelled at you. I'm going to try and do better. I'm asking God to help me with that."

"I forgive you, Grandma. And I'm sorry for making you worry so much."

She laughed. "Worrying was a choice I made. But I forgive you."

Her grandmother paused at the door, her hand on the light switch. She looked like there was more she wanted to say.

"Good night, baby."

"Good night, Grandma."

CHAPTER 46

✦ ✦ ✦

Barbara sat by Hannah in the front pew of the Harrisons'
church. Pastor Latimer had opened its doors for Thomas's
funeral. It was his last request that they have the funeral
in Franklin. The pews were full of people from Brookshire
and the hospital staff. She thought it was fitting that in
death, Thomas had brought together people of such different colors and backgrounds.

They sang songs Thomas had chosen—all of them
praising God for His mercy, love, and forgiveness. They
sang, "Open the eyes of my heart, Lord," and Barbara
smiled at the thought that Thomas was seeing again and
how wonderful his view must be.

Reverend Willy Parks, the pastor of Thomas's church in Fairview, spoke of meeting Thomas for the first time. "I didn't know him before he met Jesus. I only met him after he had lost his physical sight. But this man had spiritual sight and a hunger for God the likes of which I have never seen.

"On the day I met him, he told me he was going to pray for me every day. And he did that. I asked him if there was something I could pray for him about and I thought he would ask me to pray for his healing. But he didn't.

"On that first day I met Thomas, he had one prayer request. He asked me to pray that his daughter would come to know Jesus as Lord and Savior. I didn't even know he had a daughter. And in time, he told me the story. It's a sad one. It's heartbreaking in many ways. It was hard for him to tell it because of the guilt he felt.

"I prayed with him for almost three years about the daughter he left, the regrets he had, and this unfinished chapter of his life. We prayed together and wept together. He struggled with whether he should reach out to her after all these years and what the possible consequences of doing that might be. I have to be honest—I wanted to pick up the phone and call. But I honored his request, for the most part."

Reverend Parks looked straight at Barbara and smiled. She wiped away a tear and hugged Hannah.

"Now I look at the fruit of the prayers we prayed and the work of God in our hearts," Reverend Parks said, looking at the front row. "Hannah, your father loved you deeply. And he wanted you to know the heavenly Father's love personally. He was so proud of you. I wish you could have heard him on the phone telling me about the day you stood by his bed and told him that God had forgiven you, so the least you could do was forgive him. I got down on my knees that day and prayed with thanksgiving. God is still in the miracle business. Our God is a forgiving God. He is a loving God. And I praise Him today for you, Hannah, and for your father, Thomas.

"So now the last page has turned in the life of Thomas Hill. And the words *The End* appear on that page. But I submit to you, this is not the end of Thomas Hill. Thomas Hill is more alive now than he ever was. Thomas Hill is enjoying the relationship he began by surrendering his heart to the God who gave His only Son for him. Thomas had only one thing he wanted me to do today. He gave me only one directive. He told me to tell you about the great grace of God, who can forgive you and change you on the inside. He told me to let you know God wants to make you a new creation in Him."

Toward the end of the service, Reverend Parks gave an opportunity for Hannah to speak. Barbara told her she didn't have to, that she might not be able to get through it, but Hannah was determined, just like her father.

She rose and walked to the pulpit and spread a sheet of paper in front of her. Her voice shook as she read the words.

"I want to thank God today for my daddy. I want to thank God for the time we had together. It was short, but I'll treasure those talks and the love he gave.

"I want to thank God that He blessed my daddy in Christ. That He chose him before the foundation of the world. That He adopted him, redeemed him, and forgave him. God sealed my daddy with His Holy Spirit. God saved my daddy and made him His child.

"God created my daddy and planned ahead of time for him to do good things. And, Daddy, because you are in Christ, you were made totally righteous in God's sight. And because I am in Christ, the next time I see you, you'll see me, too."

There was not a dry eye in the church. As Hannah sat, Barbara turned and caught Coach Harrison's eyes. They were filled with tears but he was smiling.

At the graveside, a smaller group gathered. Reverend Parks stepped to the head of the casket to deliver final words.

"Thomas Hill's life is a testimony of redemption, of the grace of God and His power to change a man's heart. So we take comfort today that he no longer suffers and is now alive and well in the presence of the Lord. For Jesus said, 'I am the resurrection and the life. Whoever believes in me, though he die, yet shall he live.'"

Barbara stood next to Hannah. For years she had thought this would be a day when she would dance, finally free of the man who had shattered her life. But instead she was shedding tears—for Hannah, for Thomas, and for a deep loss she felt in her own heart.

After the service, Mrs. Harrison approached her. "Barbara, please let us know if you need anything."

"Thank you. We will."

She put a hand on Barbara's shoulder. "I know today has been one of mixed emotions for you."

"Yes, but I'm at peace," Barbara said. "I know without a shadow of a doubt that Thomas truly loved Hannah. And I can honestly say forgiveness is beautiful."

CHAPTER 47

✦ ✦ ✦

Hannah stood by the grave, staring at the pretty white carnations and ferns arranged on top of her father's casket. This was the first funeral she'd ever been to and she hadn't known what to expect. The laughter at her father's humor had surprised her—and she was glad people could smile in the midst of the grief.

She thought it fitting to wear the dress her father had picked out for her birthday party. Her grandmother agreed.

In her hands she held the folded slip of paper that contained the eulogy she had written on her own. She had thought about putting her running medal in the casket before they closed it, but she forgot to bring it. And that was fine. She would think of her father each time she saw it, remembering the look on his face when she had presented it to him the day of the race.

"Hannah, are you okay?" Coach Harrison said as he joined her.

She nodded, still staring at the flower arrangement. She wondered what they would do with it when they lowered the casket into the earth.

"I want you to know your dad was a very good friend to me. And I grew to love and respect him very much."

"Me, too," she said. "For six weeks, I had the best dad in the world."

He put an arm around her and hugged her. "I think your dad would be proud of what you said today. Proud that you stood up there in front of all those people and talked about him. And talked about your faith."

She nodded. "I think the pastor was right."

"About what?"

She put a hand on her necklace. "When he said this is not the end of the story. His life is going to speak through all of us who knew him. His story doesn't end here, Coach Harrison."

EPILOGUE

✦ ✦ ✦

Hannah kept her father's CD player on her nightstand and
wore out his collection of worship music. She continued
running cross-country for Brookshire Christian School
and won the state championship again her senior year.

Mrs. Brooks called her into the office on the day she
received a full-ride scholarship from Newhart College.
Robert Odelle happened to be in the office that day. He
stared at the floor as she passed him. Some things in life
got better, some got worse, and others seemed to stay
the same.

Curiously, Hannah's grandmother was offered a job at
Brookshire Christian School at the start of Hannah's junior

year. Mrs. Brooks said she was exactly the person they needed in the admissions department.

As soon as Hannah got settled in her college dorm as a freshman, she joined a Fellowship of Christian Athletes group and got involved in a Bible study. The leader of the group, Ethan Harrison, who was a walk-on for the Newhart basketball team, suggested she tell her story at a meeting of several campus Christian ministries. Hannah agreed, though she was nervous about public speaking. She was surprised at the response. She didn't know there were so many who would connect with her story.

Her appearances led to other opportunities to speak in front of high school groups and assemblies. She ended each talk, whether to a large or small group, with a challenge.

"At some point, you will ask yourself who you really are. I used to struggle with that. I felt like I was a mistake and had no place in this world. I felt unloved and unwanted. I got so many mixed messages from the world around me that I lived in confusion most of the time. But when I met the One that created me, I found my identity. It doesn't come from what the culture says to me, or even how I feel at any given time. The Creator is the One that gets to define His creation.

"I still have good days and bad days. I still have struggles. But through all of that, I know that the One that loves me and died for me is with me. He overcame everything for me. Sin, suffering, and death. So I walk with Him every day. I trust Him every day, no matter what. And since my identity is found in Him, I know exactly who I am."

She ran each race with the possibility of a visit from her nemesis, asthma. But she came to see even asthma as something God had allowed. He used her condition to help her depend on Him for every step, every breath.

The greatest feeling Hannah had wasn't winning races, though she did win a few in college. The times she felt most alive were when she saw that spark in some young girl who understood who she was "in Christ," as Hannah had discovered when she was fifteen.

As for John Harrison, he returned to coaching basketball. His son Will gave up his Tackle Ball Extreme idea and played point guard on the team.

John began a new tradition that first season. It seemed strange to the players that he would begin their first practice not with a drill but with a question.

"If I asked you who you are, what's the first thing that comes to mind?"

Eventually he told them the story of Thomas Hill and the impact the man had on his life. And as the seasons progressed, each player would answer the question for themselves. Each player would come to understand the power of knowing their true identity and the power available to be an overcomer.

It was on Hannah's sixteenth birthday that she discovered the surprise her father and Coach Harrison had secretly planned that Saturday morning.

On the Valentine's Day after her father's death, Hannah

opened the front door to find Coach Harrison standing on the porch with a small, wrapped package. He handed it to her and said, "Happy birthday, Hannah. This is from your dad."

She opened it and found a USB drive. *What in the world?*

"Load it on your iPod and go for a run."

She copied the file to the device, plugged in her earphones, and ran through Webb Park. She was near the basketball court when she hit Play.

"Happy Valentine's Day, Hannah," her father's voice said. She had to stop, the emotion overwhelming her. "It's your sixteenth birthday. I want to tell you that I love you and that God loves you. And I'm so excited about what's in store in your life. Here's what I've already prayed for you for this next year."

She would receive a new birthday message from her father, his words blessing her as he prayed for her, for the next fifteen years, the amount of time her father had missed before he had returned to her life. She treasured those gifts and kept them safely stored in a blue box in her nightstand.

Turn the page for an excerpt from

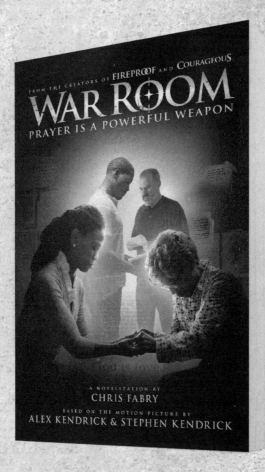

Available now in stores and online

Miss Clara

✦ ✦ ✦

She was an old woman with gray hair and dark skin, and she gave a sigh of relief as she pulled into the cemetery parking lot, as if just being able to apply the brake was an answer to prayer. She shuffled among the tombstones resolutely, nodding in recognition as she passed familiar names. It was becoming difficult to dredge up faces along with the names. Her gait was steady, and each footstep took her closer to her destination, a tombstone that read *Williams*. When she reached it, she stood and let the fresh, earthy smell wash over her. It felt like rain.

"You always loved the rain, didn't you, Leo?" she said aloud. "Yes, you did. You loved the rain."

In these sacred moments of Clara Williams's life, she

knew she was not talking to her husband. She knew where his soul was, and it was not under the green earth below her. Still, the exercise cleared her mind and connected her with the past in a way nothing else could. She could look at pictures of Leo in his military uniform and a few tattered photographs he had carried with him after he'd come home from Vietnam, and those brought her closer, but there was nothing like the feeling of running her hand across the cut stone and feeling the carved-out name and adjusting the little flag on top of his grave. There always had to be a flag there.

Clara had no concept of military warfare, except for those pictures her husband kept. She couldn't bring herself to watch war movies, especially the documentaries with grainy footage of men in combat. Falling napalm and the recoil of M16s against naked shoulders. She flipped as fast as she could past the PBS station that aired those. It hit too close to the bone.

But Clara did know another conflict. It was waged every day on six billion battlefields of the human heart. She knew enough about warfare to realize that tucked away in some place protected from the onslaught of bullets and bombs, someone had developed a strategy.

She pictured her husband staring at maps and coordinates. Sweaty and tired and scared, he and his men would analyze what the enemy was doing and mobilize resources to push back against their advance. In the years since his death, she had heard stories of his bravery, his sacrifice for his men.

"We need men with a steel backbone today, Leo," she said. "Like you. Steel backbone and a heart of gold."

But Leo's heart had given out early and left her alone with a ten-year-old son. His death had been sudden. She hadn't prepared for it. In her thirties she thought she had plenty of time and that life would stretch out forever. But life had not worked that way. Life had its own strategy and time had cut like a river into her heart.

Clara gingerly knelt by the tombstone and pulled at weeds, thinking of a day forty years earlier when she stood at this same spot with her only son.

"I wish you could see Clyde," she said. "He looks so much like you, Leo. Talks like you. Has some of the same mannerisms. The way he laughs kind of low and easylike. I wish you could see the man he's become."

Forty years earlier she had stood here with Clyde, looking at the stones covering the landscape and loved ones. "Why do people have to die, Mama?" he had said.

She had answered him too quickly. She told him death comes to everyone and quoted the verse about it being appointed unto man once to die, and after that the judgment. Then she realized he wasn't looking for theology, but something else entirely. She knelt at the same spot and told him the truest thing she knew.

"I don't know why people have to die, Son. I don't think death was what God wanted. But it sure was part of somebody's plan. I believe God is big enough and powerful enough to use it. There's more going on here than we can see."

Clyde had just looked at her with tears in his eyes. She'd hugged him and cried with him, and the more questions he asked, the tighter she held on. The words drifted high above the trees and blew with the wind. She could still feel his hug there at the gravestone.

"I never thought of myself growing older," she said to her husband and looked at the wrinkled skin of her weathered hands. "I tried to carry on and just head into life. And now four decades have passed like a strong wind. I've tried to learn the lessons God has taught me."

She pulled herself up and brushed the grass away from her knees. "I'm sorry, Leo. I wish I could go back and try again. I wish I had another chance. But it's okay now. You rest easy. I'll be seeing you soon, I expect."

She lingered a few moments, the memories flooding back, then took the long walk to the car and heard voices in the distance. A couple argued about thirty yards away. Clara couldn't hear the words, couldn't tell what the argument was about, but she wanted to shake them and point at the stones and tell them they were fighting the wrong battle. Tell them to see the real enemy. And that victories didn't come by accident, they came with strategy and mobilized resources.

The couple got in their car and drove away, and Clara shuffled back to hers and climbed in, suddenly out of breath. "If I didn't know better, I'd think this cemetery gets bigger and longer every time I come," she muttered to herself.

She could hear Leo laugh, that bittersweet echo across the years.

CHAPTER 1

✦ ✦ ✦

Elizabeth Jordan noticed everything wrong with the house she was selling before she ever knocked on the front door. She saw flaws in the landscaping and cracks in the driveway and a problem with the drainage of the roof near the garage. Just before she knocked three times, she saw chipping paint on a windowsill. This was her job. Presentation was everything. You had only one chance to make a first impression with a potential buyer.

She saw her reflection in a window and straightened her shoulders, tugging on her dark jacket. She had her hair back, which accentuated her strong face. Prominent nose, high forehead, and chocolaty skin. Elizabeth had a lineage she could trace back over 150 years. She had taken a trip with her husband and infant daughter ten years earlier to a plantation in the Deep South where her great-great-great-grandmother had lived. The little shack had been rebuilt, along with other slave quarters on the property, and the owners had searched the country for any relatives. Just walking inside made her feel like she was touching the heart of her ancestors, and she fought back tears as she imagined their lives. She'd held her daughter close and thanked God for the perseverance of her people, their legacy, and the opportunities she had that they could never imagine.

Elizabeth waited until the door opened, then smiled at the slightly younger woman before her. Melissa Tabor held a box of household items and struggled to maintain the cell phone balanced on her shoulder. Her mouth rounded into an O.

"Mom, I gotta go," she said into the phone.

Elizabeth smiled, patiently waiting.

Over her shoulder, Melissa said, "Jason and David, get rid of the ball and help me with these boxes!"

Elizabeth wanted to reach out and help her but had to duck as a kickball flew past her head. It bounced harmlessly in the yard behind her and she laughed.

"Oh, I am so sorry," Melissa said. "You must be Elizabeth Jordan."

"I am. And you're Melissa?"

The box nearly fell as Melissa shook hands with Elizabeth. "Yes. I'm sorry. We just started packing."

"No problem. Can I help you with that?"

A man with a briefcase and a work folder slipped past them. "Honey, I gotta be in Knoxville at two. But I finished the closet." He held up a stuffed bear and dropped it into the box. "That was in the refrigerator."

He passed Elizabeth on the front step and stopped, pointing at her. "Real estate agent," he said, sounding proud of himself. Not a name but a title he put on her. She was someone to put in a pigeonhole in his head.

Elizabeth smiled and pointed back. "Software rep."

"How did you know that?" he said, his eyes wide.

"It's on that folder you're holding in your hand." She was just as good at categorizing and commentating. She had to work at the connecting with others. Especially with her husband.

He looked at the folder and nodded with a knowing chuckle as if impressed by her observational powers. "I would love to stay but I have to leave. My wife can answer everything about the house. We realize it's a disaster and we've agreed to blame it on our kids." He glanced at Melissa. "So I'll call you tonight."

"Love you," Melissa said, still holding the box.

With that he was gone, down the walk to the car. He passed the kickball and didn't seem to notice.

"I understand," Elizabeth said. "My husband does the same thing. Pharmaceuticals."

"Oh," Melissa said. "Does he get tired of the travel?"

"He doesn't seem to. I think he likes being able to drive

and clear his head, you know? Instead of being cooped up in an office all day."

"While you're showing houses and dealing with people in big transitions."

Elizabeth stepped inside and noticed twelve things that would have to change if they were to make a sale. More first impressions. But she wouldn't list them all at the moment because she also saw something in Melissa's face that was close to panic.

"You know, they say that outside of death and divorce, moving is the most stressful change you go through." She put a hand on the woman's shoulder. "And this is probably not the first time you've moved in the past few years."

Melissa shook her head. "These are the same boxes we used last time."

Elizabeth nodded and saw missing paint on a ding in the wall but tried to focus. "You're going to get through this."

Right then a boy with spiked blond hair ran down the stairs, followed closely by another waving a tennis racket. Both were about the same age as Elizabeth's daughter and had enough energy to light a small city for a year. Who needed power plants and windmills when you had adolescent boys?

Melissa sighed. "Are you sure about that?"

✦ ✦ ✦

Tony Jordan had begun the day in an upscale suites hotel in Raleigh. He was up early, working out in the weight room alone—he loved the quiet, and most people on the road didn't work out at 5 a.m. Then he showered and dressed and had a bowl of fruit and some juice in the breakfast area. Other travelers hurried through, eating donuts or waffles or sugary cereal. He needed to stay fit and keep the edge so he could stay on his game, and his health was a big part of that. He'd always believed that if you had your health, you had everything.

Tony looked in the mirror as he headed out the door. His close-cropped hair was just the right length. The shirt and tie were crisp and hugged his running-back neck, strong and wide. His mustache was tightly trimmed above his upper lip, a goatee on his chin. He looked good. Confident. To tune up for the meeting later, he flashed a smile and stuck out a hand and said, "Hey, Mr. Barnes."

As an African American, he'd always felt like he was one step behind most of his white coworkers and competitors. Not because he lacked skill or ability or eloquence, but simply because of his skin color. Whether that was reality or not, he couldn't tell. How could he crawl inside the mind of someone meeting him for the first time? But he had felt the questioning looks, the split-second hesitation of someone who shook his hand the first time. He'd even felt it from his bosses at Brightwell, especially Tom Bennett, one of the vice presidents. Tony saw him as part of the old-boy network. Another white guy who knew somebody who knew somebody else and had eased into management, working his way a little too quickly up the ladder. Tony had tried to impress the man with his sales ability, his easygoing demeanor—the attitude that said, *I got this. Trust me.* But Tom was a hard sell, and Tony couldn't help but wonder if his skin color had something to do with it.

Accepting the reality he perceived, Tony vowed he would simply work harder, push harder, and live up to every expectation. But in the back of his mind he felt this unseen hurdle wasn't fair. Other people with a lighter skin color didn't have to deal with it, so why should he?

The hurdle in front of him today was Holcomb. There was no getting around the difficulty of the sale. But what was an easy sale? Even the quick ones took time and preparation and knowing and seeing. This was his secret—the intangibles. Remembering names. Remembering details about the customer's life. Things like the Ping driver he had in the trunk.

Calvin Barnes was going to salivate when Tony handed him that driver, as well he should. It had set Tony back a few hundred, but it was a small price to pay for the look on his boss's face when he heard Tony had sealed the deal.

The boardroom was tastefully decorated, the smell of leather permeating the hallway as he walked in and put his sample case on the redwood table. Calvin Barnes—who did not like to be called Calvin—would walk through the door and shake Tony's hand, so the driver needed to lean against the chair to Tony's left, out of view. He placed it there, then moved it into the chair and let the grip stick out over the back. When he heard voices down the hallway, he put the driver back on the floor. He needed to be more subtle.

Mr. Barnes walked in with another man—a familiar face, but for a moment Tony froze, unable to remember the man's name. He tried to relax, to recall the name using his mnemonic device. He'd pictured the man standing in a huge landfill with a John Deere hat on. Dearing. That was the last name. But he couldn't remember why he was standing in a land—

"Tony, you remember—"

"Phil Dearing," Tony said, extending a hand. "Good to see you again."

The man looked stunned, then smiled as he shook Tony's hand.

Mr. Barnes threw his head back and laughed. "You just won me twenty bucks. I told you he'd remember, Phil." His eyes fell on the golf club. "And what have we here?"

"That's the one I was talking about, Mr. Barnes," Tony said. "I'll be shocked if it doesn't add at least thirty yards to every drive. Your job is to make sure they're straight down the middle."

Mr. Barnes picked up the driver and held it. He was a scratch golfer who played three times a week and had designs on retiring to Florida. An extra thirty yards on his drives meant Barnes could exploit his short game, which meant that seventy-two for eighteen holes could come down to a seventy. Maybe lower on a good day.

"The weight is just perfect, Tony. And the balance is phenomenal."

Tony watched him hold the club and was certain he had the sale even before he opened his case. When they'd signed the papers and cared for the legal parts of the transaction, Tony stood. He knew he cut an impressive figure in his suit and tie and athletic build.

"I need to get you back on the course and work on that putting of yours," Mr. Barnes said.

"Maybe next time I'm through," Tony said, smiling.

"You don't mind coming all the way out here—even this early?"

"No, I do not. I enjoy the drive."

"Well, we're excited to do business with you, Tony," Mr. Barnes said. "Tell Coleman I said hello."

"I'll do it."

"Oh, and thanks for the new driver."

"Hey, you enjoy it, okay?" Tony shook hands with them. "Gentlemen, we'll be in touch."

He walked out of the room almost floating. There was no feeling like making a sale. As he neared the elevators, he could hear Calvin Barnes crowing about his new driver and how much he wanted to take the afternoon off and play the back nine at the nearest country club. While he waited, Tony checked his phone for anything he'd missed during the meeting, when he made a point of keeping it in his pocket. This was another thing he always tried to do. Value clients enough to make them the central focus. Never make your clients feel like there is anyone on the planet more important than them. They are your priority. Every. Time.

A young woman walked down a white staircase before him, carrying a leather folder and smiling. He put his phone away and smiled back.

"I see you made the sale," she said.

He nodded confidently. "Of course."

"I'm impressed. Most guys run out with their tail between their legs."

Tony extended a hand. "I'm Tony Jordan."

"Veronica Drake," she said, shaking with him. Her hand was warm and soft. "I work for Mr. Barnes. I'll be your contact for the purchase."

She handed him her card and brushed his hand slightly. Nothing overt, but he felt something click with her touch. Veronica was vivacious and slim, and Tony imagined them together at some restaurant talking. Then he imagined them by romantic firelight, Veronica leaning toward him, her lips moist and pleading. All this happened in a second as he stared at her business card.

"Well, Veronica Drake, I guess I'll be seeing you again when I return in two weeks."

"I'll look forward to it," she said, and the way she smiled made him think she meant it.

She walked away and he turned and watched her a little too intently.

As he waited for the elevator, his phone beeped and he looked at the screen.

Bank Notice: Transfer.

Here he was with the biggest sale in months, something he'd worked on and planned intricately, and right at the apex of his elation at the sale, he'd been given another smackdown by his wife.

"Elizabeth, you're killing me," he whispered.

✦ ✦ ✦

Elizabeth sat on the white ottoman at the foot of her bed rubbing her feet. The time with Melissa had been good—she'd been able to make a list of all the repairs and staging decisions that had to be done. The two boys hadn't made things easier, but children always had a way of complicating home sales. It was something you just needed to work with and hope you could navigate.

It had been a long day, with another meeting in the afternoon and then getting home before Danielle arrived from her last day of school. By the time she sat down, Elizabeth was exhausted and ready to curl up and sleep, but there was more to be done. There was always more to be done.

"Mom?"

Elizabeth couldn't move. "I'm in here, Danielle."

Her ten-year-old daughter walked in carrying something. She had grown several inches in the last year, her thin, long body sprouting up like a weed. She wore a cute purple headband that highlighted her face. Elizabeth could see her father there—that bright smile, eyes full of life. Except her eyes were a little downcast.

"Here's my last report card. I still got one C."

Elizabeth took it and looked it over as Danielle sat and shrugged off her backpack.

"Oh, baby. You have an A in everything else. One C in math is not that bad. But you get a break for the summer, right?"

Danielle leaned forward and her face betrayed something. She sniffed and then reacted like the room was full of ammonia. "Is that your feet?"

Elizabeth self-consciously pulled her foot away. "I'm sorry, baby. I ran out of foot powder."

"That smells terrible."

"I know, Danielle. I just needed to take my shoes off for a minute."

Her daughter stared at her mother's feet like they were toxic waste. "That's, like, awful," she said, repulsed.

"Well, don't just sit there looking at them. Why don't you give me a hand and rub them right there?"

"Ewwww, no way!"

Elizabeth laughed. "Girl, go set the table for dinner. When your daddy gets home, you can show him your report card, okay?"

Danielle took her report card into the kitchen, and Elizabeth was alone again. The odor hadn't been a problem until a few years earlier, and the foot powder seemed to take care of it. But maybe she was kidding herself. Maybe the odor was the sign of some deeper problem.

What was she thinking? Some disease? Some problem

with her liver that leaked out the pores of her feet? She had a friend, Missy, who was constantly looking online at various aches and pains and connecting them with her own symptoms. One day she'd be worried about a skin problem and conclude she had melanoma. The next day a headache would be self-diagnosed as a tumor. Elizabeth vowed she would not become a hypochondriac. She just had stinky feet.

She picked up one of her flats and sniffed. There'd been a cheese served at the hotel where she and Tony had honeymooned that smelled just like that. She dropped the shoe. Funny how a smell could trigger her brain to think about something that happened sixteen years earlier.

She ran her hand over the comforter and thought about that first night together. All the anticipation. All the excitement. She hadn't slept in two days and the wedding had been a blur. When her head hit the pillow in the honeymoon suite, she was just gone. Tony had been upset, and what red-blooded American male wouldn't be? But what red-blooded American females needed was a little understanding, a little grace.

She had made up for her honeymoon drowsiness the next day, but it was something they had to talk through. Tony had talked a lot in the year they had dated and been engaged, but not long after the *I do*s, something got his tongue and the river of words slowed to a drip. She wished she could find the valve or tell where to place the plunger to get him unclogged.

They didn't have a bad marriage. It wasn't like those celebrities on TV who went from one relationship to the next or the couple down the street who threw things onto the lawn after every argument. She and Tony had produced a beautiful daughter and they had stable careers. Yes, he was a little aloof and they'd grown apart, but she was sure that drift wouldn't last forever. It couldn't.

Elizabeth put her shoes away, as far back into the closet as she could, then went to the kitchen to start dinner. She filled a pot with water, put it on the stove, and dumped in the spaghetti. The water came to a slow boil, and she stirred the tomato sauce in a pan next to it.

Elizabeth watched the spaghetti, feeling something happening, something boiling inside her. A stirring she couldn't put her finger on. Call it restlessness or longing. Call it fear. Maybe this was all she could hope for. Maybe this was as good as marriage got. Or life, for that matter. Maybe they were destined to go separate ways and occasionally meet in the middle. But she had a nagging feeling that she was missing something. That their marriage could be more than two people with a nice house who rarely spent time together.

Elizabeth was busy with the salad and Danielle was putting napkins next to each plate at the table when the garage door began its hideous sound—a clacking that had gotten louder in the past year. If Elizabeth had been trying to sell their own house, she'd have suggested they get it looked at by her garage door guy. But Tony was content to let it clack and clamor.

Like their marriage.

"I just heard him pull in, Danielle."

"Will he be mad about my C?" Danielle said. The look in her eyes made Elizabeth wonder. She wanted to march out to the garage and tell Tony to affirm their daughter, say something positive, look at how full the glass was and not see the one little thing that was less than perfect.

"I already told you, baby. Getting a C is not that bad. It's okay."

She said it to convince not just Danielle, but also herself. Because she knew her husband wouldn't feel the same.

ACKNOWLEDGMENTS

Thanks to Alex and Stephen for permission to unveil a little more about Barbara, Hannah, John, and Thomas. For Brenda Harris, your prayers and encouragement are invaluable. Janet Dapper, you helped make this a better book with your observations and questions. Thanks to Karen Watson, Jan Stob, Caleb Sjogren, and Erin Smith at Tyndale for your commitment to telling great stories. And thanks to God for Your grace and mercy, for bringing us together, and for the power to overcome.

Chris Fabry

ABOUT THE AUTHORS

Chris Fabry is an award-winning author and radio personality who hosts the daily program *Chris Fabry Live* on Moody Radio. He is also heard on *Love Worth Finding*, *Building Relationships with Dr. Gary Chapman*, and other radio programs. A 1982 graduate of the W. Page Pitt School of Journalism at Marshall University and a native of West Virginia, Chris and his wife, Andrea, now live in Arizona and are the parents of nine children.

Chris's novels, which include *Dogwood*, *June Bug*, *Almost Heaven*, and *The Promise of Jesse Woods*, have won five Christy Awards, an ECPA Christian Book Award, and two Awards of Merit from *Christianity Today*. His eightieth published book, *Under a Cloudless Sky*, is a novel set in the coalfields of his home state of West Virginia. His books include movie novelizations, like the bestseller *War Room*; nonfiction; and novels for children and young adults. He coauthored the Left Behind: The Kids series with Jerry B. Jenkins and Tim LaHaye, as well as the Red Rock Mysteries and the Wormling series with Jerry B. Jenkins. Visit his website at www.chrisfabry.com.

Alex Kendrick is an award-winning author gifted at telling stories of hope and redemption. He is best known as an actor, writer, and director of the films *Overcomer*, *War Room*, *Courageous*, *Fireproof*, and *Facing the Giants* and coauthor of the *New York Times* bestselling books *The Love Dare*, *The Resolution for Men*, and *The Battle Plan for Prayer*. Alex has received more than thirty awards for his work, including best screenplay, best production, and best feature film. Alex has spoken to churches, universities, and conferences all across America and in other countries. He has been featured on FOX News, CNN, *ABC World News Tonight*, *CBS Evening News*, *Time* magazine, and many other media outlets. He is a graduate of Kennesaw State University and attended seminary before being ordained into ministry. Alex and his wife, Christina, live in Albany, Georgia, with their six children. They are active members of Sherwood Church.

Stephen Kendrick is a speaker, film producer, and author with a ministry passion for prayer and discipleship. He is a cowriter and producer of the movies *Overcomer*, *War Room*, *Courageous*, *Fireproof*, and *Facing the Giants* and cowriter of the *New York Times* bestsellers *The Battle Plan for Prayer*, *The Resolution for Men*, and *The Love Dare*. *The Love Dare* quickly became a number one *New York Times* bestseller and stayed on the list for more than two years. Stephen has spoken at churches, conferences, and seminars around the nation and has been interviewed by *Fox & Friends*, CNN, *ABC World News Tonight*, the *Washington Post*, and other media outlets. He is a cofounder and board member of the Fatherhood Commission. He graduated from Kennesaw State University and attended seminary before being ordained into ministry. Stephen and his wife, Jill, live in Albany, Georgia, where they homeschool their six children. They are active members of Sherwood Church in Albany.

www.kendrickbrothers.com

DISCUSSION QUESTIONS

1. John Harrison's basketball team is on the road to success, but because of circumstances he can't control, his life and team take a detour. Have you experienced a similar disappointment? How did you respond?

2. When Hannah prepares to attend Brookshire, she's certain she won't fit in, thinking Christians look down on those who don't follow a list of rules. How true would you say Hannah's assessment is?

3. In chapter 15, Amy has every right to be upset with John, but rather than being angry, she assures him of her love. What happens as a result? When conflict comes, how do you generally respond? Have you ever been treated the way Amy treated John?

4. Thomas asks John, "Who are you?" He's getting to John's core identity. John says he's a coach, a history

teacher, husband, father, etc. How did John's identity change throughout the story? Why? If you were asked the same question now, how would you respond?

5. After discussing Hannah's situation with Olivia Brooks, the Harrisons decide not to consult Barbara, Hannah's grandmother, about introducing Hannah to her father. Did they make the right choice? Have you ever been forced to make a similar choice about whether or not to bring someone into a decision? What happened?

6. When Mrs. Brooks talks with Hannah about her relationship with God, Hannah is ready to listen and respond. Why do you think she is open at this point in her life?

7. Reread Hannah's proclamation in chapter 31 about who she is. Which of her statements do you find most powerful? Which do you find hardest to believe about you?

8. In chapter 37, Barbara thinks, "It was one thing to believe God could forgive a sinner. It was another thing to believe that the sinner could live forgiven." Who is the person hardest to forgive in your life? Is it difficult for you to "live forgiven"?

9. With her father's voice to guide her, Hannah runs in the state championship. How would her story have

changed if she hadn't medaled or even finished the race? How does your performance affect your identity? How should it?

10. What physical, emotional, and spiritual obstacles do the characters in this novel overcome? John? Hannah? Thomas? Barbara? Ethan? Amy?

11. Are there people in your life who need a mentor? How might you begin such a relationship?

12. If you could reconnect with one person from your past, who would it be? What would you want to change about your relationship?

13. The title *Overcomer* comes from a Bible verse: "Who is it that overcomes the world except the one who believes that Jesus is the Son of God?" (1 John 5:5). In your own life, is there anything you need to overcome?